point

to make you shiver
Love, Grandad
& Nanny

THIRTEEN

13 Tales of Horror

Edited by T. Pines

SCHOLASTIC INC.
New York Toronto London Auckland Sydney

ISBN 0-590-45256-8

This anthology copyright © 1991 by Scholastic Inc.
"Collect Call" copyright © 1991 by Christopher Pike.
"Lucinda" copyright © 1991 by Lael Littke.
"The Guiccioli Miniature" copyright © 1975 by Grolier Incorporated New York. Copyright © 1975 in Canada by Grolier, Ltd. Previously published in *The New Book of Knowledge*.
"Blood Kiss" copyright © 1991 by D.E. Athkins.
"A Little Taste of Death" copyright © 1991 by Scholastic Inc.
"The Doll" copyright © 1991 by Carol Ellis.
"House of Horrors" copyright © 1991 by J.B. Stamper.
"Where the Deer Are" copyright © 1991 by Caroline B. Cooney.
"The Spell" copyright © 1991 by Scholastic Inc.
"Dedicated to the One I Love" copyright © 1991 by Scholastic Inc.
"Hacker" copyright © 1991 by Sinclair Smith.
"Deathflash" copyright © 1991 by A. Bates.
"The Boy Next Door" © 1991 by Ellen Emerson White.
All rights reserved. Published by Scholastic Inc.
POINT is a registered trademark of Scholastic Inc.

12 11   7 8 9/9 0 1 2/0

Printed in the U.S.A.   01

First Scholastic printing, October 1991

To Daddy
the only one who truly believes
that monkey hips and dumplings rule!

— TAM

Contents

Introduction
T. Pines   vii

1. "Collect Call"
Christopher Pike
     Part I   1
     Part II: "The Black Walker"   305

2. "Lucinda"
Lael Littke   49

3. "The Guiccioli Miniature"
Jay Bennett   73

4. "Blood Kiss"
D.E. Athkins   83

5. "A Little Taste of Death"
Patricia Windsor   103

6. "The Doll"
Carol Ellis   127

7. "House of Horrors"
   J.B. Stamper   149

8. "Where the Deer Are"
   Caroline B. Cooney   165

9. "The Spell"
   R.L. Stine   183

10. "Dedicated to the One I Love"
    Diane Hoh   205

11. "Hacker"
    Sinclair Smith   231

12. "Deathflash"
    A. Bates   257

13. "The Boy Next Door"
    Ellen Emerson White   279

    About the Authors   331

Introduction

WE ARE, SHALL WE SAY, THRILLED TO "DEATH" that you've decided to join us on this trip into darkness. Ask any vampire, it's so much easier to see once your eyes have become adjusted to the dark, and we have so much to show you. . . .

This anthology is a compilation of the best horror writers of the young-adult thriller genre. With the overall success of horror novels and "thrillers," it was just a matter of time before this book became a reality.

What we have here is true horror: everyday occurrences gone awry. The supernatural *is* frightening, what with ghosts, zombies, witches, and ghouls. But when you discover that your best friend has a nasty habit of doing away with the people he or she no longer likes — that is horror.

We read horror because we like to be frightened. It is a way to delve into *other* people's fears and feelings, knowing all the while that if it gets too scary we can always close the book. But what happens when we can't close the book? That is horror.

The authors who have contributed to this anthology have mastered the art of conveying horror through the written word. In Christopher Pike's "Collect Call," the going rate is a little *too* costly — it will make you think twice before accepting the charges. Patricia Windsor's "A Little Taste of Death" is a compelling tale explaining *why* your parents told you never to take sweets from strangers. R.L. Stine spins a story of a self-defeated young man who decides to let his hypnotic gaze help erase his problems . . . but it gets a little out of hand. Similarly, Ellen Emerson White tells of an average girl in a quiet New England town, neither of which are what they appear to be.

So sit back and relax. Don't worry, that creaking noise you hear is only the house settling, and that soft fluttering noise is nothing more than the turning of the pages of this book. And those footsteps . . .

— T. Pines

COLLECT CALL I
Christopher Pike

THE PARTY WAS A BUMMER FROM THE START. IT WAS an old story. Janice Adams liked this guy, and Caroline Spencer liked him, and there was only one of him to go around. . . . So there were bound to be problems.

His name was Bobby Walker, and he looked so fine. He had only lived in Chesterock a few months, the town where Janice and Caroline had both grown up. He had appeared the previous May, a month before summer vacation started, just long enough to get all the girls in Chesterock High sweating, and then had vanished until the second week in September, when classes reconvened. His hair was jet-black, his face both stern and quietly amused. He could smile and look serious, but he did not need to smile to make Janice believe he thought their high school was a joke. He had style. He didn't walk with a swagger, but he had a walk Janice was always following around. He wore faded jeans to school, a black leather jacket — the same thing every day. Bobby's jeans were tight, and Janice liked that about him, too.

A guy named Randy Claud was putting on the party. He was student body president, and he was always

having people over to his house. Janice liked Randy —
he was a social climber but he made no secret about
it. He was always telling people how he was going to
vote Republican as soon as he was old enough to buy
fine wine and play the stock market. Randy's dad had
so much money he spoke of his real estate and his son
as a long-term investment in the same breath. Janice
and Randy were old friends.

Janice did *not* like Caroline Spencer. Besides their
rivalry over Bobby Walker, Caroline was a cheerleader. In fact, she was head cheerleader, and she was
about as real as a sitcom in syndication. Caroline actually walked around school on game days talking to
kids with her megaphone. She had a big round mouth.
Everything she said drove Janice crazy. But Caroline
was a blonde babe, too, and that bugged Janice even
more. Especially at the party, and on the way home
from the party.

Yeah, Janice ended up having to give Caroline a ride
home.

It was just a bad night all around.

But that didn't happen until near the beginning of
the end. At the start of the party, and pretty much
through all of it, Janice sat in the corner drinking beer,
talking to Randy Claud, and watching Bobby Walker
slide from one group to the other without ever joining
in on any reindeer games. Bobby carried a beer in his
right hand, and a cigarette on his lower lip, but he
wasn't drinking much, and the same dark smoke
seemed to hug him no matter which way he turned.
Janice burped and raised her beer to her lips. It was

her fourth, but she always counted a six-pack backwards. She felt clearheaded, if not a little depressed.

"I wonder if he ever washes it," Janice said to Randy.

"Tell me what you're talking about, and I'll agree with you," Randy said. He had gone through plenty of beer himself, but he slushed it around inside his mouth before he swallowed. He'd read somewhere that alcohol would not eat his liver without the carbonation to make it hungry. At least that was what he said, but he was always saying something.

"I'm talking about Bobby Walker's leather jacket," Janice said. "He never takes it off. It must be filthy. The same with his pants."

"He takes his pants off," Randy said. "He's in my P.E. class."

"Really? You never told me that."

"You never told me you were in love with him."

Janice coughed. She had been smoking a cigarette earlier, but only because she thought Bobby would want to come over for a light. Her lungs were still virgin, along with the rest of her.

"I'm not in love with him," she said. "Don't say that."

"Then why are you undressing him with your eyes?" Randy asked, fixing his fat glasses on his small nose. He was blind as a bat without his glasses, but could smell a good meal a mile away. He was seventeen and already thirty pounds overweight. "I've been watching you all night, and you've been watching him. Christ, if I had feelings for you they would be hurt."

Janice smiled. "It's lucky for both of us that we're

cold and heartless." She paused. "What does he look like in his shorts?"

Randy laughed. "That's not what you're asking."

Janice hit him. "I don't care what he looks like in the shower!" People looked over. She quickly settled herself down. Bobby was at the far end of the living room. He was touching the leaf on a plant. He had not looked over. "How did this conversation get started?" she grumbled.

"You were talking about washing Bobby's jacket," Randy said. "Why don't you go offer to do it now? He's alone. He might even be lonely. You never know. It's possible."

"I can't just walk up to him," Janice said.

"Why not? I've seen you talk to him at school. He knows you."

"He knows me like he knows our school hallways. I'm just someone he passes by and smiles at."

"You're lucky," Randy said. "I don't think he smiles much. He punched a guy in P.E. the other day. Broke the guy's nose."

Janice grimaced. "What did the guy do to him to get him mad?"

"Called him a name."

"Well, he probably doesn't like being called things."

Randy shrugged and finished his beer. "Yeah, but I think the guy just called him Bobby. Guess Bobby didn't like the way he pronounced it."

"Are you saying he's a jerk?"

Randy waved his hand. "Naah, if you like him he's not a jerk."

"You are diplomatic. Why did you invite him to your party if you don't like him?"

"I didn't," Randy said. "He invited himself."

Janice continued to watch Bobby. He was still admiring the plant. Janice felt a pang of nervousness. Randy was right. If she was going to talk to him, she should do so now. Bobby wouldn't be alone long. He was, after all, the main reason she had come to the party.

"Why?" she asked. "He seems such a loner."

"I don't know," Randy said.

"Maybe he came here to meet somebody."

"It's possible. Anything is possible."

"Would you quit saying that? Here, hold this." Janice gave him her beer and stood. "I'll be back in a few minutes."

Randy patted her on her bottom as she stepped away. "I'm proud of you, Jan. Watch your nose."

"Thank you," she said.

Bobby did not look up as she approached. She took that as a bad sign. Her heart pounded in her chest, and she was thankful for the background music. For some reason — it was really a ridiculous thought — she believed he would have been able to hear the sound of her heart.

"Hi," she said. "Bobby?"

He finally looked up. His eyes were brown; that was supposed to be a warm color. But brown was also the color of the hard ground, and looking at him in that moment, Janice thought for an instant that his eyes were as empty as the barren earth. But then he blinked, and flashed her a smile, and she relaxed a bit.

"Hi," he said. "What's your name?"

She giggled. "Jan. You remember?"

He removed his cigarette from his mouth and put it out in the soil surrounding the plant. She supposed he wasn't a plant lover, after all.

"Oh, yeah," he said. "What are you doing here?"

She shrugged. "Hanging out. How about you? Having fun?"

"No."

"No? That's too bad. That's awful."

He looked about, the line of his strong jaw an unreadable shadow in the dim light. He straightened his black leather jacket over his tapered shoulder with hardly a movement.

"You know what I hate about this scene?" he asked seriously.

"What?"

He leaned closer, and she could feel his breath on the side of her cheek. It was cold. The beer he had been drinking must have been cold.

"The people," he said simply.

"You hate the people? All of them?"

That amused him. His grin grew a size bigger. "All of them except you, Fran."

"Jan."

"Janice," he corrected her.

She giggled again, nervously. "Right. Hey, this is really neat, talking to you. What did you do this summer? I didn't see you around town."

"I was here. I was around."

"But you only came out at night, right?"

He looked her straight in the eye. "You got it, sister."

Then they were rudely interrupted. One of the cheerleaders on the squad — it was Suzy McQueen, and she looked like a Suzy Q with all the white cream pouring out and making a mess of everything — flipped off the music and jumped to the center of the room and started on a loud announcement.

"Hey, everybody!" Ms. Q called. "I hope you're all having a great time. Isn't this party the best? Isn't Randy the greatest for having us all here?" Suzy began to clap her hands vigorously. "Let's hear it for Randy!"

"Jesus," Janice whispered, clapping in slow motion. She noticed Randy hadn't even bothered to stand up.

"I've got an exciting secret," Suzy Q went on. "Tonight is somebody's birthday. Whose is it?" She squealed. "It's a secret! No, just kidding. This is all so great. It's our own star cheerleader's birthday! Caroline Spencer's! Yeah! Where is Caroline? There she is! Come out here, Caroline. Happy birthday to you — come on, everyone!"

Caroline bounced into the center of the room with such blushing shyness that her cheeks looked like they needed a blood transfusion to maintain it. They sang her "Happy Birthday." Janice didn't sing. She silently watched Bobby out of the corner of her eye. He just stood there staring at Caroline with a faint grin on his lips. He stood so still, Janice would have thought he had gone to sleep on his feet if his eyes had not been open.

"It isn't even my birthday," Caroline gushed when the group was done praying for her happiness. "It's tomorrow."

"That doesn't matter," Suzy Q said, giving Caroline an affectionate cheerleader hug. "The party's tonight." Then the two of them laughed together like that was the funniest thing in the world. The rest of the party turned back to their beer and conversation.

"Well, that was special," Janice said to Bobby.

"Yeah," Bobby agreed. Then he did the worst of all possible things. He called Caroline over. "Hey, Carol. I've got a present for you."

This is not happening, Janice thought. *He likes her. No one could like her.*

But that was not true. Any guy who wanted looks would have wanted Caroline. Her long blonde hair had the sun shining through it in a dark room. Her face was as round and sweet as apple pie and ice cream. Her clear skin knew how to hug the right curves. Her green eyes may have been silly, but they could sure dance.

I look like a bookmark next to her, Janice thought as Caroline heeded Bobby's call and turned toward them. That was not true, either. Janice was a pretty girl. Her dark hair may have been short and straight and cut in simple bangs, but the face it framed was full of wit and intelligence. Her features were finer than Caroline's, her skin paler. She had a lovely smile, but the traumas of high school had forced her to add a cynical line to it. Her figure would have been fuller had her stomach been less nervous and her appetite less petite. The clothes she bought in September were usually too loose by October. The date of the party was November 2nd, and as Caroline began to walk toward them, Janice felt unusually haggard. At least Caroline didn't bring Suzy with her.

Of course, Janice had seen Caroline and Bobby talking many times at school. But it had always been for just a few minutes, and Janice had assumed Caroline fit in the same class as herself in Bobby's eyes. Someone to smile at in the hallways and maybe get to know better later.

"You really got me something?" Caroline gushed. Life was just one big gush for her. One of these days, Janice thought, Caroline would gush out her guts.

But it was just a thought, not at all mean.

"Sure did, babe," Bobby said. He reached into the pocket of his black leather jacket. Janice noted how clean the leather looked, how its fresh smell filled the air. Bobby pulled out a tape cassette and handed it to Caroline. "I would have wrapped it," he said. "But you just would have had to open it."

Caroline thought that was a riot. Janice smiled like she cared and she didn't care, trying to be cool. Bobby nodded his head and stared at Caroline without blinking. Caroline studied the cassette.

"This is so nice of you," Caroline said. "Who's this by?"

"The Black Walker," Bobby said. "Do you know him?"

"Yeah," Caroline said, but she frowned, meaning she didn't know the artist at all. "He's one of my favorites."

"He's the best," Bobby said, for once showing enthusiasm. He moved a step closer to Caroline, subtly leaving Janice out of the conversation. "Listen to him and you'll see God."

Caroline giggled. "Does the Black Walker have a video out? I thought I saw him on MTV the other day."

Bobby snorted, not pleased. "The Black Walker doesn't prostitute himself. You can feel him but you can't see him. He's never been on TV."

Caroline rolled with the remark. "That's how it is with real talent," she said gamely. "You never know it's there."

Bobby smiled again, but this time it was definitely a cold smile. He reached out a hand and touched Caroline's shoulder and squeezed it. He may have squeezed hard; Caroline grimaced slightly. "You have fun on your birthday," he said. Then he hurried to Janice and winked. "It's soon," he told her.

"Pardon?" Janice said.

Bobby didn't answer. He just walked away. The two girls watched him go. "Happy birthday," Janice said softly.

"It isn't my birthday yet," Caroline said. She slipped the tape into her pants pocket.

Janice checked her watch — eleven-fifteen. "It's soon," she said, still thinking how cute Bobby Walker was. Cute and mysterious, the way guys are supposed to be.

* * *

The girls didn't talk anymore, not till later, after midnight, when Janice was getting ready to go home. By then she was two beers drunker and feeling like a cockroach that had just been sprayed with Raid.

It was Randy Claud who cornered Janice as she headed for the front door. "Can you give Caroline a ride home?" he asked.

"No," Janice said.

"She needs a ride. Suzy left without her. I don't know why. You live near Caroline. Just give her a ride. You don't have to fight with her."

"I don't have to do anything." Janice looked around. The party had thinned, but there were still at least a dozen viable candidates for the job. She didn't see Caroline. "Why do I have to do it?"

"She asked me if I could ask you," Randy said.

"*She* asked? Caroline hates me. Don't give me that crap."

"She doesn't hate you, and you don't hate her. You're just mad Bobby gave her a present."

That was partly true. She had been hurting since Bobby had ignored her to call Caroline over. She had to blame somebody for the humiliation. Yet Caroline was a pain in the ass under the best of circumstances.

"Where is Bobby?" Janice asked. "Tell him to give her a ride home."

"He's already left," Randy said. "Come on, she doesn't have a ride. You'll be going right by her house."

"She lives two miles off Taylor. That's not near my

house." Janice shook her head, and the surroundings shook with it. She knew already she would have a thumper of a headache tomorrow, and that, too, would be Caroline's fault. "I think I'm drunk," Janice said.

"Then that's more the reason to have Caroline with you," Randy said. "She can drive to your house. Have the windows down. The fresh air will clear your head."

"Where is she?" Janice asked.

"In the bathroom. I think she's throwing up."

Janice snorted. "Right, I should have her drive." She turned toward the door. "Tell her if she wants a ride she'd better be outside in ten seconds or I'll be gone."

Caroline took more than ten seconds to reach Janice's twice rebuilt Mustang, but Janice was still parked, waiting for her car to warm up. The northern California night was brisk. Janice fumbled for her coat as Caroline climbed in.

"Thanks for waiting for me," Caroline said. She smelled of mouthwash and beer, but not vomit.

"No problem." Janice put the car in gear and rolled forward. Chesterock was a small town that went to bed early. There would be few people on the road. Janice reached over and put on her seat belt. She always put it on once she was already going. "Why did Ms. Q leave without you?"

"Who's that?"

"Suzy," Janice said.

Caroline shrugged, staring forward, her head bowed slightly as if she were wearing a fat hat. "She didn't like me flirting with Bobby Walker."

"She likes Bobby?" Janice asked.

"I guess."

"I see," Janice said.

"Why do you call her Ms. Q?" Caroline asked.

"Everyone does." Janice belched. "The name suits her."

Caroline was offended. "I don't think that's nice. She's a friend of mine, you know."

"I can't help who you choose for friends."

"You're in a pleasant mood."

"I'm giving you a ride home, ain't I?"

"I'm grateful."

"Yeah, well, it's no problem."

"You know where I live, don't you?" Caroline asked.

"Out on Taylor."

"Yeah." Caroline looked around the dark dashboard. "Does this car have music?"

Janice nodded. "But the antenna's busted. The radio's lousy. I listen to tapes." Janice paused. "Why don't you put on the tape Bobby gave you?"

Caroline shifted in her seat, fishing it out of her pocket. "He caught me off guard when he gave it to me. I didn't know he cared that much about me."

"It probably cost him a week's salary to buy it."

Caroline fumbled as she tried to slip the cassette into the player. "I really don't think so, Jan. Here it goes. I've never heard of this guy before, have you?"

"Can't say I have."

The music came on. Dark sensual synthesizers. A drum machine in tune with a disembodied spirit. Then a haunting voice as cold as gray snow, and as deep as a forgotten well. Powerful stuff.

"I come from the past.
I eat the night.
I knew you when you were young.
I tell you my story.
But I sleep with a gun.
This is my night, this is your night.
I'm a black walker, babe.
Touch me softly and you get a fright.
The stars are holes in the sky.
The moon is a thorn in the dark.
It drips white light.
Give me the knife.
Let's cut out our eyes.
Yeah, this is our night, this is what's right.
I'm a black walker, babe.
Brush my lips and I bleed you white."

"Wow," Caroline whispered when the song was done. She pushed the stop button. "That's a great song."

"It is." Janice frowned. "The guy sounds kind of familiar, but I could swear I've never heard that song before. I'd remember it."

"Bobby said that Black Walker wasn't on MTV."

"That's true, that's what Bobby said," Janice muttered, suddenly angry at the casual way Caroline was using his name, like they were the oldest and best of friends. It also bugged Janice that she was having to go so far out of her way to take Caroline home, especially since the heat in her car wasn't working, and her ass was freezing off.

A few minutes of silence passed between them, during which time Janice managed to drive out of Chesterock proper. It was such a hole-in-the-wall town. The hilly countryside surrounding the city was covered with gnarled olive trees and parched grass. The road to Caroline's house went up and down, and Janice tried her best to flow with it, but her brain was riding its own seesaw. Topping off her growing resentment of Caroline was a distinct feeling of nausea. The last couple of beers sloshed around in her stomach like they thought they were in a public washer. She didn't want to throw up in her car. She thought biting conversation might distract her.

"So what's it feel like to be head cheerleader?" Janice asked.

"I love it. You get a real rush of energy when you're out in front of all those people."

"What kind of energy?"

Caroline sat up and put a hand to her head. She didn't look so clear-minded herself. "What do you mean?" she asked.

"Is it a sexual energy? A satanic energy? A nuclear energy?"

"I don't know what you're talking about."

"It doesn't matter. I was just wondering what went through your head when you had your megaphone up to your mouth."

"I don't know if that's any of your business."

Janice giggled. "I see I hit a nerve. Don't mess with the girl's megaphone. How kinky you rah girls really are. Why did you want me to give you a ride home, anyway? Why didn't you get one of the gorillas on the football team to take you back?"

Caroline looked over at her in the dark. "You don't like me very much, do you, Jan?"

"I don't know what would give you that idea."

"I wanted to talk to you about Bobby Walker," Caroline said.

"Really? How exciting. Talk to me."

"I don't want you fooling around with him."

Janice was astounded. For a moment she couldn't even respond. But when she found her voice again, it came out far from pleasant. "*You* don't want *me* to do *what* to Bobby? Is that an order? Does God always give such authority to head cheerleaders? Jesus Christ, you are a piece of rock. Why should I do anything you want?"

"I thought I could ask you as a friend."

"But I'm not your friend. You're right, I don't even like you."

Caroline got mad. Janice supposed it was about time. "You're just jealous, that's your problem. You don't like me because I'm pretty and popular."

Janice laughed. "Don't flatter yourself. I don't like you because you're *you.* If you were a flat-nosed geek that took study hall in the janitors' closet I still wouldn't like you. But let's forget about that. Tell me about your plans for Bobby Walker."

Caroline crossed her arms over her chest. "No."

"Have you gone out with him?"

"No. But he's going to ask me out."

"How do you know?" Janice asked.

"I can tell. All the guys want to go out with me."

"Did it ever occur to you that may be the very reason he doesn't want to go out with you? Because you're such a slut?"

Caroline lost it right then. Her reaction caught Janice completely by surprise. Janice didn't expect an all-American apple-pie cheerleader — even a slutty one like Caroline — to reach over and belt her in the face.

The blow was a good one. For a moment the seesaw in Janice's alcohol-fogged brain stopped going up and down and spun in wild circles. By the time it settled back down, two seconds later, Janice had the car heading straight off the road.

They had picked a bad spot to fight. Here the road climbed and turned sharply to the right. Janice's right foot searched wildly for the brake and hit the accelerator again — hard. They raced across the opposing lane and hit the graveled shoulder. They were out in the country for all practical purposes. There were no rails. There was not even an asphalt curb. They went off the shoulder and into the black air.

It was a long way down.

Time did not slow down for Janice, but the reaction of her senses greatly speeded up. She saw and felt everything. Indeed, in her eyes, it was almost as if the dark surroundings had suddenly been lit up by a brilliant moon. As the car slowly turned more vertical than horizontal, she could distinguish the tiniest of stones below them, as well as the big ones. It was the big, sharp ones that concerned her the most. They glinted in her headlights like an unnatural maw. She knew they were going to play hell with the front end of her car. The ground rushed toward them as fast as they rushed toward it, and where they met was filled with confusion.

But before that awful moment, the tape in the player somehow slipped back into place and sang to them. It sang as they fell.

"This is my night, this is your night.
  I'm a black walker, babe."

They hit at a forty-five-degree angle to the ground, but the impact did not entirely stop them; the side they had gone over was almost as steep. They continued on down into the abyss on a wave of screams and shrieks. Janice realized almost indifferently that the two of them were crying their heads off. Maybe it was the alcohol, the shock — a combination of the two. But the accident could have been happening to someone else. Janice felt as if she observed from a distance. Loud sounds thundered up from below them. It was deafening.

Until it stopped. Then the silence rang, the stillness. The tape went off. Janice felt pressure, the hand of the world on top of her. She realized her eyes were closed and opened them. A sharp stab went through the side of her head, and everything flared a bright red. Then normal vision returned and she saw the horror of the situation.

The car had come to a stop at only a slight downward incline. In that respect they were lucky. They had made it all the way to the bottom of the cliff. Unfortunately they were not in one piece. The shatterproof windshield had cracked all over them. Janice felt glass in her hair cutting her face. The engine and everything else that made it work had been pushed practically into their laps. Most of Janice's pain radiated from her knees. They were on fire, and she could feel the liquid warmth of her blood as it seeped down toward her ankles. The space beneath the steering wheel was no more. A strong smell of gasoline choked the air.

Janice looked over at Caroline.

The cheerleader was covered in blood. She had forgotten to put on her seat belt, and Janice had failed to remind her. The top of Caroline's skull had hit the windshield. Her once sunny blonde hair was now a sad late sunset. Janice reached over and touched her, and Caroline's head rolled lazily to the right side, bumping against the mangled metal of what was left of the passenger door. Her green eyes lay open, and they stared at nothing. But Janice wondered if she saw any of these things for real. It was so dark in the ruined car. Maybe she only imagined the details. Maybe it didn't matter. She could see enough to know that Caroline was dead.

"Oh, god," Janice whispered.

What was she supposed to do now? If a car drove by above the driver wouldn't even know someone had

gone off the road. She and Caroline could sit in the
wreck until dawn before help came. She had to get out
of the car somehow. She had to go for help.

*For who? For myself. No one can help Caroline
now.*

Janice used her hands to gently pull up on her knees.
The blood flowing from the cuts on her shins acted as
a lubricant, and she was able to squeeze her legs free
from the pressure of the collapsed steering column
without hurting herself any worse. At first her lower
legs were partially numb, and she worried she had
damaged the nerves and would be unable to walk. But
as she swung them over to the side of the exploded
door on her left — despite the damage to it the door
handle was still intact and the door opened easily —
and massaged her calves, the feeling returned. The
pain was still there but it was decreasing swiftly.

She glanced above her at the dark shadow of the
edge of the road. She didn't relish the thought, but
she should be able to climb back up there. She probably
wouldn't have to walk any further, though. Eventually
someone would come along, and she would be able to
flag them down.

*Then what? They drive me to the hospital. An am-
bulance comes for Caroline. And then they take me
to the police station and lock me up.*

It was amazing, given the desperate circumstances,
how clearly the sequence of events unfolded in her
mind. But a fool could have told her she was in deep
trouble. She didn't know exactly what her blood alcohol level was, but there was no way it was below

the legal limit. She had been driving drunk, and she had killed someone. It was as simple as that. The police were never going to believe that she had gone off the road because Caroline had socked her in the face. Sure, they would say, blame the dead cheerleader. Just before they locked her in her cell.

"But it was your fault," Janice muttered, glancing over at Caroline, who looked in no shape to argue with her. Janice knew she should feel bad for the girl. Caroline may have been a flake, but she hadn't been an evil person. She'd had her life in front of her. Hell, she probably would have got rid of her megaphone by the time she was twenty-one. Still, Janice couldn't make herself feel too sorry for her. Caroline was beyond pain, and Janice was feeling too sorry for herself. She was eighteen, seven months from graduating from high school, and she had just screwed up the rest of her life.

"I wish you had been driving," Janice told dead Caroline. "Things would be so much simpler now."

Then the *idea* came to her.

She could move Caroline into the driver's seat.

She could tell the police it had been Caroline's fault. Why not? Caroline wouldn't mind.

Oh, but there might be problems. From the splattering of the blood and the wounds to Caroline's body — never mind her own wounds — the police might be able to figure out that a switch had been made. On the other hand, there was blood all over the place, her's and Caroline's. Would the police look that close? Would they have any reason to? She could call

Randy as soon as possible and get him to back her up that Caroline had been driving when they left his house. She could use the excuse that she had drunk too much beer to drive. God knows the police would be able to verify that part of the story.

It would work. It had to work. And it would be fair. The whole thing had been Caroline's fault to begin with.

Janice climbed out of the car and groaned as her legs accepted her weight. Dark stains seeped through her once-white pants. She looked up. There were no headlights on the road. There were no stars in the sky. But the cold was still there, and she shivered as she turned back to the mortal wreckage inside the front of the car. She had never handled a body before.

The first thing Janice felt when she went to take hold of Caroline was the tape Bobby Walker had given her. It lay in Caroline's lap. It must have popped out of the player on impact. Not knowing where to toss it, Janice slipped it into her back pocket. She remembered how it had come on as they had gone off the road, and she shivered once more, although she did not know why.

Janice shifted the gears of her car with a stick on the steering wheel. The space between the passenger seat and the driver's seat was, therefore, relatively unobstructed. Janice was surprised by how light Caroline felt as she took hold of the dead girl's shoulders. Caroline had kept herself in excellent shape. The top of Caroline's skull rolled and hit Janice on the chin as Janice pulled Caroline halfway into the driver's seat.

"Damn," Janice swore.

Caroline's legs were stuck beneath the crushed dashboard in much the same manner Janice's own legs had been stuck. Janice had to lean all the way into the car, pressing her chest across Caroline's lap, to pull Caroline's legs free. Caroline's bloody hair hung on top of her as she worked. The flesh on Caroline's left leg let go of a sickly tearing sound as Janice gave it one last hard yank.

"Sorry," Janice muttered.

Finally Janice had Caroline behind the wheel. Janice was debating exactly how to position the body when she again noticed the strong gasoline smell. Naturally she had seen dozens of movies where cars had gone off cliffs and exploded. When they had first jumped the edge of the road, she had briefly wondered if that was to be their fate. But since they hadn't blown up at impact, she had dismissed the idea. Yet this smell, this tension in the air, as if the fiery elements were alive and gathering. . . . it was almost as if something were about to explode.

Almost. And a little more.

Janice suddenly, instinctively, took a step back from the car.

Two steps. Staring at dead Caroline. Three steps.

The car exploded.

There was a blinding orange light and then an incredible shove. Janice literally felt herself lifted off the ground and thrown back through the air. The orange light mushroomed before her vision as she landed hard on her butt. Scalding air singed the skin on her face, and she was forced to clench her eyes shut.

Yet something forced them back open.

Screams. Caroline screaming as she burned to death.

To death?

Janice had not felt Caroline's pulse.

She had not even listened to Caroline's breathing. Not closely.

And of course Caroline had still been alive.

When Janice opened her eyes she saw the most savage of human sufferings. Every part of Caroline was on fire: her hair, her face, her chest, and her legs. Every part was trying to get out of the car. Thrashing and kicking and screaming. Janice thought Caroline would never stop making that awful sound. The blood on Caroline turned black, and smoke spun through the ash of her disintegrating hair. Janice clenched her eyes shut again and prayed that Caroline would just die.

Die. Die. Stop screaming!

Caroline stopped, finally. Janice sat in the rocks and the dirt and listened to the fire as it ate up the evidence. Now there would be no way to blame her for what had happened. Not that she was guilty.

I should have been pulling her from the car rather than pulling her into the driver's seat.

The night was filled with painful irony.

Not long after, an ambulance and the police arrived. They had seen the smoke.

Janice was at the hospital. The overhead light shone bright and white. The gown they had issued her was drafty, and the examination table beneath her bottom was cold. Her doctor had the wonderful name of Please.

Dr. Please, please.

The doctor finished putting bandages on her knees. He was a tall thin man with a bald head that looked like something that had been screwed on at birth. He was cheerful enough, however. The officer present was named Frank. Janice didn't know if it was his first name or his last. Officer Frank carried a notepad and a ball-point pen. Young and serious, he was handsome enough for a daytime soap. Janice thought he believed her story, but he was going over the details for the second time.

"Let's start again just before you went off the road," Officer Frank said. "Was there anything that startled Caroline? Anything you or she did that could have distracted her?"

"No," Janice said, thinking to keep it simple and stupid.

"Did she doze off in any way?"

"We were talking. We were both awake."

"What were you talking about?" Officer Frank asked.

Janice shrugged. "Boys. School. Stuff."

"You weren't arguing or anything?"

"No."

"You're sure?"

"We didn't know each other that well," Janice said. "We had nothing to argue about."

"Then Caroline simply drove off the road?" Officer Frank asked.

"Ouch!" Janice groaned. Dr. Please was adjusting the bandage on her right knee. She had only needed three stitches on each leg. The scratches on her face and head had only required a good cleaning. Dr. Please did not believe she would have any lasting scars.

"Sorry," Dr. Please said.

"The road turns there," Janice told the policeman. "She didn't exactly drive off the road. She just didn't turn to stay on the road."

"Do you know how much Caroline had drunk at the party?" Officer Frank asked.

"No," Janice said.

"Then why did you feel confident letting her drive instead of you?"

Janice kept her expression neutral. She had already called Randy and told him to back up her story that Caroline had been driving, should the need arise. He had immediately known what the deal was, and was not happy about it, but he was willing to support her. Anyway, he didn't know for a fact that Caroline had not been driving.

"I knew how many beers I had drunk," Janice said. "Eight or nine. Caroline wanted to drive. I let her. I thought my head would clear by the time we reached her house."

"I'm sorry," Officer Frank said sympathetically. "I know you've explained all this before. It's my job to get everything straight."

"I don't mind," Janice said. "Caroline drove off the

side. We crashed at the bottom, and I was thrown clear, and a moment later the car exploded." She paused to wipe away a tear. She wasn't sure if it was for herself or Caroline. "That's all I can tell you," she said.

Officer Frank lowered his head and spoke softly. "Was she unconscious when the car caught fire?"

Janice nodded sadly. "I'm sure she didn't feel a thing."

Officer Frank nodded in understanding and closed his notepad. Dr. Please finished with her bandages and stood back up. Together the two men helped her off the examination table. Janice winced once more in pain. Guilt weighed heavily on her heart, but she felt relieved as well. She was getting away with it.

"You've had a hard night, but you're one lucky girl," Dr. Please said.

"Yeah," Officer Frank said. "If you hadn't been thrown from the car, there would have been no one there to save you."

Janice felt a shiver go up her spine at the officer's remark. She thought of the old refrain — that some-one had just walked across her grave. But it was Caroline's grave they would be digging, not her's. She had made certain of that.

"I feel lucky," she agreed, but the words sounded hollow in her ears.

She ended up having to change back into her blood-stained pants. It was either that or go home in the hospital gown. Her parents were out of town for the weekend. Officer Frank took her back to her place in his squad car. They spoke little along the way. Janice did not know the time. Her watch had not cracked in the accident, but it was not working nevertheless.

Inside the empty house she was quick to get out of her disgusting clothes. The tape Bobby Walker had given Caroline fell on the floor as she pulled off her pants, and she set it aside. She made her way into the shower and turned on the water hot and hard. There was still blood in her hair; she didn't care if she soaked the bandages on her knees. They could always be replaced.

Back in the kitchen, while drying off with a towel, she noticed the answering-machine light blinking on and off. There was a message. It was odd; she had not noticed the light when she had come in, and she had undressed right beside the machine. She pushed the play button and turned toward the refrigerator. She was dying for something to drink.

Caroline's voice spoke at her back.

Janice stopped dead in her tracks.

"Hi, Janice, this is Caroline Spencer. I was wondering if you could give me a ride to the party tonight? Please give me a call when you get in. I'd really appreciate it."

"Mother Mary," Janice whispered, her heart pounding in her chest.

Of course there was a simple explanation. Caroline had called her earlier, before the party. The cheerleader said as much on the message. Janice quickly crossed to the answering machine and replayed the tape. Her heart kept right on pounding. Her parents' machine always noted the time a call came in. But there was no time attached to Caroline's message. Caroline could have called at any time.

So what? She must have called after I left for the party, but before she arrived at Randy's house. It doesn't matter that she was already there when I got there. I didn't go straight to Randy's. I stopped at the store and bought chips for the party.

That still didn't explain why there was a message at all from Caroline. The cheerleader had not called her once during the four years they had gone to school together. Then again, Caroline had wanted to drive home with her. Maybe Caroline had wanted to talk about their rivalry over Bobby Walker even before the party.

Janice replayed the message one more time. There was no mistaking the voice — it was Caroline's.

Janice turned off the ringer on the phone. She was tired. Tired of having to think. She lowered the volume on the answering machine. She didn't want anyone else's calls to disturb her that night. She made her way back into the bathroom. She would finish drying her hair and brush her teeth and hit the sack. Tomorrow she would take care of tomorrow.

Ten minutes later she was lying in bed when she heard the answering machine clicking in the other room. Someone was calling. It didn't matter, she told herself. It was probably just Randy. The machine clicked a minute more as the tape slowly wound and rewound. Then there was silence in the darkness, except for her beating heart. Try as she might, she could not make herself relax.

A minute later she was in the kitchen checking to see who had called.

It was not possible.

"Janice, this is Caroline again. I *really* need a ride to the party. Can't you give me one? You're my only hope. If you don't come get me, I won't get to go. Please, Janice, call me right back. I know you're there."

When the message was done, Janice stood and stared at the machine as if it were a coiled snake ready to bite. She was running out of explanations, and her nerves were running out of resiliency. Her hand shook as she reached over and turned off the machine. Someone had to be playing a trick on her. The message had not been on the tape when she had arrived home, of that she was certain. Someone — one of the girls on the cheerleader squad perhaps — must be able to fake Caroline's voice. The person must have heard what happened and be calling out of spite.

I should listen to the message again. I know Caroline's voice. I'll be able to tell it's fake.

But Janice did not turn the machine back on. She had listened to the first message three times, and it had sounded exactly like Caroline. She worried the second one would sound no different.

But that wasn't her *real* worry.

Caroline's calling me. Caroline's dead. Jesus Christ.

Janice left the light on in the kitchen and went back

into her bedroom and crawled under the covers. She hugged the blankets tight around her head so that the bogeyman in the dark corner couldn't see her, hear her, or even smell her. But the bogeyman was in the kitchen, not the corner, and she was in bed less than fifteen minutes when she heard the machine clicking again. She sat up with a bolt.

"No you don't!" she screamed. "I turned you off! You cannot take any messages!"

The machine kept on clicking, the tape spinning.

Janice got out of bed and ran into the kitchen. She switched on the phone and picked up the receiver. She got a dial tone. She studied the answering machine. The message light was blinking. It had turned itself back on. Somehow. A power surge. Some strange way. Janice reached to press the play button. Then she stopped.

I don't want to hear what was said. It will only scare me. I am scared enough. I should go to the garage and get a hammer and break the machine into a thousand pieces.

Janice pressed the play button. She had to know what she already knew. This time Caroline sounded angry.

"Janice, you know who this is. Pick up the goddamn phone. We're going to the party and you're taking me. There's no way I can drive myself. I have a fever. I'm burning up. If you don't come with me, I'll drive off the road. You got that, girl? Come get me now."

The message ended with a loud click.

Caroline had slammed down the phone.

But it had been her. Ms. Megaphone. Absolutely.
She's alive. She survived the fire.

It was the only logical explanation besides insanity.
Janice would rather believe the doctor and police had
lied to her than admit her own mind had gone over
the cliff with her Mustang. It happened all the time in
the papers that people got burned over ninety percent
of their body and survived. The people at the hospital
must have been trying to trick her into incriminating
herself.

*But if Caroline is alive she should be too injured to
call.*

There was only one way to settle the issue. She
would have to return to the hospital. She would have
to see with her own eyes the burnt patient or the burnt
corpse.

Janice put her bloodstained pants back on, her shirt,
and her jacket. She reasoned that she wanted to wear
the same clothes because they were sitting within
arm's reach on the floor. But the bloody legs had already begun to dry, and the pants cracked and poked
at her skin as she moved. She even put her broken
watch back on, for all the good it would do her. She
pulled the tape from the answering machine before she
left. She didn't want to come home to any new
messages.

Her parents had left town in her dad's car. Janice
drove her mom's car to the hospital. It was brand new,
and the radio and cassette player were of high quality.
But she left them both off.

The hospital parking lot was almost deserted. Janice

entered through the emergency doors. At first Janice thought the whole place was empty. There was no one sitting in the waiting rooms, and the nurses' station had been left neglected. The silence of the place was uncanny, as if all patients and personnel alike had died since she left. Janice moved down a long bright hall soundlessly. She was turning a corner when a hand reached out and touched her shoulder. Janice practically jumped out of her socks.

"Can I help you?" asked an old nurse. She was dressed in wrinkles and white. Her big nose hung over her pruned mouth like a witch's beak.

"Where is everybody?" Janice asked nervously.

"They're here, those that are supposed to be." The nurse gestured to Janice's messy pants. "What happened to you, dear?"

"I was here earlier. I was in a car accident with another girl. I came back to see how she was doing."

The woman didn't hesitate or show an ounce of sympathy. "She's dead."

Janice forced a smile. "I don't think so. Caroline's been calling me since I got home."

The old woman cocked her head to the side thoughtfully. "Was Caroline her name? I don't think that was her name."

"Oh, yes, she was a friend of mine." Janice added, "She drove off the road."

The nurse nodded. "I know the driver of the car was killed." She glanced down at her watch. "I have to see about a patient. You go home, you hear? There's no one here for you to see."

At that, the old woman walked away, and Janice was left alone in the empty hall with her fear. Was she surprised? She had been the one to see Caroline burn to death.

Yet who had called?

A question without an answer. Perhaps it was the mystery alone that led Janice's feet to the elevator, that made her hand push the button to the basement. The basement — where the morgue in a hospital was usually located. Perhaps it was another kind of feeling that made Janice want to see Caroline.

"I don't think that was her name."

Janice found the morgue without difficulty. It lay behind heavy twin green doors. Inside was cold and damp and filled with bad smells and gleaming stainless-steel tables, where Janice knew they cut open bodies and took things out. There was no butcher on duty. Janice's stomach rolled with unpleasant emotions and sensations. On a table on the left lay a six-foot-long green body bag.

It was occupied.

Janice stepped slowly to the table. She raised a hand to touch it, and then pulled back the hand. What was she doing? Was she going to open the bag and try to piece together what was left of Caroline's face? What if it wasn't even Caroline, but an old drunk who had rolled out of a slimy alley? The ordeal of unzipping the bag might prove nothing. Except how much she had left in her stomach to vomit.

It was then Janice spotted the tag at the top of the bag. It was tied to the easy-body-bag-carry-handle by an elastic string. Janice sighed with relief. She would just have to read the name on the tag. She reached over and held it up in the fake phosphorescent light.

JANICE ADAMS

"Sure," Janice said, and she softly laughed.

They had got their names confused upon admission. Janice could imagine the nurses and doctors hurriedly calling back and forth when the wreckage from the accident had been brought in. Was that the girl with the scraped knees or the one without any skin left? It was a simple mistake to make, Janice supposed. Caroline was dead and bagged. There had to be someone at school who had heard about the accident, and who could mimic Caroline's voice perfectly. The mystery was settled.

But maybe I should unzip the bag and look. Just a little.

"Why?" Janice asked her own mind.

No answer came to her. Only a deep cold feeling. As cold as the stainless steel where the body bag lay. She backed a step away from the body bag, just as she had backed away from the car before it had exploded in her face. Something was ready to blow up again in front of her. She could feel it. But she didn't know what it was. She didn't want to know. All of a sudden, she just wanted to get out of the hospital as quickly as possible.

Janice ran from the morgue. She ran all the way to the car, without seeing the old nurse on the way out.

Her mother's car started without a hitch, and soon she was flying down the road. Yet she did not know where she was heading. Suddenly the area looked alien, as if she had taken a wrong turn into the twilight zone when she had read the name, her name, on the body bag. She turned to the left, the right, searching for a familiar landmark. She didn't recognize anything!

I'm upset. That's all it is. I'll put music on. I'll calm down. I'll find my way home.

Janice stuck out her right hand and searched for a tape on the passenger seat. Her mother usually kept a few lying around. Her fingers chanced upon one, and she slipped it into the cassette player. It was the tape Bobby Walker had given Caroline. How odd. . . . Janice could remember putting it into her back pocket when she had moved Caroline into the driver's seat, but could not imagine how it had got into her mother's car. The only tape she had brought with her from home had been the one in the answering machine.

The Black Walker was in a dark mood.

"I come from the past.
I eat the night.
I knew you when you were young.
I tell you my story.
But I sleep with a gun.
This is my night, this is your night.
I'm a black walker, babe.
Touch me softly and you get a fright."

Yet all of a sudden Janice remembered how, when she had returned home from the hospital the first time, she had laid Bobby's tape on top of the answering machine. She had just set it there, after glancing at the machine to make sure no one had called.

And no one had called. Until a few minutes later.

"The stars are holes in the sky.
The moon is a thorn in the dark.
It drips white light.
Give me the knife.
Let's cut out our eyes."

But was that all there was to it? She had been anxious to get out of her bloodstained clothes. She had pulled them off right there in the kitchen, standing next to the answering machine. Then what had she done? She had gone into the shower and washed off the blood.

Then the calls from Caroline had started.

Wait a second. When I noticed the first call, Bobby's tape was no longer on top of the machine. I would have seen it.

"Yeah, this is our night, this is what's right.
I'm a black walker, babe.
Brush my lips and I bleed you white."

"Oh, god," Janice whispered.

She repeated the point to herself. The only tape she

had taken from home, when coming to the hospital the second time, *had been the tape from the machine.* The tape with Caroline's messages.

The tape she must have put in the answering machine.

The tape Bobby had given Caroline.

But why did I put it in? What did I expect to hear?

Messages maybe.

The tape was just full of messages.

The song ended and no new song began.

Oh, but Caroline — she was still there.

The car cassette player began to talk to Janice.

"Hi, Janice, this is Caroline. I'm glad you got my messages and can give me a ride. I know it's been a while since you've been to my house so why don't I give you directions? First, get on Winston and take it out of town . . ."

Janice passed a street sign. She was on Winston. The houses were thinning. She was heading out of town. She could hear the tape playing, the faint hiss of emptiness. Caroline had paused. For the moment. Then there was more. . . .

"When you come to Rayon, Janice, make a right. You'll take Rayon all the way out to Taylor. But you've got to watch those roads. They're dangerous at night. . . ."

Janice spotted Rayon. She made a right. She didn't know why. She didn't want to. It was just that none of the streets looked quite right, and she was lost, and she wanted to get home.

But this is insane. Caroline is not taking me home. She is taking me to her home.

And where did Caroline live now? In a body bag? Janice didn't want to go there.

"I don't think that was her name."

Janice had to concentrate on the road. It had narrowed and was going up and down. A dangerous ride indeed. An eerie ten minutes went by. Then she was out in the country, in the middle of nowhere. It was dark. But soon, she reasoned, the sun should be coming up. She glanced at her broken watch. It had begun to tick again. Ten to one.

Ten minutes before the car exploded.

What a coincidence. Caroline spoke to her one last time.

"If you get lost, Janice, you can always stop and look around. My place is not that hard to find. Thanks again for remembering to come get me. You don't know how much it means to me."

The road abruptly rose again and turned sharply to the right. Janice pulled onto the shoulder of the road. She parked and got out. For the first time in a long time she recognized exactly where she was. The night was black as spilt ink, but it was as if every little rock and bush in the surroundings were illumined by a hidden moon.

She was where they had gone off the road.

Janice crept to the edge of the cliff and peered down.

Where is the wreckage? They couldn't have gotten rid of it so quickly.

Not only was there no burnt car at the bottom of the ravine, there was no sign that an accident had even occurred on the spot. Puzzled, Janice carefully began to climb down the slope. The way was steep, but numerous jagged stones gave her ample footholds. Her puzzlement grew the deeper she went. She was sure she had the right spot, and she clearly remembered the debris the explosion had spewed over the area: the burst tires, the shattered glass, the fried metal — the garbage should have still been there. The police wouldn't have gone over the spot with a vacuum cleaner, for god's sake.

On the other hand — and this is what scared Janice the most — she felt no confusion at all. Everything was exactly as it was supposed to be. What did she expect? She had followed a goddamn ghost's directions to the place.

Janice paused to check her watch again. Still ticking toward one.

It was only right then, in that moment, and for no other reason, that Janice believed that Caroline was not dead. The name on the tag on the body bag came back to haunt her. How sad, she thought, that her own name could fill her with such dread.

A flicker of headlights shone above her. The sound of an engine.

Janice turned toward the cliff and looked up.

A car came out of the night. Off the side of the road, it sailed into the air above her head, and the screams of its occupants filled the air. Two terrified girls, plunging into god only knew what destiny. Janice watched them fall with an odd mixture of calm and agony. She could hear a tape in the car playing above the screams. Bobby's present. The car flew directly over Janice's head. Bobby must have known a thing or two when he had given the tape to Caroline. This was their night, this was what was right.

The car crashed. It did not explode. Yet Janice knew it was only a matter of time. Of seconds. She hurried down the remainder of the steep embankment. There were two girls trapped, and she had to save them.

Janice went to the passenger side first. The girl was bloody and unconscious, but Janice could tell in an instant that she was alive. She was, after all, breathing. The faint rasp of her laboring lungs reached Janice's ears as if through a psychic back door where important details could be known with a certainty beyond reason. Janice pulled open the wrecked door and took hold of the girl's limp form. There was a sudden rush of joy into the moment. Into Janice's heart. It was the first joy she had known all night.

Caroline. It's Caroline. I can save her.

Janice lifted Caroline into her arms with an ease that made no sense and carried her away from the car. She set her down gently against a boulder, then turned for the other girl, the driver, who also appeared to be unconscious.

But the girl inside woke up just as Janice reached the car. The girl stretched to open the door — just as Janice tried to do likewise. All Janice wanted to do was let the girl out. Her efforts proved counterproductive. The door handle wasn't damaged. It was one of those things — the two of them kept getting in each other's way. Janice would let go of the door handle to give the girl a chance to do it alone, and then the girl would do the same. Then Janice would try the handle again just as the girl tried it again. The end result was that the girl inside the car could not get out of the car. And Janice knew that was not a good thing. She could smell the gasoline in the air, and naturally, at the same moment, the girl inside the car also noticed the smell.

"I don't think that was her name."

Janice didn't think so, either.

Slowly, but with the practice of an act that had been done perfectly before, Janice began to back away from the car. The girl inside had frozen. Then her head turned. No, it *whirled* in the direction of Janice. She saw her, they saw each other. Something passed between them, an understanding, but it did not have to pass any further than the light between an object and a mirror. Janice saw the point of the whole night in that instant, even if the girl inside the car couldn't — as of yet — see through her eyes. It was, simply, to get Caroline out of the car first.

But that was not exactly true. No one would save Caroline, Janice thought, not according to the accounts that would be written. She would appear to have been thrown to safety. An unconscious recipient of good luck. As for the other girl, the driver . . . well, she should have known better than to drink and drive.

The car exploded. It didn't send Janice flying far away, though. It seemed to suck her inside, where it was warm, hot. Hot as a hell she no longer deserved.

Janice burned. Once more her wish had come true. All the evidence was destroyed.

Caroline awoke to the sound of someone calling her name.

"Caroline? Wake up, Caroline. You're all right."

I must not be all right if he has to tell me I am.

Caroline opened her eyes. A tall, bony, middle-aged doctor towered above her. She was in a hospital bed. White bandages covered her arms, and from the feel of it, her head as well. She tried to sit up, and a sharp pain went from one ear to the other, right through the center of her skull. She quickly lay back down.

"It would be better if you tried not to move," the doctor said.

"What happened?" Caroline whispered.

"You were in a car accident. Your friend was taking you home from a party and she drove off the road."

"Janice . . . How is Janice?"

"When the car crashed, you were thrown free. But Janice wasn't so fortunate." The doctor lowered his head. "The car exploded, and she was killed."

"Oh, god." Caroline's eyes filled with tears. "Did she burn to death?"

"The police believe she was knocked out by the impact. I'm sure she didn't feel a thing."

"That's good," Caroline whispered, although she didn't know if that was true. The doctor reached down and squeezed her arm.

"This must be very hard for you," he said.

"We weren't that close, but, yes, it's hard." Caroline

sighed, then added, not sure even where her words were coming from. "She was a good girl. She was the kind who would do something for you if you really needed it. Do you know what I mean?"

"I do indeed." The doctor glanced at his watch. "It's two in the afternoon. You've been asleep all day. Your parents have been here since late last night, but they just stepped out for a bite of lunch. I could see you were coming around and told them you were going to be fine. But there is a young man here who's anxious to see you. He's been here all night as well."

Caroline was dumbfounded. She knew tons of boys at school, but she could not imagine that any one of them cared enough about her to stay up all night.

"What's his name?" she asked.

"Bobby Walker. He can come in and see you for ten minutes, if you'd like, but that will have to be it. You need rest now more than anything. You have a bad concussion and several broken ribs."

"Bobby," Caroline whispered, amazed. Hadn't she and Janice been arguing about Bobby just before they crashed? Vaguely Caroline could recall them fighting about something. "I would like to see him."

"Fine," the doctor said, moving for the door. Caroline had a room all to herself. "It may be a few minutes before I see him. I have to check on a patient next door. By the way, my name is Dr. Please if you ever want to have me paged."

Caroline smiled faintly, dabbing at her tears. "Dr. Please, please."

The doctor grinned. "I hear it all the time." He

opened the door. "I'll see you soon, Caroline."

"Thanks," Caroline said. Dr. Please left, and she was alone with her aches and pains, and her sorrow over Janice. She wished to god she hadn't insisted Janice give her a ride home. The poor girl had drunk too much beer to see straight, never mind drive. A fool could have seen that.

Caroline spotted the phone on the stand beside her bed. She wondered if many people knew about her accident. She doubted if any of them would have called to see how she was doing, but, just in case, she decided to pick up the messages on her answering machine. She still couldn't believe Bobby Walker had stayed up all night for her. He must really like her. Not many people did, she realized sadly. She was the most unpopular popular person in school.

She had two messages. The first one was from Bobby Walker.

"Hi, Carol, this is Bobby. Wanted to know if you loved the tape. If it did something for you. I'll see you soon, if you're still alive, that is."

Caroline was confused. When had he left the message? Immediately after the party? Before he knew about the accident? That must have been the case. It would have been in extremely bad taste to say what he had when she was lying unconscious in the hospital. Yet it wasn't exactly a sweet message even if he hadn't known about the accident. His voice had sounded cold, like the voice of the singer on the tape he had given her.

In fact, it hit her right then, he sounded *exactly* like the singer.

Bobby Walker and the Black Walker. Interesting.

There was a long pause on the answering-machine tape.

The second message was from Janice.

"Hi, Caroline, this is Janice. You called me so I'm calling you. But don't try calling me back. I can't answer the phone. The fire burned off my hands. But don't worry, I'll be in touch . . . soon.

Caroline dropped the phone and screamed. She was still screaming when Bobby Walker entered the hospital room.

He was smiling.

LUCINDA
Lael Littke

I HAVE THIS MEMORY OF LUCINDA. *IT'S LIKE A
dream, and in it I'm ten years old again, and I'm
hiding in some bushes watching her. She's standing
on the edge of the lake, dressed in her red graduation
robe because it's commencement night and a bunch of
the graduates are having a party there at the lake.*

Lucinda is quarreling with my brother Brandon.

*"If you don't come back to me," she's saying, "I'll
swim down to my secret place and stay."*

*Brandon just stands there miserably, his shoulders
hunched.*

*Lucinda scrubs at her face with her sleeve. "It's
Holly, isn't it?" she cries. "I knew I couldn't trust her.
Or you."*

*"Well, what about you and Kevin?" Brandon de-
mands. "Seems to me you've been a pretty hot item."*

*"I just turned to him because you left me!" Lucinda
sobs for a moment, then flings herself out into the lake,
wading out where it's deep, her red robe floating on
the water around her.*

*Brandon watches her, then turns his back and walks
away.*

51

*Lucinda changes her mind and starts to come out.
Suddenly there is something there in the water with
her.*

That's where my memory fades away. I was just a
kid and couldn't deal with whatever it was I saw.

Lucinda disappeared that graduation night and
was never found. Brandon told everyone she'd
drowned herself, but I think that someone made her
drown.

I never told anybody that I'd been there. That other
person could have been any of the seniors at the party.
But then again, it could have been my brother Brandon.

Now it was six years later, and Brandon and I were
standing in that same spot on the lakeshore. But the
lake wasn't there anymore. After several years of
drought it had shrunk to a murky puddle off in the
distance.

We hadn't been there to see it happen. Mom and
Brandon and I had moved away soon after that tragic
graduation night, away to Newland where Brandon
could get therapy to relieve the guilt that kept him
from sleeping and made him babble terrible things in
the dark. He said *he'd* been responsible for Lucinda's
death, that he'd turned his back on her when she'd
needed him. He said she was down there under the
lake in her secret place, waiting for him to come get
her.

Mom was dead now, and Brandon and I had moved
back to Lake Isadora.

I knew Brandon had come back to look for Lucinda, and I didn't like it. But what could I do? I was only sixteen, and Brandon was twenty-three. He was the adult. He called the shots.

But if he became obsessed with Lucinda again, if he totally flipped out, what would become of *me*?

He seemed rational enough as he gazed out over the broad valley where the lake had been.

"Look over there, Kate," he said. "That's where I started school."

He was pointing to a low cement foundation down in the lake bed. There'd been an old town in the valley before the river had been dammed and the whole area flooded as a conservation measure. The buildings had been moved to the new town site when Brandon was a child, but the foundations were still there, like the stumps of a cut-down forest. They'd been under the lake for years, until the waters receded.

"We used to dive down and explore the old streets," Brandon went on thoughtfully. "Lucinda and I and Holly. Holly was such a great diver."

Now we were getting into dangerous territory. It had been the diving that had started the split between Lucinda and Brandon. Lucinda had lost interest in exploring the underwater remains of the town, but Brandon kept on going down there with Holly.

"Brandon," I said, "let's go home. We've still got lots of unpacking to do."

"No." He shook his head. "Not yet," he said softly. "Let me show you where our house was before it was moved."

He started down the dusty path that led to the floor of the valley.

I didn't want to go down there, not now in the twilight of the late summer day. Darkness hung in the tall stands of willows that had grown up all over the valley except where there'd been pavement. A slight breeze rattled the dry leaves, dead now because of lack of water.

It was an eerie place, and I couldn't leave Brandon there alone.

I had another flash of memory as we walked between the clumps of willows on what had once been a street, our footsteps silent in the deep silt left by the lake. I remembered a painting Holly had done after she and Lucinda and Brandon had dived down to the old town. She'd painted willows, tall, pallid sticks with long, twisted leaves floating in the water. Behind them were the spectral shapes of buildings that were no longer there, but worst of all were the faces caught in the willows, faces with huge, vacant eyes and open mouths.

She'd called the painting "Drowned Town."

I peered at the dark dead willows as Brandon and I walked through them now. What if we found Lucinda there, or what was left of her, caught in the brush like those faces? Lucinda, in her red graduation robe, her flesh gone, and her long, blonde hair tangled with leaves.

Perhaps Brandon was thinking the same thing because he began talking then, in a soft, feathery voice. "The willows grew up *after* the town was dead," he said. "Did you know, Kate, that they grow under water? We'd dive down here, and we'd see them growing, waving and swaying in the currents." He shifted his gaze to me, and I saw that his eyes were not quite focused. "Do you believe what they say about how hair grows on a dead body?"

I grabbed his arm. "It's time to go home, Bran. We'll come back here tomorrow, during the day, when we can see."

He pulled his arm away. "No. Lucinda's here."

"Bran, listen." He was walking so fast I had to trot to keep up to him. "If you'll just wait for a while, they'll find her. When the waters drop down some more, she'll be there. Remember that article Keith sent?"

My friend, Keith, with whom I'd exchanged a few letters since we'd left Lake Isadora, had sent us an article about the disappearing lake. It had said the lake was yielding up all of its dark secrets, and it told about a small airplane that had been missing for over ten years. When the waters dropped, it was found there in the lake bed, with two skeletons still sitting in the cockpit.

I think it was that article that gave Brandon the idea of moving back to Lake Isadora and looking for Lucinda.

I wondered why Keith had sent it. He must have known it would disturb Brandon. Maybe that was the reason. Lucinda had been Keith's sister, and I wasn't at all sure his family had ever forgiven Brandon for what happened.

Brandon didn't say anything now, but he slowed his

stride, peering through the willows at the old foundations that stood well back from the street.

"Here," Brandon said suddenly. "This was where Lucinda's house was."

Walking slowly toward the stumpy foundation, he climbed five porch steps leading upward to nowhere and stood staring down into what must have once been a basement.

"It's here somewhere," he whispered.

I walked along one side of the foundation, barely able to see over the cement wall into what looked like a huge open grave. The old basement was filled with brush and decayed tires and other debris. A snake slithered through the deep silt on the floor and disappeared into some hidden cavity in the foundation.

I shivered. "What do you mean, Bran? What is it that's here?"

"Lucinda's secret place." His voice was wispy and dry, like the rattle of the willow leaves.

He used to babble about her secret place, back in those days when he was crazy with anguish about her death. He said she'd talked about it when they were kids playing together. But she never showed him where it was.

Maybe I should look for that secret place, too, I thought. If I found it and Lucinda was really there, Brandon *couldn't* have put her there. He didn't even know where it was.

But where could I begin to look? I peered through the gloom at the area around the old foundation.

That's when I saw it. It was a damp spot in the dry,

dry dirt. An underground spring, maybe? I stamped at it, my feet making hollow thuds as if I were tromping on a drum.

The dust underneath puffed up, showing it was just surface dampness, as if somebody had stood there dripping after coming out of a rainstorm.

Or out of the lake.

There was something else, too. Right there by the damp spot I smelled the light, sweet scent of flowers.

"Brandon," I started to say, but then I stopped. Did I want him to know this?

He still stood there on the steps that had once led into the house. As I watched he lifted a hand to knock at a phantom door. "Lucinda," he whispered. "It's Brandon. Come out!"

He swayed, and I could see he was about to collapse.

"Brandon," I yelled, leaping onto the steps.

"Shhhhh." He put a finger to his lips. "Listen."

I stopped. All I could hear was the dry rattle of the leaves. But wait. Faintly, almost unheard under the whisper of the willows, came another sound. A voice. "Braaaaaaaandon," it wailed. "Braaaaaaaandon."

Brandon's legs buckled then, and I grabbed hold of him. If he'd fallen into the old basement where the snakes were I'd never have gotten him out.

I helped him to sit down, and he hung his head between his knees.

A brisk wind suddenly puffed at the dusty old streets, and the clattering of the willows became almost cheerful. The ghosts were gone. Had never been there, I assured myself. It was easy to let your imagination run away with you in a place like this.

The wind restored Brandon, too, and in a few minutes he was all right. It was as if the little block of time just past had never really happened.

Standing up abruptly, Brandon said, "Well, I guess we'd better get back to our unpacking."

Keith was waiting on the porch of our house when we got there. He didn't look much like the ten-year-old I'd left. He was tall now, and looked as if he lifted weights or something every day.

"Hi," he said shyly, and I couldn't imagine that there'd been any malicious motive to his sending us the clipping about the lake. I would have seen it in his face, wouldn't I?

"Just came to welcome you back," he finished.

"Hi," I said. We smiled foolishly at each other, neither one of us knowing quite what to say.

Brandon made it easier for us. "I just took Kate on a tour of the old town under the lake," he said. "I guess a lot of people come to look at it these days."

Keith pulled his eyes away from me. "People are all over the place, poking around. You'd think it was an archaeological dig or something."

"What do they find?" Brandon's voice was casually interested.

"Old rusty bicycles. Tin cans. There was an old car somebody had pushed into the lake." He laughed. "There was even a dog skeleton, and Herb Howard — remember him? — claimed that his neighbor killed his dog and dropped him into the lake. Caused quite a fuss."

Brandon cleared his throat. "Have they found anything of . . . ?" He paused.

"Of Lucinda?" Keith finished for him. His face was sympathetic. "No, nothing. Except . . ." Now it was his turn to pause.

"Except what?" Brandon prodded.

"Well . . ." Keith looked at both of us as if he wondered if he should go on. "Just a week ago somebody found a red graduation robe at the edge of what's left of the lake."

Brandon sank down onto a chair.

He didn't have time to ask any more questions because brisk footsteps came tap-tapping up our walkway. We couldn't see who it was until she came up onto the lighted porch.

"Holly," Brandon said weakly.

"Well, don't sound so thrilled to see me," Holly said, laughing.

Brandon tried to get up from the chair, but sank back again. "I didn't know you were still here in Lake Isadora."

Smoothly Holly pulled up a chair and sat down close to him. She tried to make him forget that he'd been too weak to stand up.

"I came back here after college," she said. "I teach art at the high school."

I wondered if she still had that picture she'd done of the drowned town. Maybe she'd thrown it away after Lucinda's death.

I'd always liked Holly. She'd written Brandon dozens of letters after we moved away, beautiful love letters. I knew because I'd sneaked into Brandon's room and read them before he threw them away. As far as I knew, he'd never answered any of them. He couldn't seem to forgive either himself or Holly for Lucinda's death.

"Why is everyone so solemn?" Holly asked now, glancing around. She looked almost the same as she used to, with her glossy black hair and tall, athletic figure and those strong, long-fingered artist's hands.

"Keith just told me about somebody finding Lucinda's red robe," Brandon said. His skin was waxen in the porch light.

Holly studied him for a moment, then said, "Who's to say it was Lucinda's? It could have been ditched by almost any overexuberant high school grad. They still use red robes, you know."

Brandon seemed to consider that. "Does it look like something that could have been under water for six years?"

Holly shrugged. "Don't know. Tomorrow's Saturday. We could go down to the police station and take a look at it."

"No." Keith shook his head. "It's gone. Somebody took it."

"Took it?" Brandon sounded bewildered. "Who would take it?"

Holly reached out to touch his arm. "Look, I've got this theory. Maybe it's nutso, but I always did say

Lucinda didn't really die. Wouldn't they have found something of her by now if she had?"

Holly looked around at us for confirmation, then went on. "You know how she was always saying she'd like to run away. Well, I think she saw her chance and went, letting us all think she was dead."

"That's crazy," Keith objected. "She was my sister. If she were alive, she'd get in touch with Mom and Dad and me."

Holly shrugged again. "Let's forget it," she said shortly. She turned toward Brandon. "Look, you can't go on forever blaming yourself for her death. If you do, then you have to include me. I was as much to blame as you were. It was *me* she was jealous of."

Brandon shook his head. "No," he said. "No."

I appreciated Holly's saying it was her fault, too, but I didn't think she could convince Brandon. Oh, how I wished her theory about Lucinda being alive could be true. It would release Brandon from all of his guilt and allow him to go on with his life.

But I didn't believe it any more than Keith did.

It took me a long time to fall asleep that night. I could hear Brandon thrashing around in his room next door, too.

But somewhere around three I slept, only to be awakened near dawn by the sound of rain dripping from the roof.

But there'd been no sign of rain when we'd gone to bed.

Then I realized with horror that the sound was right

there in my room. Water was dripping from something and splashing on the floor.

I leaped out of my bed and across the floor to the wall switch.

But when the light went on, no one was there. On my bare wood floor was a spreading puddle of water.

My heart was hammering wildly, I looked all around to see if there were wet footprints or some other clue.

There weren't. But there were drops of water leading out into the hall and through the living room to the front door.

Rushing back to my room I threw on my jeans, a sweatshirt, and shoes. Should I wake Brandon? No. I didn't want him to see this. I didn't know what it would do to his fragile hold on reality.

Grabbing my flashlight, I ran to the front door, unlocked it, and went out.

The watery trail led down the street four blocks to the old lake bed, and on to the foundations where Brandon and I had been earlier the day before. They stopped beside Lucinda's old house, and I saw that the damp spot I'd seen earlier was bigger. And again there was the light, sweet scent of flowers.

What was somebody trying to tell me? And why *me*? Why not Brandon?

Maybe because Brandon *knew* what had happened on that commencement night six years ago. Maybe because Brandon was the something I'd seen in the water with Lucinda.

"No," I cried aloud.

I shone my flashlight around the foundation, then

down into the gaping pit of the basement. Down there, in the deep silt, I saw another wet spot, dark, like blood.

I saw the bright glitter of rats' eyes down there, too.

Suddenly I was running, my legs pumping, my breath coming in gasps. Running down the street past the stumps of the vanished houses and the old schoolhouse. Running to get away from . . . what?

But I was lost in the avenues of willows. A morning breeze blew through the dry leaves, making them clack like the dead tongues of old ghosts, telling me to hurry, hurry, hurry out of there.

But which way was out?

At one intersection I stopped, uncertain of which way to turn. It was then that I saw the flash of red off through the willows to my right.

Red, like Lucinda's graduation robe. It was moving quickly toward me.

I couldn't run any farther. If Lucinda was coming after me, I'd just have to face her.

I stood there in the silence of early dawn, my breath coming in sobs, waiting.

The flash of red came closer, and I could see more of it. Then, as it came around a stand of willows, I saw it was a red jogging suit, and inside it was Holly.

She stopped abruptly. "Kate," she exclaimed. "What on earth are you doing here at this hour?"

"What are *you* doing here?" I stalled for time, trying to think of a good reason. How would it sound to say I'd followed a trail of water drops?

"I jog here every morning," she said. "It's quiet and peaceful." She peered closely at me. "You look pale. Is something the matter?"

I tried a small laugh. "It's just your red jogging suit. You know — we were just talking last night about Lucinda and her red graduation robe."

I thought she would laugh, but she didn't. "I'm sorry," she said instead. "No wonder you were frightened." She came over to me and took my arm. "I'll walk with you out of here."

We started off, but then Holly pulled me to a stop. "Listen," she whispered.

I listened but could hear nothing but the breeze in the willows.

She stood with her head cocked to one side, straining to hear. "Someone's calling," she mouthed. "Don't you hear it?"

I didn't.

"Braaaaaandon," Holly said. "That's what it's saying." She started walking again. "Let's get out of here."

She walked me all the way home. Neither of us spoke.

It was only after Holly had left and I was unlocking the front door that I remembered I'd had to unlock it to go out. That meant that whoever — whatever — had left the water drops had gone right through the closed door.

"Brandon," I called out. I hurried to his room.

But he wasn't there.

"Brandon," I called again.

Had the voice in the lake bed called to him, too, enticing him out, away from me, off into the dawn to the lake perhaps? Would he swim out into the murky water, looking for her?

"Braaaaaandon!" I bellowed.

"Kate." His voice was weak. "Kate, I'm here."

I followed the sound to the back door and looked out. Brandon was huddled there on the back steps, clutching something red.

"Brandon," I cried, "how long have you been out here?"

"A long time," he whispered. "She was here. Lucinda. I saw her face. I ran after her, but she got away. I grabbed her robe." He held up a red graduation robe. It was dripping wet.

"Just let her go," I said desperately. "She was trying to tell you to let her go."

I convinced Brandon to come back inside and lie down on the couch. Eventually he fell into an uneasy sleep, mumbling and groaning to himself.

I had to do something, and quickly, before it was too late for him.

It wasn't until I'd gone over every single thing I'd seen at Lucinda's old house, including the snakes that slid into the foundation, that I remembered the sound my feet had made when I'd stamped on the damp spot yesterday, that hollow, echoing sound.

Was there a cavity under the ground there where the snakes had gone? Some empty spot near the old foundation?

Who could I ask? Who could I trust?

I waited until a decent hour, then walked down the street to where the house stood now. Keith answered the door when I knocked.

We both blushed again as we greeted one another, but I managed to say that I'd been fascinated by the site of the old town and wondered if his family had pictures of when their house had been there.

"Sure," he said. "Come in. Mom and Dad aren't here, but if you don't mind being alone with me I'd be glad to help you."

I followed him into the living room where he pulled a photo album from a cabinet. "Remember how we used to look at these pictures and imagine that the old town was still there under the lake?"

I'd forgotten, and as that memory came into mind another one came with it. On one picture there'd been a funny-looking pipe coming up out of the ground near the house, and we used to speculate about what it was. We'd asked Keith's mother once, and she'd said it was a ventilation shaft for an old root cellar.

A root cellar.

Keith watched as I examined the pictures. I found the one I was looking for and saw that the pipe was right next to the old foundation.

Right where the damp spot had been.

Keith saw how closely I examined that photo. He didn't say anything, but his eyes narrowed ever so slightly as he watched me. Did he know what I was looking for?

I went home as soon as I could gracefully leave. I couldn't go back to the lake bed until after the day's souvenir hunters left. But I couldn't stay there with Keith, either. Not when he was watching me with that thoughtful, guarded look on his face. What was he thinking?

Brandon slept most of the day, getting up now and then to go out to the red graduation robe, which I'd hung outside to drip-dry. He wanted to look at it, touch it, smell it.

"It smells like Lucinda," he said. "Like flowers. It's her perfume."

Flowers? I remembered the faint, light scent by the damp spot in the lake bed. But when I put my nose next to the robe I smelled nothing except mildew.

Finally evening came.

In the light of a pale half moon, I set off once more for the old town. I couldn't even let myself think about what I had to do.

When I got to the old foundation of Lucinda's house, I shone the flashlight I'd brought around to see how I could get out of the basement once I got into it. To my relief, I saw a crumbling set of narrow stairs in one corner.

Before I lost my nerve, I scrambled down those stairs, praying that both the rats and snakes were asleep and would stay that way.

It was worse down in that pit than I'd expected. My feet sank deep into the silt and debris, and a rat skittered out of an old tire, staring at my light with glittering, hard eyes. But I gritted my teeth and began my search for the root cellar.

I looked at the wall closest to the damp spot. The

wall was overgrown with brush, but I cleared some of it away. There was a warped, decayed wooden door in the wall, and suddenly I smelled the faint, sweet scent of flowers.

The old, forgotten root cellar was Lucinda's secret place.

It took me quite a while longer to clear away enough brush and dirt so that I could yank at the door. Its wood crumbled as I worked at it, but soon I had it open enough to shine my light inside.

Taking a deep breath, I looked at as much as I could see.

All I saw in that first glance was greenish slime. There was something slick and shiny hanging from the ceiling, and I didn't even want to know what that was. Now the scent of flowers was overpowered by the stench of foul decay.

Suddenly, I heard a sound on the old porch steps. Swinging the light up there, I saw what made my heart stop.

"Lucinda," I gasped.

She stood there in her red graduation robe, her long, blonde hair falling over her shoulders. Her face gleamed like ivory in the light. She was smiling.

Holly was right. Lucinda was alive.

"Lucinda." My voice choked in my throat.

She said nothing, just continued to smile that set, unmoving smile.

She isn't alive at all, I thought. This is a ghost!

I began easing myself toward those crumbling stairs that led up out of the pit, but suddenly Lucinda leaped down there in the basement with me, still smiling into my light.

Without warning she grabbed my arms, twisting my hands behind my back and tying them with a narrow, cutting cord. I dropped my flashlight somewhere in the deep silt.

This was no ghost. Strong human hands were doing this to me.

"Lucinda!" I screamed. "Why are you doing this?"

Still she said nothing. But now she began to push me toward that open door into the rotten ooze of the root cellar.

She was going to put me inside.

I screamed. Frantically I wondered what I could use to bargain with. "Lucinda," I gasped. "I won't tell. You can go back to wherever you've been, and I'll never tell a soul."

She shoved me another foot forward — toward the reeking cellar.

Before I knew what was happening, she'd swooped down and snatched my flashlight. Holding me firmly with one strong hand, she kicked the cellar door all the way open and shone the light inside.

What I saw made my stomach lurch up into my throat. There was a skeleton, brown and hideous from the putrid filth in that hole. It was partially covered by some tattered threads of what must have once been a red graduation robe.

A snake, awakened by the commotion, thrust his head through one of the empty eye sockets of the broken skull and flicked his forked tongue at us.

The realization that came to me then was almost worse than the sight my eyes saw. Lucinda, or what was left of her, was in that cellar. Somebody else held me captive and was forcing me to join her.

I should have known. That smile was too set, the face too porcelainlike. It was a very cleverly made mask.

Who was behind it?

The person was strong. With a grunt, whoever it was pushed me still closer to my doom.

"Look," I pleaded. "I know you're not Lucinda. So tell me why you're doing this."

No answer.

"This isn't going to work," I said. "They'll find me, and you'll go down with two counts of murder."

Behind me I heard a chuckle. "No, they won't find you. Nobody has found Lucinda's secret place for all these years. Nobody has been here since I dived down and left her here."

"Holly!" I knew her voice. "You're the one who's been leaving that robe around and calling to Brandon and all the rest."

"It drove me crazy that Brandon wouldn't answer my letters, after all I did for him," Holly said. "So I thought I'd return the favor and drive *him* crazy."

A memory was returning to me now, one that I'd tried so hard to bury. "You hit her with an axe, there in the water. There was blood all over, and you kept hitting her."

"Somebody had brought the axe to cut firewood." Holly's voice was reasonable, calm. "I saw my chance,

and I took it. Brandon would have gone back to her
eventually, you see. She could wheedle him into anything, if she kept on long enough. So when I heard
her threaten to go to her secret place, I just made
sure she did. She'd shown it to me once when we'd
dived down there."

She pushed me forward. "I can't let you tell all this,
you know. If you'd kept your nose out of it, you'd be
home safe in bed now."

One more shove and I'd be in that gangrenous cellar.
I could feel Holly gather strength for one final heave.

I was close enough to the opening of the cellar now
that I could brace my foot against its side. Quickly I
did so, and with strength born of pure panic, I shoved
myself backward.

Holly fell. I got up and raced to the crumbling stairs,
but she was too fast. She caught me, just as someone
shone a light down into the basement. Someone who
stood on the porch stairs, outlined against the pale
sky.

"What's going on here?" demanded Keith. Before
he even had the words out, he was down there in the
basement with us.

Holly was strong, but she was no match for Keith.
And me. I helped, too, once Keith helped me out of my
cords. I bound up those powerful artist's hands that
years ago had created the "Drowned Town" painting
with the hideous, anguished faces caught in the willows.

Later Keith said it had taken him nearly all night
to figure out why I was so interested in that old picture

that showed the ventilation pipe. When he did, when he remembered his mother mentioning the root cellar, he guessed what I was up to, just as I'd guessed he might, and he'd come to see if I was all right.

Thank goodness he came. I couldn't have fought Holly alone.

I received a message from Lucinda right after she was finally laid to rest in a proper grave. I awakened one morning to find a small puddle on my floor, as if someone had stood there dripping. In my room was the faint, sweet scent of flowers, and a small bouquet of rosemary, for remembrance, was at the foot of my bed.

THE
GUICCIOLI
MINIATURE
Jay Bennett

IT WAS PAST MIDNIGHT, AND THE ORCHESTRA HAD stopped playing. He got up from his seat at the table in the café and walked across the huge Piazza San Marco. He turned and went past the façade of the cathedral, past the Doge's Palace, which gleamed white with all its tracery, and then down between the two high pillars to the water's edge. He stopped and looked out at the canals. With his eyes he followed the gliding of a gondola, and then he saw an empty *vaporetto*, ghostlike and fast-moving, far out in the center of the channel. And he was looking out across St. Mark's Canal to the dim outlines of San Giorgio Island when a shadow fell across the pavement and he heard a man's voice.

"You American?"

Jerry nodded silently.

"Just come to Venice?"

The stranger was a tall, lean man with a haunted look in his eyes. Even though the night was damp and hot, he wore a coat and an old hat with the brim turned down. His hands trembled as if he had a fever.

Out in the channel the *vaporetto* vanished into the darkness.

"Been here a few days," Jerry said.

The sleeves of the man's long coat were frayed, and his lean face had a stubble of beard on it.

He's down and out in Venice, Jerry thought. And so he wasn't surprised when he heard the man say, "Maybe you can help a fellow American?"

Jerry waited.

Then he saw the man put his long hand into his coat pocket and draw out a small object that glistened in the half-darkness.

"Give me ten for it and it's yours, kid."

"What is it?"

"A miniature. I painted it myself. It's worth a good hundred. Two hundred. More. But give me ten dollars and you'll have something to take home to your girl."

He put the miniature into Jerry's hand, and it was cold, almost icy to the touch.

"Ten dollars. You're about eighteen, right? You have a girl, right? Bring her something from Venice." Then he asked, "How long are you going to be here, kid?"

"Till tomorrow afternoon."

"Then you're going home?"

"Yes."

"Home," the man said — and was silent.

And all the time they were talking the icy miniature lay between Jerry's closed fingers. Suddenly the man spoke again.

"Give me ten dollars. It'll be the best buy you'll ever make."

His hand grabbed Jerry and pulled him to a little pool of light. "Take a good look at it."

Jerry lifted the miniature into the spill of light. He saw that it was beautiful.

"The Guiccioli miniature," the man said in a hushed voice, "a copy of the Guiccioli miniature. The original is in the Pitti Palace in Florence. I stood there and copied it, day after day until they wanted to throw me out. The Guiccioli miniature."

It was the face of a very beautiful woman with brown, liquid eyes and auburn hair. Her features were small and perfectly shaped. But it was the eyes that haunted Jerry — the amazing eyes.

He looked up slowly.

And now the eyes of the man were glittering.

"I came here years ago to be a great painter. And I'll soon die and all I have to offer is a copy. My whole life is nothing but a copy. Nothing. Nothing. Give me ten bucks for the picture."

Jerry looked down again at the miniature and then, suddenly, with a shock, he remembered. Teresa Guiccioli . . . Lord Byron, the great romantic poet . . . the two of them had been in love. Byron must have had the miniature painted to carry with him when they were apart. And so this was Teresa Guiccioli, Byron's Countess Guiccioli.

"How about it?"

Jerry hesitated. "I've got very little money left m\

self," he said. "I came over here with only a little money. I'm a college student. So, you can see, I . . ."

His voice trailed off into silence. The look in the man's eyes pierced him. The stranger seemed so desperate, so alone, so filled with dread. He began to plead.

"The original is priceless. Go to the Pitti and compare it with this copy. You won't be able to tell the difference. Byron had it painted by one of the great artists of the day. The original is worth a hundred grand — a hundred grand, kid. And I'm offering it to you for ten bucks. I'm broke. Nobody wants to buy it from me. I need money. I need it badly — anything I can get."

Out on the glimmering canal the lean form of a gondola wavered into view and then slowly faded into the darkness. The sound of a boat whistle came from a great distance. It was a haunting, mournful sound.

"All right," said Jerry. "I'll buy it."

They moved out of the pool of light, and Jerry gave the man the money. He dropped the miniature into his pocket.

"It's the best buy you ever made." The man's voice was now mocking and bitter.

"What are you going to do with the money?" Jerry asked.

"Eat. And then get a ticket out of here."

"Where to?"

"Where can a doomed man go?"

The man's eyes glittered and then faded into the darkness.

Jerry stood there a long time. Then he turned and made his way back, across the great square and past the empty tables of the cafés. He went into a long, gloomy arcade and from there along the quiet alleys and narrow streets. He passed over a narrow bridge and came at last to his *pensione*, the little boarding-house he was staying at. The whole time he walked he felt as if he were being followed. He felt as if a long, lean shadow were walking behind him. He turned to look over his shoulder a number of times on the way. No one was there. There was nothing behind him but the empty alleys and streets — and the night.

Jerry Moore went into the *pensione* with its peeling walls and climbed up the dark flight of stairs. He opened the door of his little room and went in. He turned on the light and looked again at the miniature. He thought of Byron and the lovely poetry he had written — "She walks in beauty, like the night. . . ." He could still remember that from English class. He looked at the terrifying beauty of the woman in the miniature. Subtly, the strange, glittering eyes of the man came into his consciousness. He heard the despairing words again, even though he tried not to:

"Where can a doomed man go?"

Suddenly, the miniature grew even icier to his touch. The beautiful face of the woman began to seem almost repellent to him. His hands became clammy.

Jerry got up and went to the old, streaked mirror that hung on the wall. It was his own face that looked back at him — but it had changed somehow. His face was now white and drawn with fear. His eyes had become two black pools.

Where can a doomed man go?

And now Jerry felt that for some strange, inexplicable reason, with the passing of the miniature to him, he, too, had become a doomed man. The painter had passed the curse to him.

Jerry turned out the light. He went over to the window and opened it wide. He stood there, looking down at the dark waters of the canal. He knew that these were the same dark Venetian waters that Lord Byron had looked into in 1819, when he had first seen the miniature of his beloved countess, Teresa Guiccioli.

Beloved?

No! Repellent. Terrifying.

Jerry's face was tight with fear. He looked as frightened as the poor painter had looked when they had made their bargain near the canal.

Then Jerry shivered slightly and turned away from the window.

His sleep that night was restless. He awoke several times. Once he was sure he heard something. He sprang right out of his bed. He stared straight ahead and broke out in a cold sweat. He knew he could not stay in this room any longer. He dressed in a panic. He stood for an instant in the center of the room, stock-still.

His eyes fixed on the doorknob. He could have sworn that it was beginning to turn, slowly.

Then he screamed. And the knob stopped turning.

After a while, Jerry went to the door. He turned

the lock very carefully and very slowly. He opened the door cautiously, an inch at a time. He peered out.

The hallway was dim but he could tell it was empty. There was no one outside.

Jerry closed the door. He went to the window of his room and stood there, looking down at the canal as he had earlier in the evening.

It was then that he made his decision.

He went to the bureau and picked up the miniature. He looked at it for the last time. Then he went over to the open window and threw the tiny painting down into the black water.

There was a splash and then a vast silence.

And in that silence Jerry felt — for the first time since he had met the mysterious painter — like himself again. He felt as if a great weight had been lifted from him.

He was free of the curse — if there was one.

Then he began to laugh silently, and said aloud, "Silly superstitious fool!"

He went back to bed. This time he slept soundly and didn't wake until the sun was streaming in through the open window.

Just before his plane took off that afternoon, the stewardess came around with a selection of magazines and newspapers for the passengers to read. Jerry took one of the Italian newspapers. He settled back in his seat and began to read it. It always gave him pleasure to speak and read Italian. That was one of the reasons he had come to Italy — to improve his Italian. There was a slight smile of pleasure on his face as he began to read. He slowly turned the first page. Then the smile slowly left his face.

He had come upon a picture of the man — the man he had met by the canal, the sad painter. The painter was lying on his back on a cobblestone street, his face turned up to the sky.

Jerry read further.

The "painter" had been one of three men who had stolen the Guiccioli miniature from the Pitti Palace. Then he had double-crossed his partners and had run off with the treasure. His partners had finally caught up with him in Venice, after chasing him all over Italy.

The police had captured the murderers and were now searching desperately for the priceless miniature.

Jerry slowly put down his newspaper.

"Is anything wrong?" the stewardess asked him.

Jerry did not answer.

BLOOD KISS
D.E. Athkins

"OH, GROSS!" THAT WAS DELIA. EMPHATICALLY. Everything Delia did was emphatic. You could hear her coming a mile away. You knew her opinions right up front.

"Eww . . ." Valerie wasn't as emphatic. In fact, Val was practically a disappearing act. Frail. Waiflike. Big eyes like on those hokey sympathy cards. Only she wasn't frail. Or waiflike. Not really.

"No way." That was me. Chiming in as always. I'm Elizabeth. My parents named me Elizabeth along with hundreds of other kids from my generation. Dare to be the same. . . . I've tried to think of nicknames that might be distinctive. But the other Elizabeths in the school beat me to it long ago: Liz Greg, she's a cheerleader. Beth Dvorak, she's going to be a model — to pay her way through MIT, probably. Eliza — nah. Betty? I don't think so.

So just Elizabeth.

"Still . . ." Valerie was rising to consciousness. Her big, big eyes narrowed.

We were looking at the new boy. Ken. An unfortunate choice for a name, if you ask me. Like Barbie and Ken, you know?

But what's in a name?

And he *did* look like a Ken doll might look, if it had come to life. Gorgeous, but pale. Carved, rugged, but somehow delicate, features. Straight dark brows. Perfect, black, black hair.

A living doll.

Maybe that was how the rumors had started. He definitely had an air about him. He wore dark glasses, long, long coats that looked somehow from another century — maybe what a rocker might wear on stage. Hats.

He defiantly played to the rumors, and it should have looked phony, but it didn't. At least not to me. I'd die before I'd say it out loud, but I thought he was the most gorgeous guy I'd ever seen. I, Elizabeth Smith, little, plain, pale Elizabeth Smith had fallen in love.

What was it about him? The way he chose to stand up, stand out, when I'd spent my whole life fixated on being normal? The fearless way he was what he was (or what he'd like to be) while everyone else moused along, hating whatever was different without thinking, afraid of their own shadows?

Whatever it was, *whatever he was*, I was attracted to him. Drawn to him. Drowning in love for him.

And there was nothing I could do about it.

Except talk about him every chance I got. Which wasn't hard, not only because of the way he looked and dressed, but because of the rumors.

"Maybe . . ." whispered Valerie.

Delia said, "There's no such thing, okay? Valerie? Are you in there?"

"Well . . ." Valerie never lets go, once she's got a grip on something. That's the real survival of the fittest for you.

"Valerie," I said. "It's a gag rumor."

"Yeah, as in 'to throw up.' " Delia still hadn't taken her eyes off Ken.

"A joke, Val," I said before Val could get caught up in any double meanings.

Val smiled her demure, close-lipped little smile, secret as the Mona Lisa's. "Still, wouldn't it be sexy if he were a real, live vampire?"

"If he were a real, live vampire, it would be life-threatening," snarled Delia, suddenly switching her attention back to Val. "Because he would put his teeth into your neck and suck out your blood, and you'd be dead."

That got to Val. "Gross," she said, her perfect little smile turning into a perfect little pout. And then, proving that she was all there at least some of the time, she added, "What's it to you, anyway, Delia? Since when were you a vampire expert?"

Delia blushed. And I was grateful that Val had decided Delia was the competition (not counting every other girl in school). Because, like I said, when Val gets something in her head, there is no stopping her. And I didn't want Val getting anything in her head about me — like me being hopelessly in love with Ken.

After all, Barbie might have had the figure for it. I didn't. I just didn't quite fit. I was always on the outside, looking in. Saying things that were just a little off. Trying things that were a little uncool. A barely tolerable sort of person, except that I was a master (mistress?) of disguise. So they didn't know I was a gawk, a misfit, a dumb dweeb. They just thought I was average.

See what I mean? If I'd been the kind of girl who fit in, I wouldn't have had to work so hard just to be average, right?

Anyway, however remote my chances of someone so gorgeous paying *any* attention to someone like me, I couldn't get him out of my mind. Which is how I ended up at the local library behind a stack of — you guessed it — vampire books, hoping no one would see me. Not that it mattered (see above). Seeing me at the library wouldn't damage *my* reputation. And if we're going to do true confessions, I actually went there pretty often.

Where do you think the girls who aren't cheerleaders and class presidents hang out, anyway?

I learned a lot. I even took some notes. It was pretty fascinating stuff, if you like that sort of thing. Of course, everybody knows I have a weak stomach. But love makes you strong, right? So I read about vampires being afraid of garlic, and vampires not having any mirror images, and killing vampires by driving stakes through their hearts, and vampires frying in the cruel, cruel sunrise. It was pretty gruesome. Stupid, but gruesome.

Except that none of the authorities really agreed. I

found myself mentally echoing Val's words to Delia: So who made you an expert on vampires, anyway?

Ken.
Ken.
Ken.

I caught myself doing all the stupid things I swore I'd never do. Writing his name in my notebook. Writing my name and his. Making anagrams of his name and mine. Elizabeth and Ken. Why not? It certainly sounded as good as Barbie and Ken.

Ken, on the other hand, wasn't wasting any time doodling. He started dating Liz. She probably promised to teach him all her cheers. I'd see them in the corner during lunch practically locking lips. Of course, it ruined my appetite. Not that I'm a big eater, but what does it matter? It's the thought that counts, right?

But it didn't last. One day they were a my-locker-or-yours couple, the next day they were looking in opposite directions when they passed. Liz wouldn't talk about it.

The rumors started up again.

"Nonsense," said Delia, but she had the light of a different kind of battle in her eye. "He goes out in the daylight, doesn't he? Vampires can't go out in the sun."

"Maybe they can when they're young," argued Val. I looked at Val with new respect.

"Besides, Liz's wearing a turtleneck."

Now Delia was looking at Val. "You're from outer space, you know that?"

"Maybe I am," said Val. "So I should get along just fine with a vampire."

She wafted away, leaving me and Delia standing there.

"Uh," I said to distract her, "maybe he *is* a very young vampire. Like *Young Frankenstein*, the movie?"

"Elizabeth," said Delia. "You're getting as bad as Val." And she walked away in the other direction.

So I had time on my hands, and I went to math early and grabbed a seat in the back as usual — but it was a better than usual seat. Because he always sat in the same place in the room, the back corner, and this time I was sitting one desk away.

It was the darkest corner, come to think of it.

He came in with Louise Murao on his arm. She was looking up at him; he was looking down at her. It was sickening. And she got a better seat, right in front of him.

They flirted all through math, not that I watched them. But I couldn't help but notice one thing. Louise got out her mirror at the end of class to study her perfect face. She frowned a little and at about the same time Ken jumped up.

"Coming?" he murmured. Oh god, it was sexy. Louise frowned just a little more, then remembered that frowning was not in the most-beautiful-most-popular handbook and stopped. She jumped up and reattached herself to him, and they went out hip to hip.

"Coming?" I sneered to myself and looked up to see

Mad Math McGee looking at me. Teachers. You have to watch them every minute.

"Going," I said more loudly, and gathering up my books, hurried out of class before he could ask if anything was wrong, did I need help, what about a parent-teacher conference? My parents wouldn't come, I could explain it all to them, no problem, but what's the point of borrowing trouble as my mother would say. Besides, just imagine how puzzled they'd be: "But she's never given us a minute's trouble," my mother would say earnestly. "She's always been such a *good* girl." My father would look hurt, bewildered.

I remembered when my mother had tried to have her little girl-to-girl talk to me about "things." She never did get around to defining "things," and the questions I had probably weren't in her definition anyway. I mean, imagine me asking her how you could tell if someone was really a vampire? And what you would do to get him to fall in love with you. Right.

Besides, if "things" like my mother imagined ever came up, I could always ask Delia.

But getting back to other things . . . Ken and Louise lasted through several very nice weekends. The sort of weekends where you go to football games and parties and parking, at least in our town. We're so all-American it could make you sick. But I wanted more than anything to be a part of that. And not with Delia and Val. With Ken.

Who, if anything, was getting *more* pale and romantic and interesting and gorgeous. Delia and Val, of course, kept talking about him, watching him, but what had once been a pleasure was now a pain. I was afraid I'd give myself away. But I couldn't not talk about Ken, the most perfect guy I'd ever seen. Because even if Val did miss that little distinction, Delia would catch on and make my life miserable. And whatever else Delia was, I wanted her on my side. Because if Delia decided you were a potential gossip victim, then that was the end of your social life forever. You were outside the pale. You might as well really be a vampire.

When Ken and Louise broke up, Delia broke in. One minute we were standing in the hall arguing about guess who being guess what, and the next, she was cutting across the traffic and planting herself firmly in front of him. He smiled down at her, a neat, tight-lipped little curl of the mouth, and I felt my heart take a dive.

"He's definitely a vampire," said Val.

"You won't know until you wear some garlic around him," I said without thinking. How can you think when your heart is breaking? *Eat garlic and die, Delia,* my broken heart was thumping out in my chest.

"Well, don't tell Delia," said Val in an aggrieved tone. "Let him just rip her throat out, for all I care."

"Val!" I exclaimed, surprised by her vehemence.

The next night, against my better judgment, I let Collin Harper take me to a horror movie. I thought I was going to throw up. It was so crude. All that spurting blood and ripping flesh and vampires turning into bats. Puh-lease. Give me a break.

I know, I know, I was supposed to shriek and bury

my face in Collin's manly shoulder. But suppose I poked my eye out on that collection of pens he carried in his pocket? I just couldn't do it. I let him squeeze his hot hand around my cold one, but when the movie was over I said, "I have a weak stomach, Collin. I'm sorry but you'll have to take me home."

Of course, it didn't help seeing Delia and Ken on the way out. Delia didn't see me. She had her head thrown back, laughing. She was wearing something very un-Delia like. Low-cut. So with her head back, she was practically offering Ken her whole neck.

Everything started swimming around in front of me. It was so unfair.

"Take me home now," I told poor Collin. And that was that.

What happened between Ken and Delia? No one knows. One day she appeared at school, a major scarf tied around her neck.

"He got you!" gasped Val.

"Don't be ridiculous," snapped Delia. "It's just an act."

"Why do you have that scarf on, then?"

"Why does anyone wear a scarf after a date, Val? Think."

Val thought. She got really wide-eyed and went "Oooh."

"He's a creep," said Delia.

"He dumped you, didn't he," said Val. "Why?"

"Oh, shut up," said Delia and turned on her heel and stomped away.

"He's such a gentleman," cooed Val.

"What?" I said. "What are you talking about?"

"He never talks about the girls he goes out with. Don't you think that is awfully polite?"

"I'd think he was a pig if he did," I said.

Val giggled. "Not pig, silly. Vampire."

Val was his next victim.

I just couldn't figure it out. Liz wasn't talking. Louise wasn't talking. Delia wouldn't say anything. The rumors were still flying, but they were mostly old stuff now.

Was he or wasn't he a vampire?

With Delia sulking and Val busy, I had plenty of free time, so I went back to the library. I checked out some more books and found out a lot more interesting stuff. Including the fact that it took more than one bite (some people believed) to turn you into a vampire. Of course, there was the one-bite school, too, and the all-in-how-he-bit-you school — which I thought of as the vampire's kiss school. The kiss that made you his forever.

Naturally no one talked about how a vampire kissed a vampire. (When you've never been kissed, you think about it a lot, right?) Like, what did they do with their teeth? Was it like wearing glasses or having braces? Could a vampire write to Ann Landers about it? Anonymously of course?

I giggled, then sobered up.

Was Ken just feeding off his victims? Or was he testing them somehow? Looking, maybe, for his one true love, the girl who would be willing to . . .

Oh, Ken, I thought to myself. You just haven't kissed the right girl.

"You're sick," I said to myself aloud.

"Shhh," said someone else, so I gathered up the books. And that's when I noticed it.

Val. Val's name was on all those books, too.

She'd checked them out. Val, class space cadet, had actually checked out and possibly read not one but many books. On vampires.

Calm down, I thought. I mean, how is anyone supposed to know anything about vampires if they don't look it up? Even if no one seems to know the truth.

But, Val???

The next few weeks were interesting. Val showed up right away with a scarf *and* a turtleneck. But she didn't look pale.

If anything she looked rosy. Glowing. Positively full of life.

Or life's blood.

It was Ken who looked paler and paler. He even seemed to recoil a bit when Val came toward him.

Had he made her a vampire?

Had he created a monster?

"Have some pizza," I said to Val one day. I'd secretly loaded it with garlic.

"Mmm," she said, scarfing (if you'll excuse the expression) it all down.

So either she wasn't a vampire, or two more vampire laws were proven false: vampires hate garlic, and vampires can only eat blood.

Whatever it was, it was killing my appetite. I pushed my pizza away.

Val snatched it right up. "You never eat," she said happily. "Your poor weak stomach."

And then over Thanksgiving, they broke up.

Val drifted back into our threesome, vague as ever. She wasn't wearing a scarf or turtleneck. I inspected her neck as closely as I dared. It looked fine.

"What happened?" I asked as Delia glared.

"He's . . . not . . ." she let her words slide off.

"Not a vampire?" I asked.

Val sighed. "I don't want to talk about it," she said in a long-suffering way that made me want to throttle her. But it wouldn't do any good. I knew that was the last I'd get out of Val.

So I did what any red-blooded all-American girl would do. At least I *think* I did. I mean, I don't know the rules, and who could I ask?

What I did was ask Ken. Basically. I just sort of threw myself at him.

I waited for him by his locker.

"Hi," I croaked, leaning against it, holding my books up in front of my chest as if I had something to hide.

"Hello." He smiled. A little.

"Elizabeth," I said. "Not Liz. Not Beth. Just Elizabeth."

"Hello, just Elizabeth," he said. I stared as hypnotically as I could into his eyes. For some reason, it worked.

"So, just Elizabeth, what are you doing Saturday night?"

* * *

For my date, I went for a more sophisticated look. It's one I actually feel more comfortable in, but I think he was a little startled at the radical departure from my usual pastels all over. But if you're going to date a vampire, I think you should dress the part.

Of course, I didn't invite him in to meet my parents. I couldn't. They'd look at me, they'd look at him, what would they think?

Our little girl, is what they'd think. After all we've done, where did we go wrong?

And what could I tell them?

So I slipped out for my date with an alleged vampire with a quick, guilty good-bye, and my heart breaking and racing at the same time. I guess that is true love. Isn't it?

"Wow," he said, after he got used to my new look. I could feel his eyes on the low-cut, square neck of my basic black dress (my mother's actually, but she wasn't using it, and what she didn't know would hurt her).

We went to a horror flick, and I screamed and buried my face in his shirt. It felt so good. I imagined kissing him, and I could almost taste it. I held his hand so tightly, and that was hot, too. It felt as if his hand was on fire. Like dry ice. . . .

We drove up to the Point where everyone of every generation has gone parking since the town was founded. (I told you we were an all-American town.) He stopped the car and turned out the lights.

He began to trace the edge of the neck of my dress with one finger. No other touching, just that.

I shivered.

"Cold?" he asked, smiling. I saw a milli-flash of white teeth in the dark.

I shook my head.

"Scared?" he asked, leaning closer.

I shook my head again. I leaned back.

"Ken," I said softly. "Ken, tell me . . . is what they say, true?"

The flash of white teeth again. "What do they say?"

"That you . . . that you're a vampire."

He laughed softly. Deliciously.

"What do you think?" He leaned over, paused. I waited. His breath touched my throat.

Then I felt it. The sharp pinch, the needle point of teeth on my neck . . . a schoolboy nibble, the kind that goes with parked cars and steamy windows. Nothing more.

When he was finished he leaned back.

I was shaking. I was so ashamed. I felt like such a fool in my vamp-the-vampire clothes. I'd practically told him I thought that he was really and truly a vampire . . . Oh god, I wished I was dead. . . .

"Well?" he said.

"I think all I have here is a world-class hickey," I said as neutrally as I could.

I mean, I would have been lying if I'd said it was what I'd expected. That I wasn't disappointed.

He started to laugh.

"Don't," I said, holding out my hand as if I could push away my embarrassment.

He grasped my hand and begin to nibble on each

finger. And suddenly my courage came back. Sometimes, you just have to take a chance, right?

"What about Liz?" I said, almost to myself. "Louise? Delia? Were you just teasing them, pretending, leading them on? Did you give them a good sharp bite and a little scare, so they felt like fools for believing you?"

The nibbling stopped. I could feel him staring at me, but I didn't look. I stared into the darkness as I went on.

"And Val? Was she a wild card? Did she take you up on it — and then leave you because you weren't what she wanted you to be?"

His breath suddenly felt hot. But my hands stayed icy cold.

"Well, well," he said. "There's more to you than meets the eye, just Elizabeth."

"Is that how it was?" I persisted. "A bad joke? Tell me. Tell me the truth."

He watched me for a long, long moment. I could hear him breathing. I could hear me breathing. It wasn't like in the movies at all.

His voice, when he finally spoke, was a voice I hadn't heard before. Soft. Eerily beautiful. "They thought it was a fun game. It made them sexy — to be able to say they'd once dated a vampire. But when I got serious, they got angry. Them! Angry! As if by being what they wanted me to be, I'd betrayed them.

"As if *I* was using them. As if I was the perverse one. . . ."

"Val?" I breathed. My hands were suddenly freezing against his lips.

The glint of teeth again. "Val. Oh, she wanted to play. She loved it, a nibble here, a nibble there. She was almost inhuman the way she teased me, led me on . . . and everyone envied me for being with Val. . . ."

He paused, then went on, smoothly, expressionless. "In the end, I quit. Not Val."

His voice changed. "So, what now, just Elizabeth?"

He was mocking me now. But it was okay. I understood. I knew the real truth, and I loved him all the more for it.

I would love him forever.

"You . . ." I hesitated a moment longer. Surely he could hear my heart. Surely he could see it beating. "You *really are* a vampire?"

I looked up then, into his eyes. They burned suddenly red, red as blood rubies in the dark.

I saw it in the night that is never dark for those like him. Like me.

I felt my own eyes flame red with joy and promise and relief and hope for the future as I looked back into his.

He tilted his head back. Half closed his glittering eyes. I leaned forward tentatively. I felt him stiffen as my breath touched his neck. I felt his pulse beneath my lips. I felt his skin yield. Just a little.

I stopped. I'd been clumsy. A thin trickle of blood slid down his pale throat.

But he touched the shining track of blood, then reached out and touched my lips.

I leaned forward again. I opened my mouth over the

blood, and it was as if I were taking a deep, deep breath for the first time, sucking, feeling its salt sweetness beneath my teeth, against my tongue.

I heard him sigh. And then I heard him whisper, "Yes . . . yes."

I sat up slowly. Slowly, I tilted my own head back, imagining my neck, pale and smooth.

He smiled at me. A real smile.

I smiled at him as he pulled me close.

"Gimme a kiss," I said.

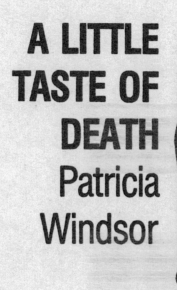

A LITTLE
TASTE OF
DEATH
Patricia
Windsor

Louey HAD TAKEN TO READING THE NEWSPAPER AT breakfast every morning. She woke to the sound of it hitting Gran's front porch at eight o'clock. At that moment her day began, and the paper was there to help the morning pass.

It was a flimsy newspaper, nothing like the Atlanta newspaper her daddy read every evening. The *Dolonga Morning Press* took less than twenty minutes if Louey read real slow. The classifieds could stretch it out a little more.

Breakfast was served in the dining room, complete with linen cloth and napkins. You had to refold the napkin into its silver holder for the next meal. You had to be careful not to wipe your mouth too vigorously or your napkin would be filthy before the week was out.

Gran, frail and refined, didn't say much in the morning. It took time to get her motor started, she said. Gran sat at the other end of the table, staring out the window at her garden. She didn't read the *Dolonga Morning Press* until the afternoon. She had instructed Louey to fold it back up as neatly as the napkins; and

Louey had perfected the technique of running her fingernail along the creases to make them look fresh.

The first thing Louey read in the classified section was the funeral notices, mostly for very old people. After that came lost-and-found pets. Louey's heart ached over these. She memorized descriptions of the dogs and cats just in case one might stray into the garden or cross her path on the street.

After that were ads for jobs, like home typist or experienced waitress. Then came used cars, real estate, and finally the personals.

Remember the lollipop? Louey read this morning. *The man in a white hat?* Louey sat up straighter and squinted at the fine print. Those who remembered were asked to call a local number immediately. *It could save your life.*

A shivery feeling crept over Louey. She looked up, thinking the sun had gone behind a cloud. The garden was brilliant in yellow morning light. Louey read the ad again.

Well, it's just a joke, she thought. What was wrong with taking a lollipop? Certainly not a matter of life and death.

For the first time Louey did not finish reading the paper to the end. She put it down in an untidy heap. She sat for a moment. It was funny how the telephone number kept repeating in her head.

She did a quick calculation. More than ten years ago, it must have been. Was there some kind of poison that took ten years to work? Or maybe it was a cancer recall, the way they did with cars.

"Louey, dear," Gran said tenderly. "Do ask to be excused."

This meant she'd been fidgeting. "Sorry."

"And . . ." Gran gestured at the messy newspaper.

"Yes, Gran, yes," Louey said, suddenly impatient. She took the paper away with her and went into the other room.

The day was interminable. There was nothing to do in Dolonga except sit in the garden drinking cocolas and reading the books she had borrowed from the county library. She didn't know anybody. She couldn't talk much to Gran who was mostly distracted and vague, although at night she pepped up some. Louey hadn't wanted to spend a summer in Dolonga. But she had promised not to complain, not even to herself. Her parents deserved their anniversary vacation, and Louey would not spoil it.

But now she felt as if she might jump out of her skin. The trouble was, aside from refolding newspapers and linen napkins, there was nothing she *had* to do. She suddenly wished Gran was a cranky old lady who made her mop floors and wash windows. Instead there was Clara in the kitchen and Ned in the garden and any number of other people Gran called in to do chores. Gran's idea of work was embroidering pillow covers. Louey was hopeless at that.

She went out to the garden and came back in again. She walked into the hall and looked at the black, old-fashioned telephone sitting on its stand.

Why did she keep remembering the number? It was as if it were asking her to dial it.

Finally, she did.

She expected to hear some idiotic recording trying to sell her something. Instead a businesslike male voice said, "Can I help you?"

Louey stifled a screechy laugh. "Um . . . your ad . . . I — "

"How old are you?"

Her age was on the tip of her tongue but she held it back. "Why?"

There was no answer from the other end.

"Fifteen," Louey said, defeated.

"That's about right. How are you feeling these days? Any symptoms?"

"What kind of symptoms? What's this all about?"

"There's a meeting Thursday night." He gave her an address. "Why don't you come?"

"Why should I?"

"It could make a difference," the voice said, overriding Louey's attempt at more questions. "Really, it's in your best interest. Maybe you haven't noticed any changes yet, but you will. When you ate that lollipop, you ate death."

"Oh, sure," Louey said and banged the receiver down.

Gran, coming from the kitchen, looked at her curiously. Louey mumbled about a friend back home, and Gran went mildly on her way. Doesn't know I'm alive, thought Louey with unexpected venom.

Louey had no intention of going to the meeting; she was too smart to be suckered into schemes that were supposed to make you rich selling vitamins or kitchen cleaners door-to-door. She decided to help Ned in the garden and got a sunburned nose, which clinched it; she looked too ugly to go out. But on Thursday night, things conspired against her resolve.

For one thing, her nose had healed; it wasn't even peeling. For another, Gran was going out herself. It was ladies club night, and she fretted about leaving Louey on her own. Club nights were Clara's nights off.

"I don't need a baby-sitter," Louey said.

"But what will you do?"

As if they did anything thrilling anyway, Louey thought. Gran didn't have a television. Usually she and Louey sat in the living room and read, unless Gran was peppy, and then they talked.

"The same as usual. I've got my new library book."

Gran looked uncertain. "Really," Louey said, her annoyance showing, "I'm not a child."

Gran shrank back a little, and Louey felt sorry. She had never before raised her voice in this well-modulated household. She was about to apologize but Gran obviously felt the matter was closed. At seven-thirty she came into the living room to say good-bye. Louey was reading in her favorite chair. "Have a good time," she told Gran, and snuggled down. But as soon as she heard the front door click, she was full of nervous energy. As the phone number had done, the address pounded in her head and wouldn't quit. Easy to slip out; no one to ask where she was going. It wasn't far.

Louey left the lights on and locked the door. She told herself she would walk over and take a look, just from the outside. She'd be back before Gran came home.

The sun was disappearing behind the live oaks and sweet gum trees. Louey walked as fast as she could on the uneven brick streets. The address was on the border of what Gran would call the unrefined section of town. Across the street, the houses were already squatter, the gardens less tended, a hint of backyard junk in the air.

It was dark now, and Louey could comfortably stare without being seen from inside. It was an austere house, with cast-iron decorations. The iron balconies had leaked rust stains beneath the windows. Not a friendly house, Louey decided.

"Are you going in?" a voice asked. Louey whirled around. "Didn't mean to scare you."

A boy about her own age was standing there, greenish eyes darting from Louey to the windows and back.

"Did you get a lollipop, too?" Louey asked him, trying to make it sound funny.

He nodded.

"You look so serious," Louey told him, wishing he would laugh. "What is it all about, anyway?"

"Let's go see." He took her hand and pulled her toward the curving iron staircase. Louey held back only a moment.

"Well, if you're game, so am I," she said breezily, but her stomach churned.

Inside it looked like the kind of dull old meetings

her parents had, to discuss building variances or sewage. People were sitting around on sofas and straight-backed chairs. They looked ordinary, about Louey's age, some a little younger, some older.

One of the older ones was in charge. Louey guessed it was his house because he was offering sodas and coffee. He cleared his throat, and everyone quieted. "Hi, I'm James," he said, and Louey recognized the voice on the phone.

"Hi, James," everyone said back.

"I see we have two newcomers tonight." He nodded at Louey and the boy she'd come in with. "Let's introduce ourselves to them."

All around the room they announced their own first names: Keith, Dawn, Mary Beth, Curt, and Darrell. Louey gave her name reluctantly, then wished she'd made one up. The boy next to her was Bobby Lee.

"Okay," James said. "Louey, Bobby Lee, we'd like to tell you about our experiences. That's what we do here; share to give each other support. All of us have been called."

Called. Louey stiffened at that word. If it was going to be some kind of revival meeting, with chest beating and hymns, she was leaving right now. She twisted around to look at the door, just to make sure it was there. She heard them start telling stories, about bad feelings they had, nasty stuff they'd done. It didn't seem right to tell things so personal. Louey tried not to hear. Then she realized they were waiting on her.

She felt her face getting red. "I don't have anything to say, I mean nothing like that."

"Just start at the beginning, hon," Dawn said. "You know, tell us how you got your lollipop. No need to feel shy here. We're all in the same boat."

Gloomy chuckles.

"But I don't know . . ." Louey stammered. It was hard to remember it all. They had been on the train to Fayetteville, to visit some relatives, she and her mama. Louey felt excited and proud. Mama dozed off, but Louey kept her eyes on the window, watching the scenery roll by, mostly trees and, once in a while, a small town. The man had come up the aisle, swaying with the rolling motion of the train. He stopped at the double seat Mama and Louey shared. He smiled pleasantly at Louey. Louey smiled back. He reminded her of a good cowboy in a movie, with his big white hat. He had twinkling green eyes. But she noticed that one of his front teeth was brown.

"Look what I've got for you," he exclaimed heartily and handed Louey a big red lollipop.

"Oh, I'm not sure . . ." Mama said, waking up.

"It's quite all right, ma'am," the man said, tipping his hat.

"Don't eat that," Mama whispered when he walked away.

Louey knew all about not taking candy from strangers but surely this was different? The lollipop looked fine, a brand she recognized, and it was all wrapped up. Cherry-flavored, too. Louey felt the inside of her mouth begin to water.

"Get rid of it. Stick it down there between the

seats," Mama said, looking back over her shoulder, as if afraid to be seen rejecting the gift.

Louey obeyed. But when Mama fell asleep again, she retrieved the lollipop and hid it in her jacket pocket. And later, in Fayetteville, when the relatives were busy talking to each other, she went outside and unwrapped the lollipop. It had tasted better than any other lollipop she had ever licked.

Louey stopped, embarrassed to have been talking so long. "How about you?" she challenged Bobby Lee. "Your turn next." She wanted to put him on the spot but he jumped right in, telling a tale similar to her own.

"All of us here ate our lollipops, too," James said. "And now we've been called, and we're going through the change. You might not feel it yet, but when you do, don't be afraid. You have us."

Mary Beth leaned toward Louey. "Coming here makes it easier to bear, takes the edge off the evil, so to speak." She smiled weakly at the rest of them, as if fearing they might disagree.

"Helps not to bottle up the guilt inside," Curt advised. "You come here, talk, get it out."

There was lots of nodding, but then Keith's angry voice broke in, "I'm sick of talk. Talking doesn't make it go away. I want to stop it. This is no way to live."

"You can't fight it," Darrell said.

"So, do we just give up and die?" asked Mary Beth.

"Face it, hon, you're already half dead," Dawn said. Louey hadn't noticed before how pale her skin was, how feverish her eyes.

The mood turned sour, and people stared at the floor.

"You all know talking about dying does no good," James admonished. "The only way we can fight this is to keep on living."

"No," Bobby Lee said. Everyone looked at him. "The only real way out may be in death."

People perked up; this was something new.

"I've been thinking about it a lot," Bobby Lee said. "We should kill ourselves now, before it gets worse. It's the only thing we can still do by our own free will."

Louey was mad at herself for not making her legs move. She felt like a lump of lead. But if her feet wouldn't work, her mouth could. "My daddy always told me to speak straight and plain," she said. "What changes are you talking about exactly? What's supposed to happen to me?"

They ignored her, like she wasn't even there.

"Bobby Lee's right," Keith was saying. "Do it now, get it over with. Take charge of our own destiny. Makes a lot more sense than talking. Talking gets us nowhere. At least dying will get us someplace."

"Yeah. Get us some peace," said Darrell.

There was a moment of heavy silence. And then, to Louey's amazement, they started talking about killing themselves as if they were planning their summer vacations.

Louey found her legs at last. She stood up and tore for the door. The iron stairs thundered under her feet. She made it two blocks without a breath. Then stopped and gasped and laughed. Crazier than a bunch of pickled goats, her daddy would say. She stopped laughing and felt cold as ice for a moment. But it passed. It left her with an anxious feeling she couldn't shake. But then, she was anxious for having stayed out so long. What if Gran had come back? She ran along the deserted streets and took a shortcut through the square. A little black-and-white dog appeared from underneath an azalea bush and just about tripped her.

Lost, black-and-white older male cocker spaniel wearing red collar, Louey remembered.

The dog whimpered and held up an injured paw.

Louey stared at him. He wagged his tail feebly, looking up at her with hopeful eyes. "Stupid," she said and shoved him away. The dog squealed and limped back into the shrubbery.

I'm in a hurry, no time for stupid dogs. She pounded down Gran's street. She let herself into the house. Just moments later, there was the sound of a taxi. When Gran came inside, Louey was back in the living room chair.

"Have you had a nice evening, dear?" Gran asked.

"Just peachy."

Gran frowned. "Well, then, I'm a bit tired. I think I'll turn in early tonight."

Turn in permanently for all I care, Louey thought. She waited, her nose stuck in the book, until she heard Gran go upstairs. Then she threw the book across the room and turned out the lamp. She sat in the dark for a long time, glaring at a thing that burned behind her eyes. It wasn't until the faint light of dawn began to seep into the room that she got up from the chair and went, cold and stiff, up to bed.

Louey woke to the sound of the newspaper hitting the porch with its unassuming thump. She felt as if she'd had a very bad dream. Or worse. She felt as if she'd done something she should be ashamed of, but she couldn't think what.

For the first time since arriving at Gran's, Louey wanted to stay in bed. Maybe she was getting a cold. She felt her forehead; she sniffed a few times. Gran's quavery morning voice came wafting up the staircase. "Louey? Breakfast is served."

You couldn't come down in your pajamas in Gran's house. Louey hurriedly pulled on some clothes and swiped at her short hair. Gran would be sure to notice if she hadn't brushed her teeth. She grabbed a mint to suck instead.

In the dining room, Gran had poured the coffee, but was waiting to begin, her plate still protected by its silver warming cover. "Sorry," Louey said and sat down to uncover her own plate. Gran gave a slight nod and began to eat.

But halfway through, she put her fork down and delicately patted her lips with her napkin.

"Something upsetting has happened," she announced.

Louey felt a pang of guilt. Had Gran discovered she'd been out? "What?" she asked, keeping her eyes lowered.

"In there," Gran said, and Louey had to look up to see the gesture toward the living room. "A terrible mess."

Louey remembered throwing the book. Gran was a stickler but this was too much. "I guess I dropped it and forgot."

"What are you talking about, dear?"

"My library book. I left it lying on the floor."

"I didn't notice."

Well, then what was it? Louey got up from the table to see. "Oh, I wouldn't," Gran said, but Louey walked across to the living room door, which had been pulled shut. The old wood stuck a little. She gave it a push and was about to step in. The smell stopped her. Cloying and sickly sweet, and some undercurrent of the unmentionable; smells that shouldn't be in living rooms.

Gran was behind her, pulling at the door. "Come away, you don't want to see. Some degenerate, the police said. I wouldn't let them wake you." Gran's mild face creased with concern. "Are you feeling well? You were sleeping so sound."

"I didn't see anything," Louey said, aware that her voice was rising strangely. "I went to bed the usual time."

"Thank goodness you did! You might have been harmed."

"Was anything stolen?" Louey asked.

"Nothing at all."

"Something *must* have been stolen," Louey said.

"No. They just left that . . . mess." Gran was trying

to behave like a lady. She suddenly looked much older, more fragile. Thin as glass, Mama would say, crisp as a dead leaf. Pathetic really, Louey thought. Ugly, too. Whiskers sprouting on her chin. Wrinkled-up chicken neck wobbling like Jell-O every time she talked. Louey felt like giving Gran a shove. It was a lucky thing that Clara came in, to say that Ned had arrived to clean up.

Louey didn't read the newspaper that day. She spent the morning in her room, trying to push down the feeling that she had done something wrong. She regretted running away last night. She should have stuck around for the facts. She wished she could talk to Bobby Lee again. In spite of his crazy suicide idea, she trusted him most. Maybe he'd only said that to humor them. That was it, of course. Bobby Lee had just been playing a joke on that bunch of maniacs. They could have laughed together afterwards.

By the afternoon, she couldn't stand it and told Gran she was going for a walk. The living room had been thoroughly cleaned, and the hall smelled of disinfectant. Gran said it was a good idea to get some fresh air.

Louey retraced her steps in search of the house, worrying that it wouldn't be there. But as she rounded the corner, she saw it right away. She couldn't miss it. There was a commotion going on. Police cars and an ambulance.

She joined the throng rubbernecking at the curb. "What happened?" she asked no one in particular.

"Man killed hisself," someone said.

"Missus Blane's son," said somebody else. "Slit his throat in the tub. Water overflowed, blood come down into the kitchen where she was making biscuits. Ruined the biscuits!" Snickers and then solemn silence as the front door of the house opened and a woman was helped out, hunched over, sobbing, leaning on a policeman. She passed close enough for Louey to smell her perfume, even touch her. "Why would he do it?" she was asking. "Give me one reason why!"

Louey melted back into the crowd, afraid the woman would see the guilty knowledge on her face.

Louey went back to reading the newspaper. She woke up long before eight o'clock, anxious for its arrival. She was dressed and ready before Clara even put the breakfast on the table. First thing, Louey turned to the funeral notices. She didn't know their last names, but she could tell by their first names and their ages. She'd already read about James Blane. The obituary didn't mention suicide. A day later, there was one for Dawn Whitaker. Had to be her, only seventeen. Died suddenly and unexpectedly. Sure, Louey thought. As sudden and unexpected as a razor slicing across your throat.

One morning she looked up and was startled by Gran's troubled gaze.

"Are you feeling all right, dear?"

"Of course I am."

"Get out in the fresh air more," Gran said. "Better than dwelling on morbid things."

Louey felt furious, she wanted to push the whole dining room table, silver, china, crystal and all, onto Gran. Instead she got up and stomped out into the garden to finish reading the paper. But somehow, she never got herself past the obituaries these days.

Louey thought she might be in love with Bobby Lee. Could you fall in love on such short notice? She remembered his pretty eyes and his nice smile. She hoped she wouldn't see his name in the paper one morning.

That week, they picked themselves off with uncanny regularity. First James and Dawn, then Keith and Darrell. She wondered if she should tell the police, to try to save the few left. But it was so crackbrained; who would believe it? Anyway, it was their business. Hadn't they wanted to remain anonymous? Suicides Anonymous, she thought and laughed, spewing toast crumbs across the tablecloth.

"Something funny?" Gran asked with a frown.

"No," Louey said rudely and saw Gran swallow hard.

"You're not yourself today, dear," Gran said.

"I feel fine."

"But you haven't been sleeping well."

"I sleep fine." Louey glared at Gran until the old woman's gaze dropped. Then she threw the newspaper down on her unfinished plate and tramped out of the room.

Okay, there were the nightmares. Louey had never been one for bad dreams but now they came every night. Bobby Lee figured in all of them. Which was why she thought she had fallen in love. But he was different in the dreams. He said strange things.

"What causes your heart the most pain?" he'd asked last night when they were riding on his black motorcycle. She had felt the wind sting her face and had smelled the leather of his jacket as she pressed her face into his back.

"What is the worst thing?" he'd screamed at her. "Come on, tell, Louey, tell the very worst most private thing!"

Louey had not answered. She had been busy trying to think of the worst when he stopped in a deserted lane. Mean brick row houses with narrow backyards. An animal foraging in the garbage cans.

"Use this," said Bobby Lee.

The coffin-shaped handle fit easily into her hand. The massive bowie blade glinted in the light of the moon. She hefted its weight. She ran her finger down the steel, and her own blood gleamed back. "It's sharp," she said.

"Sssssssharp." Bobby Lee smiled. "You'll do anything for me, won't you?"

"Yes, yes," she'd replied, breathless with the closeness of him, remembering the feel of his muscles rippling under leather, oh Bobby Lee, I want you to kiss me.

"Then kill that," he'd said and pointed.

Of course, it was funny that when she woke up she actually had a cut on her left index finger, just where she'd dreamed she'd run her finger along the blade.

And she'd been a little ashamed of those feelings and hoped, even in the dream, that she hadn't said them aloud to Bobby Lee, about wanting him to kiss her. Now that she remembered it, his smile wasn't quite the dazzle she had first thought. There was something the matter with one of his teeth.

"Louey! I've been talking to you," Gran said in the living room that night.

Louey's head felt heavy, as if it had grown too big.

"I was saying that tomorrow we'll get the doctor to take a look at you. Now why don't you go up to bed?"

The mantel clock said a few minutes past eight. "It's too early."

"Not for the state you're in," Gran said, her voice sounding stronger, more determined than it ever had before.

"It's too early," Louey cried out as if in pain, and Gran's papery face paled.

"I'm sorry," Louey said, feeling suddenly sly. "Yes, yes, it's time for me to sleep."

"Pleasant dreams," Clara said as Louey went past her in the hall.

Louey laughed. She heard Clara go in to Gran and say, "Whatever's come over that child? She's *changed*."

Louey ran up the stairs to drown out the word. She threw off her clothes and got into bed. Now it seemed urgent that she go to sleep, quickly, quickly, to dream.

* * *

Bobby Lee was waiting, looking cross. Louey hoped he wasn't really mad.

"I'll forgive you," he said. "Maybe."

"Please, Bobby Lee," Louey cooed at him, running her hands up and down his leather sleeves. "I'm sorry I couldn't do it last time. Please . . ."

He pulled away. She had to run to get on his motorcycle before he took off without her. Hanging on, they rode like the speed of night in the light of a fluorescent moon. Bobby Lee asked again: "What is your worst most private thing?"

Louey felt he might see into her heart even when she didn't know what was there. She was afraid of him, but overwhelmed by the thrill of him. She never wanted their wild ride to stop. She closed her eyes and let herself go. I don't care anymore, she thought. I give, yes, I give, I'm ready for you.

She felt the thing in her hand again. She gripped it hard to the hilt.

"Do it for me," said Bobby Lee.

My worst thing, Louey thought. The thing that makes my heart hurt. My private mind has been invaded, and I am complying, not minding, I am going, not retreating, I am, I am . . . doing it.

She could feel the rush of blood on her fingers, warm and thick. The smell of it made the salt in her own mouth twinge. If only there wasn't this horrible bleat of dying.

"Good?" Bobby Lee asked, his voice hoarse and urgent.

"I'm not sure," Louey said.

Bobby Lee was cross. But he laughed. Bitter laugh. Long piercing scream of a laugh that cracked the face of the moon, skidded them around a corner, and threw Louey off the bike. She landed hard, heard herself make a sound like *ooof*. She opened her eyes. Flinched at the raw smell of sweat on her.

The dream scream went on and on. Until she realized it was coming from downstairs.

She threw on her robe and ran, and wondered at how her shoulders ached as she clutched the banister.

Gran was standing at the door between the kitchen and dining room, a bony white-knuckled hand pressed to her mouth. The outside kitchen door was open and through it Louey could see Clara in the garden, hands covering her eyes, walking blindly through Ned's neat borders, as if trying to run away.

On the stove, a big, black iron soup pot was bubbling. It had always been stored in the cellar, a relic of a bygone era, big enough to soak a whole hog. But there it was, chortling away, its lid dancing in escaping steam. A tantalizing smell wafted out, like roasting oranges and fatback pork. Louey walked over and lifted the lid.

When she looked into the dog's eyes, boiled away now to a white glaze, she knew. Her private heart had been cracked open. The knowledge was in her sore shoulders, on her stained hands.

She had no time for retching or crying. With strength she didn't know she had, she lifted the pot clear off the flame and carried it outside. Steam rose up to sear her eyes but she moved on, walking the thing down to the bottom of the garden where she threw it on the compost heap.

She helped Clara back inside; she sat Gran down in a dining room chair. She didn't mind the pain of blisters forming on her scalded hands; there was a promise of healing goodness in it.

She expected the pounding that came on the door.

"I'll get it. It's for me."

He was standing there. A twinkling in his green eyes, one brown tooth in his dazzling smile.

He lifted his white hat. "I've come calling," he said.

She blinked and he was Bobby Lee. Blinked and he was the man on the train again.

"Got 'em all, except you," he said genially. "Time to go now."

"I'm not going," Louey said.

She could almost hear him saying it: *Oh, yes you are*.

"See, it's this way," Louey began in a conversational tone. "I just remembered. When I took that lollipop outside? When all my relatives were busy talking? I unwrapped the pretty red paper. I put that lollipop to my lips. And I gave it one good lick. But Mama came out then and saw what I was doing. She grabbed me and gave me the whipping of my life."

"You hated her for that," he said, leering.

"Sure I did. That's why I forgot. But see, I never ate the lollipop. Mama threw it away."

It unsettled him, made him look angry but helpless at the same time.

"So I don't have to go with you now," Louey said, slowly closing the door on him, " 'cause I only had a little taste of death."

THE DOLL
Carol Ellis

THE MAN HAD BEEN OUT SINCE SUNRISE, WALKING along the narrow strip of sand at the base of the rocky cliff. It was a beautiful place to walk, except for the garbage. Drivers up on the cliff road tossed down everything from greasy fast-food bags to broken beach chairs. The man usually ignored it, but something caught his eyes this morning, wedged in a wide space between two big boulders. Curious because it looked different from most of the stuff people dumped here, he walked over and pulled it out. It had been scratched up a little, and there was one big crack along the bottom. But it had survived the fall from the clifftop, which was something of a miracle. He slid his fingers over the latch, but it was tight, and his hands were cold. He sat down on a flat rock and blew on his fingers. When his hands warmed up, he'd try again.

Three months earlier, a few miles away from the cliff road, sixteen-year-old Abby Rodgers and her family had moved into their new house. It wasn't new at all, really. Abby's mother, Deanna, thought it must

have been built in the 1870s, although it had obviously
been redone several times.

"It looks ancient," Lindsay grumbled. Abby's sister
was ten and thought anything old was *disgusting*, her
favorite word for things she didn't like. "I still wish
we'd moved into that condo. The swimming pool was
fantastic."

"And the condo was fantastically expensive,"
Deanna pointed out. She hefted a cardboard box onto
the small front porch and pushed her hair out of her
eyes.

"The condo didn't have any trees, either," Abby
said. "There's that huge one out back, remember,
Lindsay? Maybe you can build a tree house in it."

Lindsay's frown faded.

"Good idea," Deanna said. She turned the key in the
lock and pushed open the front door. "This is great,
isn't it? Our first official night in the house."

Abby hadn't been crazy about moving. She couldn't
do anything about it, though. Since her parents had
divorced four years ago, making the payments on the
old house had gotten harder and harder. And she kept
reminding herself that it wasn't like they were moving
out of town. She'd still go to the same school and have
the same friends. She'd still wonder whether Mark
Helpern would ask her out this year.

Still, Abby had been reluctant to leave their old
neighborhood, so she was surprised and a little confused by her reaction to the house. The first time she'd
seen it, she'd felt drawn to it. She wasn't sure why.

It was old, and it sagged, and the yard was mostly weeds.

But there was something about the steep roof and tall old windows, something that made her feel like the place was reaching for her.

Once she'd seen it, she couldn't wait to move in.

At dinner that first night, Deanna flattened a paper bag from the deli and wrote a list of chores on it. Unstick the windows, paint every room, pull up the kitchen linoleum, clean out the attic.

"I'll do the attic," Abby said without even thinking.

"Are you sure?" Her mother looked at her curiously. "It's going to be baking hot up there. And it's completely unfinished, no windows. I thought you hated closed, stuffy places like that."

"I'll still do it." Abby didn't blame her mother for being surprised. Small, airless rooms, elevators, closets, always made her feel panicky.

But the attic, even more strongly than the house itself, seemed as if it were pulling her to it.

The next morning, shortly after her mother had left for work, Abby tied a scarf over her fine blonde hair, opened the hatch in the upstairs hall, and climbed up. Her mother had warned her about the heat, but Abby was still overwhelmed. It was like a living thing, thick and so heavy that she felt as if a hand were pressing down on her, squeezing out her breath, making her knees buckle, making her dizzy. She leaned against the flaking bricks of the chimney and closed her eyes for a moment. Sweat was already beading on her face

and rolling down her sides in tickling rivulets. She
wiped her arm across her forehead and tried to breathe
slowly. From outside, she could hear the faint thump
of a hammer on wood — Lindsay had started working
on her tree house. She heard the chirping of birds,
too, and the occasional swish of a car. In a few more
seconds, she opened her eyes.

Sunlight crept in where the roof met the floor, and
dust motes danced crazily in their shafts. A single bare
light bulb hung from the center of the roof, its long
string dangling within Abby's reach. She pulled on it
and a weak light spilled down into the middle of the
room, leaving the far corners in shadow.

The heat, the closeness, the thought of spiders, any
one of them would usually have made Abby give up
before she'd even started. But something was waiting
for her here. She could feel it, sense its presence in
the airless shadows.

With a strange sense of urgency, Abby waded into
the piles of sagging cardboard boxes, stuffed paper
bags, and rolled-up rug remnants. She had to find
whatever it was that was waiting. She searched for
an hour, frantically, until her hands were black with
grime and her clothes were covered with dust.

At last, she found what she'd been looking for.

The moment she pulled it from a paper bag so old
it shredded to pieces in her fingers, she knew this was
it. In her hands was a rectangular wooden box, thick
with dust like everything else. It was a handsome box,
or would be, when the smooth wood and the tarnished
brass catch were polished. Abby could feel an energy

pulsing through the thick wood of the box and into her hands, hands that shook as she fumbled with the catch and lifted the lid.

Inside the box was a doll.

Bedded on white satin that had yellowed with age, the doll lay like a small dead child. Its shiny black hair was piled high on its head, and its dress of lilac satin looked like something a woman would have worn a hundred years ago. The skirt was long and full, the waist was tight, and the high neck and long sleeves were edged with lace.

The dark-lashed eyes in the china face were as blue as the sky, as blue as Abby's, and they were wide open.

The staring, sky-blue eyes seemed aware, alive, and filled with an emotion so powerful that Abby gasped.

For a moment, she thought she saw hatred in those eyes.

But it was only a moment. Abby blinked and lifted the doll from its box. The eyes were empty, lifeless. It was just an old doll with blue glass eyes glittering in the feeble light of the dingy attic.

Later, after she'd cleaned out half the attic, Abby took the doll downstairs to her room. Smoothing its satin skirt, she put it on a long shelf where she kept a few stuffed animals, another doll her father had sent her from Mexico, two lopsided clay pots she'd made in art class last year, and a bunch of shells she'd found at the beach. The doll sat on the shelf like a queen, imperious and cold, its face turned toward Abby's bed.

"I don't see what you want o keep it for," Lindsay

said that night, after Abby had put the doll in place. "It's so old it's disgusting."

"I don't see why you care," Abby told her. She was lying on the bed, staring across at the doll. "But she happens to be beautiful. Mom thinks it might be an antique, maybe valuable."

"So why don't you sell it? I would."

"I know *you* would," Abby said. "But I don't want to. Think of it this way, Lindsay — I just liberated her. She's a free woman now."

"Yeah, right," Lindsay snorted.

"Why don't you scram?" Abby suggested cheerfully.

After Lindsay left, Abby switched out the bedside lamp and stretched out to sleep. The light from a street lamp filtered in through the thin white curtains, and across the room Abby could see the doll's eyes shining in the shadows. The eyes wouldn't close. Her mother said they must be stuck, probably because they were so old, or maybe they were never meant to shut. The only way to know would be to take the doll's head off, but it was delicate and there was always the chance it might break. Abby couldn't do that, any more than she could have left the doll in the attic. Now that she'd found it, she couldn't risk destroying it. She'd just have to live with the doll's strange staring eyes.

School started a week later and so did Abby's dreams. She thought, at first, that it must be **all the** changes in her life. New house, new room, new classes. By the time Abby learned the true cause of the dreams, it was too late.

She tried to forget the dreams, but they stayed with her, shadowing her days like clouds and keeping her awake late at night, staring across the room into the doll's sightless eyes.

The dreams were eerie, strange little scenes that made no sense but filled her with dread as she watched, twisting and turning in her sleep. But it was what happened after she woke up that was so frightening. She began to wonder if the face looking back at her from the mirror every day was an Abby she'd never known, an Abby who dreamed of danger but was powerless to stop it.

The first victim was her friend, Erin Gray.

It was Friday night, the end of the first week of school. Erin was sleeping over at Abby's after the two of them had gone to the movies. Before they went to sleep, around one in the morning, Erin tried to convince Abby that Mark Helpern wasn't her type.

"I know he's cool," Erin said from her sleeping bag on the floor, "but he never sticks with anybody. He's with a new girl every week."

"Well, I don't want to marry him, Erin," Abby said. "I just want to date him."

"Oh, Abby." Erin stood up and walked across the room. She took the doll down from the shelf and absentmindedly turned it over in her hands while she talked. "You know you'll be miserable when he dumps you." She was flipping the doll up and down. "What's wrong with this thing? Its eyes won't close."

"It's a doll, not a thing, and I don't know why," Abby said. "Anyway, you're wrong about Mark."

"I just don't want to see you get hurt, okay?" Erin plunked the doll back on the shelf and snuggled into the sleeping bag. "I also don't want to have to say I told you so."

Abby laughed and switched out the light. A few moments later, Erin's sleepy voice came wafting up from the floor. "Abby?"

"Huh?"

"That doll's eyes give me the creeps. Do you mind if I turn it around or something?"

"Go ahead." Abby watched sleepily as Erin moved across the room, her long white T-shirt a pale blur in the shadows. As Erin came back, Abby's eyes were drifting closed. For a second, she woke again with a jerk, feeling an icy touch on her back, a touch that made her shiver even though the room was warm. But then the touch was gone, and Abby sank into a deep sleep.

She saw a hand. A small, pale hand out in the hall. She didn't know, or couldn't see, what it was doing. But she knew it was the hall outside her room because she recognized the peeling, ivy-patterned wallpaper that they hadn't stripped off the walls yet, and the painted baseboard that her mother wanted to sand down to the original wood.

The hand was delicate and fine-boned. A girl's hand. Like a pale, fluttering moth, it hovered near the floor at the top of the stairs for a moment, then pulled back gently into darkness.

Abby woke up to the sound of a scream.

The room was dark, but a sliver of light came under

the door from the hallway, and she heard muffled voices out there. It was Erin, talking to Abby's mother. Abby swung her legs over the side of the bed and went to the door.

"It's okay, I'll live," Erin was saying. "I think."

"What happened?" Abby blinked in the hall light. "Are you all right? I heard you yell."

"You'd yell too if you almost broke your neck," Erin said. "I wanted to get a drink. So I was going to go downstairs, but I didn't make it to the top step, even." She bent over and rubbed her knee. "I tripped."

"On what?" Abby's mother was looking around the top of the stairs. "There's nothing here to trip on."

"I don't know." Erin frowned. "But something was there. I felt it."

The three of them stared at the top of the stairs, then at each other. Abby felt something nudging her memory, some thought or image, but she couldn't catch hold of it. Finally, they all went back to bed.

"That was scary," Erin said as she lay back down on the sleeping bag. "But at least I didn't fall all the way down. Those stairs are steep."

"I know. I'm glad you're all right." Abby got in bed and closed her eyes, then opened them again when Erin got up. "What are you doing?"

"Turning this doll around," Erin said from across the room.

"I thought you already did that."

"I did, but I guess it slipped because I can see the eyes again."

It wasn't until the next day, after Erin had left, that

Abby remembered her dream. The pale hand hovering, almost floating, at the top of the stairs, in the very spot where Erin had fallen. Had the hand been trying to point, to let her know that something was going to happen there?

Almost a week later, Abby and Erin and Holly Roselle, another friend, were sitting around the table in Abby's kitchen, studying for a test in social studies. They'd tried to study in Abby's room, but like Erin, Holly couldn't stand the doll's eyes. "They're awful," she'd said. "It's like they're watching me all the time." So the three of them had taken their books into the kitchen.

"I never do any good on these essay tests," Holly complained. "How do we know what to study for if we don't know what the questions are going to be?"

"I know what you mean," said Erin, who was at the refrigerator, pulling out a bottle of soda. Abby stood beside her at the counter, refilling the bowl of popcorn.

Holly was still sitting, her elbows on the table, her chin in her hands. The light from the hanging lamp overhead made her dark hair gleam. Abby turned to say something to her, and that's when it happened.

There was no time for a warning. One second the stained-glass lamp was hanging from its chain above the tabletop, and the next second it was dropping straight down, crashing with a shattering of glass onto Holly's head.

It was Erin who pulled the lamp away, Erin who started to wipe the blood away from Holly's face and then ran to get Abby's mother. Abby had screamed when the lamp fell, but after that she was silent, paralyzed, looking on in horror as her mother calmed Holly down so she could look at the gash on her head. Abby heard her mother say she didn't think it was as deep as it seemed, that head cuts always bled badly. She watched as her mother and Erin helped Holly up, heard her mother say she'd take her home. She watched it all, but at the same time she was remembering.

The lamp was spinning, spinning so fast that the light from the colored glass panels swirled and blended together into a crazy pool of color on the shining tabletop. Abby watched it go around, faster and faster, until she was dizzy from watching and had to look away. Then she heard the sound. Not a gasp, really, just a soft intake of breath, coming from somewhere near the lamp. She looked back, and there was the hand, white and delicate, reaching toward the lamp. At the touch of a slender finger, the lamp stopped spinning. Then Abby heard another sound. A sigh, as soft and delicate as the hand. A sigh of satisfaction.

She'd dreamed it the night before. Now, looking at the books spattered with dark-red drops of Holly's blood, Abby shuddered and closed her eyes. She'd been warned. She'd been warned in her dream, but she hadn't remembered in time to help.

Holly needed four stitches in her head, but she was all right. Even so, Abby couldn't forget what had happened, or what she'd dreamed.

That was when the dreams began to haunt her, when

she tried to keep her eyes from closing at night, afraid of what might happen after she dreamed again.

But she had to sleep, and when she did dream again, it was worse, much worse. Not the dream, but the reality. The horrible reality that Abby didn't see until it was almost too late, until she woke one night to the sound of her mother's voice, hoarse with fear, shouting for Abby to come help her.

Abby stumbled across the room and pulled open the door, saw her mother's back disappearing down the stairs. Barefoot, her mind still cobwebbed with sleep, she followed Deanna down and out the back door into the cool night air.

The crackling sound was soft, almost soothing. The smell reminded Abby of summer camp. But there was nothing comforting about the sight of the flames licking at the bottom of the boards. Abby stopped, frozen in horror for one painful second, then rushed after her mother across the weedy backyard toward the burning tree house where Lindsay lay sleeping.

For Lindsay, the reality of Abby's third dream was agony, the agony of scorched flesh on her shoulders and back and hands. Deanna cried when the doctors said Lindsay was lucky — they were first-degree burns. She could have died, but she'd live.

No one knew how the fire had started. The tree house was close to the street that ran near the backyard, and Deanna thought some idiot must have tossed a match from a car.

But Abby knew better, because she'd seen it. She'd

seen it in her dream. Hours before her mother's cry
had pulled her from sleep, she'd seen the match. Not
tossed from a car, but torn from a matchbook and
struck into flame by a slender white hand.

Sitting in the hospital room, with Lindsay sleeping
in the bed and her mother dozing fitfully in a chair,
Abby tried to gulp back the tears, but she couldn't.
Her shoulders shook, but she cried silently, the tears
spilling from her eyes and dripping from her chin onto
her clenched hands. After a while, she wiped her
cheeks and held her hands in front of her face. Small
but wide, with blunt, squared-off fingertips like her
father's. Not like the dream hands, delicate and pale
and deadly. Whose hands did she see in her sleep?

Another week went by before Abby dreamed again,
a week when the weather turned cooler and the leaves
on the trees dropped down in bushels. Lindsay was
much better, but she didn't go in the backyard, and
there was no talk of building another tree house. No
one talked of the fire, but everyone remembered the
horror of that night, and how close Lindsay had come
to death.

Abby went to bed each night afraid to sleep, and
dragged through the days wondering what she'd see
when she did sleep. She knew she'd dream again, and
she was terrified of what would happen. Mark Helpern
bought her a Coke after school, and Abby was too tired
and worried to even try to have a good time. No one
was more surprised than Abby when he asked her out
for Saturday night.

"I'll pick you up about seven-thirty," he said as they stood on her front porch in the late afternoon. He smoothed back his dark blond hair and smiled at her. "A movie and some food, does that sound okay?"

Abby was about to say it sounded great when the front door opened and Lindsay stepped out. She was carrying the doll by one leg. "It fell," she said defensively to Abby. "I was walking by your room and I saw it on the floor."

Abby took the doll and smoothed down the heavy lilac skirt. "So why didn't you put her back on the shelf?"

"Because I heard you talking and I wanted to know who was with you." Lindsay looked at Mark, smirked, and went back inside.

"You like dolls, huh?" Mark asked.

Abby laughed a little. "I found her in the attic. She's really old."

Mark took the doll in his hands, hands still tan from the summer, and looked it over. "Nice," he said. He raised his eyes to Abby's face. "But not as nice as you." He shook his head and chuckled, as if he realized how corny he'd sounded. But then he leaned close and touched his lips to Abby's.

Abby supposed it was an awkward kiss, with the doll stuck between them and Abby herself so surprised she didn't do anything but stand there. But it didn't seem to matter. Mark smiled at her again, put the doll in her hands, and headed for his car. He folded his long legs into the tomato-red compact, tooted the horn once, and then he was gone. Abby stood still a moment, hugging the doll against her chest, before she headed into the house.

She dreamed again on Friday night.

She woke at midnight, her legs tangled in the sheets, the blood pounding in her ears. The sense of danger had been overwhelming, and it stayed with her through the night, snapping her awake every hour until she finally gave up and watched the sunrise through the kitchen window.

She could see the hands again, but not only the hands. She could see an entire figure, a small one, maybe a child's. The figure was in shadow, though, and she couldn't tell much about it. Just the delicate hands and the curve of a pale cheek. But it was moving, walking. Abby heard a crunch of gravel on a road, the swish of a dress, saw the tip of a shiny black shoe. And she heard another sound, the sound of breathing that broke into a soft, excited giggle as the figure skimmed quickly along.

Then the figure was running, running down the road, scattering pebbles under its feet, its breath coming faster and faster. Abby could feel her own breathing speed up. She didn't know what was coming, she only knew that it was going to be bad. But she didn't know how bad until she saw the glare of headlights, heard the hum of the engine turn into a roar as the car got closer and closer, saw the small shadowy figure step deliberately into the path of the oncoming car.

Then came the screech of brakes, and the sickening sounds of crunching metal and shattering glass. There was a moment of silence, and then came the last sound

Abby heard before she woke — a soft, whispery giggle.

It was Saturday now, a day when she should have been counting the hours until Mark came to pick her up. Instead, she drifted through the day in a haze of depression, the memory of her dreams hanging over her like a dark weight.

Erin had been lucky — she could easily have tumbled to the bottom of the steep stairs and broken her neck. Holly had been lucky, too. The glass could have sliced into her eyes or neck, blinding or killing her. Lindsay might have died in the flames, charred and blackened like the boards of her tree house.

And now this fourth dream. Would Abby read about the crash in tomorrow's newspaper? Would she see the words telling her what she already knew — that there'd been a car crash, that someone had been hurt, that maybe a child had been hit?

Tired and edgy, Abby spent most of the day moving from room to room, gazing out the windows at Lindsay and her mother, who were raking leaves. There had been frost on the ground this morning. Soon the grass would turn brown and brittle, the trees would be empty and skeletal, and darkness would come earlier and earlier.

At seven, Abby took a shower and washed her hair. Under the sharp, hot needles of water, she felt her tense muscles relax a little, and the dull headache she'd had all day started to ease. Wrapped in a thick terry robe, she padded back to her room.

She was staring into the closet, her eyes roving over and rejecting shirts and skirts and pants, when she heard the sound . . . that childish giggle. It was so clear, so close, that without thinking, Abby whirled around, expecting to see someone right behind her.

But the room was empty.

Shaking her head as if to clear it, Abby turned back to the closet. She was reaching for a dark orange blouse, soft and silky to the touch, when she noticed the time. Eight o'clock. Mark was half an hour late.

An hour later, Abby brought the cordless phone into her bedroom and called Mark's house. If she'd stopped to think, she might have wondered about her pounding heart and shaking hands. She might have realized that they were caused by something much more horrible than the fear that Mark stood her up. But she didn't stop to think. So when Mark's mother answered, and Abby asked to speak to him, she was completely unprepared.

Abby stood frozen in the middle of her room while Mark Helpern's mother, her voice thick with tears, told her that Mark was dead, that he'd died in the hospital that afternoon.

"He was driving home from a friend's house," Mrs. Helpern said. "He's a good driver, a careful driver. But of course, he had to swerve, and . . ." She stopped a moment, and Abby heard her swallow several times. "He was only going thirty-five, at least that's the speed limit there. But the police told us that even at that speed, when you hit a tree . . ." She stopped again.

Abby's mouth was dry and when she spoke, her voice cracked. "Why?" she asked. "You said he had to swerve. Why?"

"Because of the little girl," Mrs. Helpern said. "When they were putting him into the ambulance, he told them he'd seen a little girl run into the road. He was very clear about it. They looked and looked, but they never found her." Her voice broke completely then, and all she could say was good-bye.

Abby switched off the phone and closed her eyes. A wave of dizziness hit her. She knew she ought to sit down before she fell, but she couldn't move, she could only stand there, so dizzy she felt herself swaying.

That's when she heard the giggle again. A happy, impish, childlike giggle. And it was close, so close Abby could hear the indrawn breath before it came a second time.

Abby opened her eyes, but didn't move. She held her breath, waiting, knowing she'd hear it again. When she did, when that eerie, whispery giggle drifted toward her across the room, she slowly turned around and stared into the doll's glittering, sky-blue eyes.

A little girl.

A little girl in a purple dress, with slender, pale hands and shiny black shoes. Just like the doll Abby had freed from the rubble in the attic and . . . what? Brought to life? Brought to life so her fine china hands could trip one friend on the stairs, send a lamp crashing onto another friend's head, strike a match and set the tree house ablaze with her sister inside it?

Brought to life so she could dash into the road and kill an innocent sixteen-year-old boy?

Then, as Abby stood there, she watched in terror as the doll's eyes changed, came alive, shifted in the lifeless china face and focused directly on Abby. In the eyes was a look of triumph. It lasted only a second, but that was enough. There was life there, some kind of life, some kind of deadly force that had killed and would go on killing until somebody stopped it.

Abby knew what she had to do. Swallowing a scream, she strode to the shelf and snatched up the doll. She didn't look at its eyes again. If there was life there, she didn't want to see it. Sobbing in her need to get rid of it, she thrust the doll into the beautiful wooden box that she'd polished until it gleamed.

It looks like a coffin, Abby thought, as she slammed down the lid and pushed the shiny brass catch in place.

A satin-lined coffin for a doll.

Ten minutes later, Abby pulled her mother's car to a stop up on the cliff road. The box was on the seat next to her. As she reached for it, she heard a sound coming from it. A faint, pattering sound, like pebbles. It wasn't pebbles, though.

It was tiny china fists battering against wood.

Then Abby was out of the car, the wind tearing at her hair, standing at the edge of the cliff with the box in her hands. She didn't hesitate. With all the strength she had, she threw the box over the cliff and watched it, turning over and over, its brass catch winking in the moonlight until it disappeared into the darkness below.

Abby stood alone at the top of the cliff. She was shivering from the cold, but she had to wait, had to be sure. Straining her ears, she listened until she heard, faint but distinct, the clattering sound as the box struck the sharp boulders at the base of the cliff. She heard it hit once, twice, three times, and then there was silence.

It was over. The doll was gone, and Abby turned to go home, knowing she could sleep and never see those pale, deadly hands again.

The man had finally pried the latch open and as he looked inside, he smiled, surprised and pleased. It was funny, what some people threw away. He was sure this was a genuine antique, probably worth a lot of money. The hands and face were fine china and he bet the dress was real satin. They didn't make dolls like this anymore.

Antique or not, though, he wasn't going to sell it. Not with Christmas on the way. Not when he had a daughter who was nine years old and still crazy about dolls. Yes, this would make a perfect gift for her.

With a satisfied chuckle, he tucked the box under his arm and headed home.

HOUSE OF
HORRORS
J.B. Stamper

M ARK STARED AT HIS REFLECTION IN THE MIRROR and, for a moment, was startled by what he saw. His face was deathly white with black shadows under his eyes and cheekbones. His dark hair was slicked back off his forehead like a shiny, black cap. And when he smiled, remembering that he was supposed to look like this, he saw the fangs that he had capped onto his teeth just an hour ago.

"Mark, shape up," a voice yelled from across the room. "They'll be coming in soon."

Mark turned away from the mirror to look at Eliot, the head usher, who was smirking at him near the entrance door. Eliot's handsome face was distorted by the scar he had drawn across it. But the girls who came through the House of Horrors still stared at him wistfully and giggled nervously when he made eyes back at them. Mark never got more than a quick glance at his thin face and awkward body in its black usher's uniform.

Mark snapped his mind to attention as the heavy oak doors of the House of Horrors slowly began to creak open. As they did, he heard the familiar music start up from the speaker system. It sounded like the sound track of a horror movie and still made an uneasy shiver crawl down his spine. He waited in the shadows of the room for the people to pass through the doors and begin their tour.

One by one, they walked into the entrance hall, their faces lit by nervous anticipation. Predictably, they all jumped as a flash of lightning seemed to cut through the room and thunder rumbled over the loudspeaker. Then Eliot began his smooth welcome to the House of Horrors, warning them to watch for the dark shadows and lurking terrors of the rooms. Mark watched with envy as the faces of the girls turned to watch Eliot, and their eyes fixed on his rugged features. Then, he heard the high-pitched, eerie scream on the sound track, his cue to speak to the group.

"This way, ladies and gentlemen," he said in his deepest voice. "Follow me into the sitting room." The crowd of people stared at him expectantly for a moment, and then began to walk through the entrance door that he held open, motioning them through with his flashlight.

A blonde girl who had bravely walked into the sitting room first now screamed so loudly that the rest of the group huddled closer together, smiling nervously as fear flashed in their eyes. Mark pulled shut the door and walked after them into the dark sitting room where spotlighted wax corpses were sprawled on the chairs and sofas in various grotesque postures of death. The tourists began murmuring and gasping as they moved along the railings of the sitting room.

Mark tried to avoid looking at the corpse that bothered him most — a thin, young man who seemed to have four puncture wounds in his neck. But, as always, his eyes gravitated to his face, twisted in a horrible death spasm. He pulled his eyes away and checked to see if any sightseers were straggling in the shadowy darkness of the room. There was only one girl who jumped in terror as he tapped her shoulder and told her to move on.

Mark's hands began to tremble with anticipation as he reached for the door that led to the next part of the House of Horrors — the library. He opened it and motioned the crowd through, peering into the room to catch a glimpse of the library tour guide, Lisa. She was staring back at him with her dark eyes heavily lined with black makeup. Her blood-red lips curled into a suggestive smile. Then, like a cat, Lisa slipped through the shadows to Mark's side.

"Party tonight, Mark," she whispered into his ear. "After hours . . . don't be late."

Mark felt his heart begin to pound against his rib cage as he breathed in the smell of her heavy perfume. She gave him a last, long look with her liquid, brown eyes and then slipped off into the darkness of the library where waxen readers sprawled dead with faces frozen in masks of terror.

As the last tourist in the group walked into the library, Mark slowly pushed the door shut, reluctantly closing out the sight of Lisa. He suddenly felt dizzy with excitement. After weeks of working in the House of Horrors and being ignored by the other guides, he was finally going to a party with them — after hours!

Never had a day's work passed so slowly for Mark. As each group of tourists moved from the sitting room into the library, he would meet Lisa's eyes. Each time, she smiled back at him, seeming to suggest that she, too, couldn't wait until the long day was over and the party would begin.

Finally, Mark saw by his luminous watch dial that it was 8:45, fifteen minutes until closing time for the amusement park. There would be just one more group going through the House of Horrors. Then the spotlights would be turned off, the doors to the building would be locked until the next day, and the guides would go home for the night. Suddenly, Mark wondered how the guides could have a party after hours without being caught by Mr. Hiller. He was the tough-minded manager of the House of Horrors, and he never let any of the guides step out of line.

Then, just before the last group of the day came through the oak doors of the entrance hall, Eliot pulled Mark aside.

"Did Lisa tell you about the party?" he asked.

Mark grinned and nodded his head, suddenly liking Eliot for the first time.

"Just make sure Hiller doesn't see you," Eliot said in a low voice. "As soon as you usher through this last group, hide behind the sets in the sitting room some-where, and stay hidden. Hiller comes through every night with a flashlight, checking to see that nobody damaged the wax figures. When he finally leaves, we all come out."

Mark was about to ask where they'd meet, but the oak doors began to creak open, and Eliot rushed away to his post. As the eerie music started up for the final time that day, Mark felt a chill run through his body. Suddenly, he realized that tonight might not be all fun. To go to the party would mean risking his job. But it would be worth it, Mark told himself, thinking of Lisa's eyes and perfume. It would be worth it.

Mark felt his heart pounding as he motioned the last group of visitors through the sitting room. This group was wild and giddy and screaming at everything they saw. Mark's nerves were on edge by the time he opened the door to the library and saw Lisa staring at him, her lips curled into a tantalizing smile. As the last visitor walked by, Lisa came up to him and ran a finger down his cheek.

"It won't be long now," she whispered. Then she floated away into the shadows of the library.

Mark's knees had gone weak, and his heart was beating even faster. He shut the door between the library and the sitting room and then shined his flashlight around the dark corners of the room. Usually at this time of night, he quickly made for the exit of the House of Horrors along with the last group of tourists and then hurried home. Suddenly he realized that he wouldn't have a chance to call home to say he'd be late. His mother would probably worry, but Mark wouldn't miss this party for anything.

Mark stepped over the railing that kept visitors from going near the sets of the sitting room. He found himself only inches from the waxen heads of two women who seemed to have died of fright. With a shudder, he crept into the shadows behind them, shining his thin light at the velvet curtains that made a backdrop for the sets. Mark realized he'd never thought about what was behind those curtains before, and now he had to find out. Hesitantly, he pulled the edge of the curtain aside and aimed his light behind it. There was a scurrying sound, like a rat on the floor. Mark jumped back and looked for someplace else to hide. But behind the curtains was the only concealed place in the room. He hesitated to step into their mysterious darkness; but, then, he heard the door from the entranceway begin to open. Quickly he slipped behind the curtains and then froze as a switch was flicked, and the room was flooded with light.

Mark looked down at his watch. It was just 9:00. Hiller must have walked into the room, starting his nightly rounds to close up the House of Horrors. Shifting his head slightly, Mark peered through a narrow opening in the curtains and saw the manager walking along the carpeted aisle, carefully inspecting each of the waxen figures and peering behind pieces of furniture. Mark felt as stiff as one of the wax figures by the time Hiller had finished his inspection, switched off the lights, and walked into the library.

Mark heard, again, the scurrying sound of a rat in the dark and felt its body brush against his leg. Holding back a scream, he pushed the curtains aside and ran across the sitting room set. In the dark, he bumped into one of the waxen figures, which felt strangely

warm to his touch. Finally, Mark turned on his flashlight with trembling fingers and crept toward the edge
of the set near the brass railing. He sat down and
flicked off his light again. Now all he could do was
wait, wait for Hiller to finish his inspection and for the
party to begin.

In the dark, Mark smiled to himself, thinking about
Lisa hiding in the dark in the next room. He wondered
if she was thinking of him, too. He was tempted to
sneak to the library door and open it to join her. Surely
Hiller must be finished in there by now. But caution
stopped him. Mark decided to wait for Eliot or Lisa
or another of the guides to come get him from the
sitting room. After all, they hadn't told him to meet
them anywhere else.

The minutes seemed to drag by like hours as Mark
sat in the dark, his body tense and his senses alert.
He tried to imagine where Hiller would be on the path
through the House of Horrors. By now he must have
finished upstairs and was walking through the last
room — the dungeonlike cellar. Mark checked his
watch and saw that it was 9:45. He shivered, suddenly
realizing that the air-conditioning had been turned
up. He had heard that the building was made colder
at night — to harden the wax figures for another day
under their spotlights.

Mark stood up and began to pace back and forth on
the red-carpeted aisle of the sitting room, wondering
where Eliot and Lisa were. He pulled up the collar of
his black usher's jacket as the air temperature grew

colder and colder. Finally, at 10:00, he decided to open the door to the entrance hall where Eliot must be waiting.

Mark pulled open the door and shined his flashlight around the small room, expecting Eliot to jump out at him at any moment. But the room was completely empty, and its dark, paneled walls had no hiding places. Feeling a stir of panic in his mind, Mark walked over to the double doors that the visitors came through. There were padlocks through the handles of each one, and when he pushed against them, they didn't budge. Cold fingers of fear crept around Mark's mind as he ran back through the sitting room into the library, no longer worried that Hiller might still be around.

"Lisa!" he shouted into the darkness. His voice echoed hollowly back at him and then died down into the velvet blackness of the room. Mark stood perfectly still as another wave of fear washed over him. Either Eliot and Lisa were playing a game with him, or he had misunderstood what they'd said. In panic, he tried to remember their words. He was sure Lisa had said a party tonight, and Eliot had told him to hide until Hiller left.

Mark let his flashlight move across the wax figures in the room. He looked into one grotesque face after another, and then suddenly held the light on a blonde woman whose beautiful face shone out of the darkness. For a second, he thought it was Lisa. The wax face had the same liquid brown eyes and full lips as she did. But then Mark noticed the four white fangs curving over the lips. With his flashlight playing on her face, the woman looked so real that Mark swore her eyes were staring at him and her lips were moving in a mocking smile. With a shudder, he moved the light away from the woman's face and ran from the library through the door that led to the dining room.

"Eliot! Lisa!" he called out in a trembling voice. There was no answer, only the deep silence of the empty House of Horrors. His flashlight picked out the faces of the diners gasping for breath over their poisoned food. Mark began to run, faster and faster, up the stairs to the bedrooms, all filled with grizzly scenes of death and murder. As he opened each door, he held on to a slight ray of hope that he would be greeted by the happy shouts of the rest of the guides having a party. But each room he looked into was empty, and, finally, he had only the dungeon downstairs left to investigate.

Mark walked down the creaking stairs, his shoes sounding on each of the old boards. The dungeon door loomed in front of him, his last hope. But when he pushed it open, he saw only darkness, a darkness that mocked him.

Mark felt anger flood through his body like a hot liquid. They had set him up like a fool, Eliot and Lisa. There never was any party tonight. They had just wanted to trick him into staying on alone, in the House of Horrors. They were probably together somewhere, right now, laughing at him. Mark pointed his flashlight down onto the red-carpeted path that wound through the dungeon. Carefully, he avoided looking at the scenes of torture on either side of him. He only wanted to get to the exit doors and leave this place as fast as possible.

Mark turned the last corner where the path ended abruptly in front of a set of red curtains. He pulled them back and pushed angrily against the doors that led out of the House of Horrors. They didn't budge against his weight. Mark beat on them with his fists and slammed his body into the doors. Finally he accepted the awful truth: He was trapped inside the House of Horrors for the night.

Mark slumped against the doors and held his aching head in his hands. Terrible thoughts flew like black bats in and out of his brain. In his mind, he went through the rooms in the house, one by one, trying to decide which he should spend the night in. The thought of each one disgusted him, but he knew that the dungeon where he stood was the worst of all. Slowly, like an animal wary of its predators, he crept back along the red-carpeted path through the dungeon toward the stairway that led up to the bedrooms.

Halfway through the dungeon, he heard a sound rise out of the darkness in front of him. It made his blood run cold with terror. Mark strained his ears, but the sound didn't come again. He tried to tell himself that it was another rat, but part of his brain refused to believe it. The sound had been human, like footsteps coming softly toward him in the dark.

Mark began to run through the dungeon, flashing his beam of light from one side to another and glancing quickly at the twisted features of the wax figures. One face caught his attention — it was the face of the beautiful blonde woman with dark eyes and full, red lips. Mark had never noticed her in the dungeon before. Hadn't she been in the library only a few minutes ago?

Reaching the stairs, Mark stumbled up the steps on his trembling legs. He fell hard at the top, hitting his head against an iron statue of an executioner. For a moment, he lay stunned on the floor, too confused to move. Then, through the haze in his mind, he heard the sound again, the sound of footsteps coming up the stairs below him.

Mark scrambled to his knees and frantically searched for his flashlight. Somehow, he had dropped it when he fell, and the light had gone off. He groped in the darkness, feeling for the flashlight, but it seemed to have disappeared into the House of Horrors.

The sound of the footsteps was coming closer and closer up the stairs. Mark couldn't wait any longer. Stumbling forward, he ran along the carpet through the upstairs rooms. At the end of the hallway, he pressed his body against the wall, breathing heavily, and waited. The darkness felt as thick as velvet and was as quiet as a tomb. Slowly, Mark began to relax and breathe more regularly. It had been his imagination, he told himself. All his imagination.

Then the sound of the footsteps echoed down the upstairs hallway. They were coming toward Mark, slowly but intently, through the darkness.

Mark choked back a scream and began running down the stairs that led to the dining room. He heard the footsteps following him more quickly now. They

seemed to be running, too. He forgot about a turn in
the aisle and slammed his body into the brass railing.
A cry of pain rose from his lungs, echoing in the vast,
hollow room. Mark staggered back, dizzy with pain;
then he heard a laugh — a low, evil laugh — come out
of the darkness. Fighting down the panic that was
spreading through his body, he ran toward the door
that separated the dining room from the library.
Throwing it open, he rushed into the library and
screamed, "Lisa!"

His voice echoed back, mocking him. Mark ran toward the door that led to the sitting room, but before
he reached it, he heard footsteps come into the library.
They were steady and sinister and seeking him in the
dark. As his fingers began to claw against the door,
Mark felt warm breath against the back of his neck.
Then a low, throaty laugh came from behind him in
the darkness. Just as he began to scream, the sharp
fangs plunged into his neck. Then Mark sank to the
floor, another victim for the House of Horrors.

The next afternoon, Lisa came into the library to
begin another day's work. She wondered if Mark would
show up; she couldn't wait to hear how scared he'd
been last night. Shining her flashlight across the wax
figures in the library, Lisa noticed that the woman
with the long blonde hair was in a new place, leaning
over a body on a sofa. For a second, Lisa's heart
seemed to stop. She was sure nothing had been there
before.

Walking closer, Lisa looked down at the wax figure

of a young man whose face was twisted in terror. For a crazy second, she almost screamed. The figure looked just like Mark. But then Lisa reached out and touched the face. And all she felt was the cold smoothness of wax.

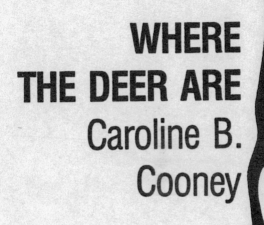

WHERE
THE DEER ARE
Caroline B.
Cooney

THE HOUSES ON FAWN HILL WERE DEEP IN THE woods.

Tiffany hated the woods, and the woods knew it.

Other people could find a path and follow it. But for Tiffany, the trees lifted up branches like a teenage boy's leg in the aisle, and tripped her.

For other people, the woods sang quiet songs of nature and beauty.

For Tiffany, the horrible tops of their grim gray branches rasped together like sore throats. Infections that made it impossible to swallow.

Whether she looked out the bedroom window, the kitchen window, the living room window, or any other window, her view was the same: tall, thin, armless bodies of trees. So thin. Like teenage anorexics. Gray complexions, peeling skin. In winter you could see through the trees, but all you could see were more trees. In summer, green leaves closed up the woods, as dense as tent walls.

Each school day, the neighborhood children left their homes and walked down long, rutted driveways.

Fawn Hill was the name of their road.

Tiffany had never seen a fawn. All the deer in the woods on Fawn Hill were the same, as if cut from mangy brown fake-fur cloth and stuck through with pencil legs. In the way that doll babies are neither male nor female, but just person-oids, the deer on Fawn Hill were not bucks and not does: They were deer-oids.

Deer terrified her. They were supposed to be so pretty, but they weren't. Those deep brown eyes were no liquid pools. They were flat but full of knowledge.

People shot the deer in season. Cars hit them year-round. Just last week her father had hit a deer. The deer had tried to cross Fawn Hill Road in the thick fog, but her father's Wagoneer was there first, and the deer was nothing but a dent on the fender now. It lay there, sunken, its brown eyes open and unchanged, looking just as alive, and just as not-alive, as before.

Deer-oid.

Deer seemed to be in her backyard more than anybody else's. Matthew said it was because of all the leafy shrubs and tasty flowers. Patrick said it was because Tiffany had a more open yard, a more relaxing passage from deep woods to meadow.

But she knew better.

It was because of her.

They had their eyes on her.

Even in the dark, Tiffany could feel their eyes on her.

Those muddy snow-melting deer-oid eyes.

At the bottom of Fawn Hill Road, the children

turned left onto Schoolhouse Road. The school was a quarter mile away. The road wound to the right, curving steadily, until it seemed certain to have made a complete circle. On the inside of the circle was a jagged rock face from which slabs of stone often fell.

Trees grew sideways, their roots thrust into the cliff like pitchforks.

Bushes clung to slick rocks with little green fingers. High up were ledges, from which a fourteen-year-old could see the world. But fourteen-year-olds knew better than to climb the ledges.

For this was Dead Kid Curve.

This was where Kenny Morgan vanished and was never seen again.

This was where Laura MacMarkham paused to tie a shoelace. Her friends sauntered on, headed for school. Laura MacMarkham screamed once, and only once. Her friends ran back, but Laura was not there. Laura was never there, or anywhere else, again.

Dead Kid Curve.

Of course, no one really knew if Kenny or Laura were dead. They knew only that Kenny and Laura were gone. But that was a quarter of a century ago. Nobody who lived on Fawn Hill now knew the Morgans or the MacMarkhams.

Parents said that way back then kids ran away from home a lot. Reporters had exaggerated things. Probably television had gotten in on it, and made it appear scary, when all it was, was that Kenny decided to run away and Laura had a boyfriend who picked her up in his car.

None of the parents thought twice about it.

But the children thought twice.

And they knew.

Walking under the cliff, they could feel what had happened to Kenny Morgan and to Laura Mac-Markham on Dead Kid Curve.

Janie walked below the cliff now.

And Matthew.

Kelso.

Tiffany.

Patrick.

These five walked to school.

Nobody else followed the wrapping cliff.

"One of us is chosen," said Janie. She had a slow, fluty voice, so high it was unnatural. Tiffany disliked the sound. She always wanted to clear her throat when Janie spoke.

"The cliff has decided," said Janie, her voice fluttering like wings in trees. "It just hasn't told."

"Told what?" said Patrick nervously.

"Which of us goes next," said Janie. Her voice ended, still high, like an unfinished story.

They never talked about the cliff. They were afraid of setting something off. Who knew what had made the cliff take Laura? Or Kenny? Who knew why it had waited a quarter of a century for another child?

Tiffany never permitted herself to look up at the cliff.

She never looked across the road into the woods, either; the tightly bound bare trees of that woods, like gray soldiers linked arm to arm. Sometimes a deer

materialized, and Tiffany would bite back a scream.
You never saw a deer coming. Never. It was just
suddenly there.

You saw a deer leave, though. It signaled you with
its white tail. But it always vanished when it should
still have been in sight. It seemed to be swallowed by
the trees, as if a door had opened and the deer entered
another room, or another world.

Where do the deer go? Tiffany always wondered.
You never see a fawn, thought Tiffany. It's as if they
don't have babies anymore; it's the same grown-up
deer, being recycled.

Tiffany was one of the race that shot them and ran
over them. But mostly she was one of the race that
built on their land and cut down their woods and put
pavement on their meadows.

She said, "Janie, don't talk about the cliff."

Or the woods.

Or the deer.

"It's today," said Janie dreamily. "One of us will go
today. I *know* it."

Treetops rasped together. It sounded like cellar
doors opening. Tiffany whirled, to look behind her. For
one breath, for one heartbeat, she knew. She saw.

It *was* a door opening.

She could see down the black hole, feel the horror
and the emptiness. She tottered, as if trying to back
away from the long fall.

"Janie, shut up," said Kelso. Kelso was the leader
of the group. He was smaller than the rest, but braver
and stockier. They all liked to walk next to Kelso when

they circled the cliff, but Kelso liked to walk alone.

Tiffany ran after Kelso and tried to take his hand. Kelso shook it free and shoved it into his pocket. Tiffany hung onto his denim jacket instead. "Don't stretch my jacket," said Kelso sternly.

"Look," whispered Matthew, who rarely spoke. "There's a deer." Of course everybody else wanted to stop and look; everybody else thought deer were beautiful; everybody else never tired of saying how graceful, how swift, deer were.

Again the treetops creaked and groaned.

Again Tiffany whirled, quickly enough to see the cellar door open. She could see down, looking into truth and history. Now she knew. Somebody paid for everything. One generation paid for what another generation did. From ancient times, from the earliest story in the Bible, this was true.

It didn't matter that you were innocent.

The deer hit by the car was innocent, and it paid.

She was sobbing and clutching.

It was harder and harder to breathe. The air was being pumped in, shoved down her throat into her lungs.

She could see where the deer were: among creeping roots and strangling branches, past dead moths and road kills.

"Don't step on my ankle, Tiffany!" snapped Kelso.

"Sorry." She jumped to match stride with Kelso. This way she could walk only an inch behind him and yet not tread on his ankle.

Kelso gave her the look only he could give a girl,

filled with disgust and loathing, but being polite anyway.

She was caught in a fever of trees.

A paralysis of deer.

"Where do you suppose they go?" said Matthew.

"Missing children?" said Kelso. "Laura and Kenny?"

Matthew shook his head. "Deer."

Kelso was scientific in his answer. "They have their own little paths and thickets."

"But they just vanish," said Matthew. "I remember when my dad went hunting last fall. The deer ate our entire garden, and we saw them every day. But when we went up on top of the cliff — because that's where they have to live, you know, I mean, there are houses and roads and swimming pools everywhere else — we never found one. Never saw a trace or a dropping. Where do the deer go?"

Patrick said, "Your father killed a deer last week, didn't he, Tiff?"

A weird laugh percolated like drunken coffee in her throat.

Her skull and the cliff quivered, as if pounded by the hooves of a thousand deer.

Tiffany could look nowhere; or she would see the eyes of the deer, or the woods, or the cliff.

Where are my fawns? Where is my wilderness? Why are there beer cans in my woods and tracks of dirt bikes through my leaves?

Matthew tried to lead them over to the woods side of the road instead of the cliff side. Here, debris lay like a fence: discarded hamburger wrappers, old liquor bottles, pieces of newspaper, and strips of tires. You had to look over the trash to see the woods, and as deep in as you looked, the woods was not pristine forest, but full of junk. There was even an old armchair, its stuffing spilling out like vomit into the winter leaves. A car door, without the car, was propped up against a twisted old evergreen.

"We can't walk on the woods side of the road," said Janie firmly. "We wouldn't be facing traffic; we'd have our backs to oncoming traffic. It'd be Dead Kid Curve for real. We'd all be smashed by a truck."

Janie knew her safety rules. Janie always knew things like where the fire extinguisher was kept. Janie was the sort of girl who wore a white jacket if it was the least little bit dark out, so cars would see her, even if she was in her own backyard and the only cars were parked in the garage.

Kelso said he was going to climb the cliff and sit on the ledges up among the twisted pines. He would bring along his camera, said Kelso, and photograph the cliff from all angles, even the very top where nobody had ever been. That would set this Dead Kid Curve nonsense to rest.

"It's not resting," said Tiffany. "Don't you feel it quivering?"

Kelso scoffed. "Sympathetic vibration from the train tracks."

But the train tracks were miles away.

"Dragons, maybe, Tiff?" said Kelso, raising his eyebrows to make Tiffany feel infantile. "Evil spirits? So

Kenny Morgan and Laura MacMarkham had a bad year. It's been twenty-five years! What's this evil spirit been doing all that time?"

"Don't say their names out loud," whispered Janie. "Today is the day the cliff chooses."

"I won't mind so much," said Patrick, "what the cliff does, as long as we all go together."

It wouldn't work that way, Tiffany knew. It would single one of them out. The rest would neither see nor understand. All their lives, the other four would wonder, and wake screaming, and weep in the night. But they would not know.

Kelso sighed heavily. "You guys can worry about anything you want, but I personally am going to worry about whether I make the soccer team."

Tiffany stopped short, and Matthew bumped into her.

"You know we don't stop on the way to school," said Matthew urgently. "Keep going, Tiff."

"Do you hear that?" breathed Tiffany.

"Hear what?"

"That sound. Do you hear it calling?"

Kelso was irritated. "The wind is right. You can hear the marching band practicing."

But Tiffany could hear nothing except her own leaping heart.

She looked up where groping pines blocked the sky, tilting over the road, losing their balance. "It's calling me," she said.

Janie was right. It had been decided. Tiff could hear

her name, spun in high, airborne notes like dead leaves. The leaves of last year. But she did not think it was the cliff after all.

It was the deer.

Tiffany's eyes opened very wide. They were bluer than before; they had become part of the sky. Her thin jacket was the hard green of the pines, and her fingers were mottled, like the rocks she pressed against.

Kelso grabbed Tiffany's arm. "We'll be late for school," he said. He looked fiercely at Matthew, who obediently took Tiffany's other arm, and the two of them marched her forward like a prisoner.

It doesn't matter, Tiffany thought. The cellar door opened. I'm the one who saw. I'm next.

Patrick was skipping ahead, looking out the corners of his eyes to be sure the others were right behind. Tiffany clung to Matthew and Kelso. She would even have held hands with Janie at this point, although Janie was the worst sort of girl, whiny and always worried about ruining her shoes by stepping in a puddle.

Finally!

The roof of the school appeared. It was slanted, with reddish-brown tiles, the only tiled roof Tiffany had ever seen; there was something about terra-cotta that was warm and safe; and Tiffany said, "There's school!" She had been holding her breath and not even known it. "We're here," she said, removing a quiver from her voice. "There's school," she repeated, feeling warm and safe.

Kelso said, "Where's Janie?"

* * *

Time to run into the school, slam and lock the doors behind them, and call the police, the fire department, the FBI, and their mothers.

Matthew stood very still, apparently feeling that whatever it was would pass him by, mistaking him for a telephone pole or a tree.

Patrick giggled. His face didn't match. His face was frowning and sobbing while his mouth giggled.

Tiffany kept busy with a demented combination of whimpering and gulping.

Kelso said, "Shut up. Come on. We're going back to find her."

He strode away, marching back to Dead Kid Curve. Patrick, Matthew, and Tiffany stood desperately, eyes swiveling back and forth between the warm red-tiled safety of school, and the cold rock tower of the cliff.

"Rats," said Patrick gloomily. "I hate when you have to be a hero." He ran after Kelso. Matthew uttered a tiny cry, like a bird hitting a windshield, and joined the boys.

Tiffany thought: Nothing will make me go back there. Nothing!

It got Janie. It was calling to me, but the boys held onto me and I escaped, and it had to take her instead.

Tiffany ran into school, into the safe warmth, into the wonderful homey smell of lockers and pencil lead, copy paper, and old sneakers.

They'll find Janie, she promised herself. Janie just — well — something reasonable. And they'll just — well — find her.

Tiffany's chest was rising and falling with such rapidity that she no longer felt human. Perhaps she was a hummingbird, whose tiny heart beat two hundred times a minute.

She was burning hot and freezing cold at the same time. Her clothes were slithery and alien, like reptile skin.

She staggered to the nearest girls' room to look at herself.

The varnish on the door had split, alligatoring the finish. The five letters were stenciled off-center, and tilted, as if the door had been through a convulsion.

G I R L S

She pushed at the door.

How heavy it was. How slowly it yielded. She had to use her entire body to wedge herself in. The lights were not on. With her right hand, Tiffany fumbled over the wall for the switch. She found nothing. The bathroom tiles were slimy.

She stepped further into the room.

The door closed behind her with the breathy thud of a perfect fit.

The room was fat with silence.

She felt her body expanding, like the dead deer on the road going bad — felt herself balloon — and — felt the switch, and turned it on.

One fluorescent ceiling tube trembled with effort and half-lit the space.

Shadows crept up, feeling the backs of Tiffany's legs.

Three mirrors over three sinks leered at her, dark and blind as stones.

There was a deer in the mirror.

Not Tiffany, who stood in front of it.

But a deer.

Soft and brown and muddy.

She tried to scream but her lips were knit together.

She tried to back up but her feet had swollen, making movement almost impossible.

Her sky-blue eyes opened wide enough to burst, but the eyes that looked back were flat and deer-oid.

And then there was something sharp and dark in the mirror. Something —

— climbing out.

A dainty hoof coming right out of the mirror, pointing at Tiffany, pursuing her. First one deer leg, thin as a broken pencil, and then the next.

Tiffany fell out of the bathroom like cereal from a box.

Into the hall.

An empty hall in an empty school.

The door closed in its heavy mechanical way.

The school was silent.

There was nobody there. Nothing happening. Not a sound. Not a breath. Not a creak.

There's no school today? thought Tiffany. I'm alone in here? But —

The girls' room door began to open.

Out came a single leg, like something cooking in a stew pot.

She could hear little sounds now, and she knew they were her, whimpering.

She ran.

Ran out of the school, across the wide parking spaces, over the soggy grass, onto Schoolhouse Road.

No traffic.

No cars.

No humans.

But yes. Deer.

In the woods, among the trees, all the deer that had vanished during hunting season stood still, staring at her.

Their eyes were like brown hubcaps: huge and glistening.

I'm innocent, she thought.

But the deer neither saw nor understood; their flat dead eyes just reflected more deer.

Home, thought Tiffany. I have to go home.

Home would be warm, and have four walls, and a radio playing.

Home would be human, and it would last, and there would be cookies.

Home would have no deer, no woods, no cliff.

She began to run, with the cliff on her left now, and the woods — woods thick with deer; woods that hardly had trees, so full of deer they were — on her right.

The cellar door rasped.

It's treetops. Don't look. It's just trees.

She tried to stare only at the road: the man-made road: tried to think man-made thoughts, nothing of woods, nothing of deer.

But the death of the deer and the demise of the woods was also man-made. There was no getting away from what was man-made.

She would disappear. And that would not be man-made. It would be deer-made.

Far, far away, she saw Kelso. Matthew. Patrick.

Far, far away, as if through binoculars, she saw Janie with them. Perhaps Janie had forgotten her homework. Or her freshly laundered gym suit. Janie had to be perfect or else.

Tiffany heard the hum and the rhythm of the woods.

For a moment, she was all of it: hunter, hunted, and remains.

She was the road kill.

She was the deer that had been hit and left.

"It's not my fault!" she cried. "I didn't build the house. I didn't drive the car!"

The trees rasped.

She tried to close her eyes. If she did not see the cellar door opening, she could not go in.

This is where the deer are, she thought. They have their own doors, to their own world.

The trees rasped.

The hands of the woods were rubbing together with glee. They had another one. They had Tiffany.

She tried to call to Kelso, who would save her.

Kelso waved.

She tried to call to Janie, who had known one of them was going today.

Janie shifted her book bag.

The door opened.

Tiffany tried to step around it.

It just spread wider, like a smile.

"I'm sorry I scared you," said Janie.

"No problem," said Kelso.

"My mother gets angry if she makes me a sandwich and I forget to bring it," said Janie.

"No problem," said Kelso.

Tiffany saw the laughing deer, the sneering underside of the road, the strangling vines above the ground and beneath the soil. The trees closed around her, like shovels full of dirt on a coffin.

Her feet struggled with the edge of the cellar, so for a moment she seemed to be dancing with the deer.

Tiffany began the long fall. She knew the fall would never end. She would never catch up to Kenny Morgan or Laura MacMarkham. She was alone, and falling, and in the dark, forever and ever.

The trees rasped.

The wind breathed.

The deer vanished.

"Where do you suppose the deer go?" asked Janie.

Kelso shrugged. "Who cares?" he said. "In a few years, there won't be any deer around here anymore, anyway." Kelso finished the soda he had taken from the bag lunch his mother had carefully packed. He threw the can into the woods.

It glittered, scarlet and silver, like a marker on a grave.

THE SPELL
R.L. Stine

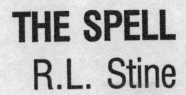

I KNOW I SHOULD CALL THE POLICE ABOUT WILliam. But I'm just sitting here staring at the phone. It's as if someone has cast a spell over me or something.

William will be here soon. I don't know what he's going to do to me. I really should call the police.

But I keep thinking this just isn't the way it's supposed to be. I mean, we were all such good friends. All five of us.

Erica and Stan were my friends first. But when I started going out with William, it was like the four of us had been close forever. Marty, too. Sure, Marty was always teasing William, always making jokes, always giving William a hard time. But Marty was like that with everyone.

With his curly red hair and his chubby, freckled face, his laughing blue eyes, Marty was a real Huck Finn type. You just had to like Marty. And even William, who is so serious, so earnest, so . . . intense, thought Marty was a great guy.

At first, anyway.

The five of us went to all the basketball games together. And we used to drive out on the River Road in Stan's old Pontiac and just hang out at the Falls, sitting in the tall grass, watching the water trickle over the rocks or staring up at the slow-drifting clouds.

Sometimes we had impromptu softball games there on the flat grass on the other side of the road. It was usually Stan and Erica against William, Marty, and me. Long, lanky Stan was so good in sports, he and Erica usually won even though we outnumbered them.

Stan was so funny about the baseball bat he always brought. He claimed it really had belonged to Pete Rose during his rookie season in Cincinnati, and Stan treasured it. When we batted with it, he was always yelling at us to make sure the label was up so we wouldn't crack it.

William didn't like our softball games. He isn't very athletic. Sometimes when it was William's turn to bat, I'd actually see a glint of fear in those strange, slate-gray eyes of his.

He usually struck out. Or sent a weak grounder to the pitcher and was tagged out at first. And then Marty would really get on William's case. We all thought it was very funny. And William was always a good sport about all the ribbing. At least he didn't *seem* to mind.

One really hot Saturday afternoon, William hit the ball up, a high fly that sailed over Marty's head and kept going. William just stood open-mouthed, staring at it. He'd never hit the ball that far before.

"Run, William! Get moving!" I shouted. And then I saw that Marty was chasing the ball, running at full speed, staring straight up, his glove outstretched, his sneakers pounding on the ground. He chased it right into the river, made a desperate dive for it, but just missed.

What a splash he made. When he came up sputtering, he gazed into his glove. He couldn't believe he hadn't made the catch.

Before I realized what was happening, the four of us were running into the river to join Marty. The water was freezing! And our sopping-wet clothes weighed a ton. But we had so much fun ducking each other and splashing, tackling each other and mainly acting crazy.

That was one of the best days of my life.

I'm not sure when things started to go wrong.

It may have been when William got so interested in hypnotism. This was about the same time that Marty got the lead in the school musical, *The Music Man*. A major disappointment for William.

William is really very shy. He usually speaks very quietly, and he blushes easily. But he can be very intense, too. Those weird gray eyes of his light up, and he starts to talk very rapidly, very excitedly, raking his large hands back through his long, wavy, white-blond hair.

What I'm saying is that William has a theatrical side, too. I guess that's part of the reason he became so interested in hypnotism. He can be very dramatic, and there's a side of him that likes to show off.

That's why I wasn't surprised when he stopped me at my locker on the day of *The Music Man* auditions and said, "Jennifer, I can't go home with you this afternoon. I've decided to try out."

William really wanted to be the star. It meant he
had to compete with Marty, who had been in the
Drama Club all year, and who the drama coach thought
was wonderful. Marty was just so popular.

But William auditioned anyway. And then when
Marty got the part — big surprise! — William never
talked about it again.

About a month later, Erica, Stan, and I went to see
Marty in the play. He was really good. William said
he wasn't feeling well, so he didn't come.

None of us saw William as much as before — not
even me. He was so involved with his hypnotism studies. He had stacks of old books about it that he had
bought from some grungy bookstore downtown.

I have to admit I was a little hurt that he was spending more time up in that attic room of his, poring over
those dusty, old books, than he spent with me. I tried
to get interested in it, too. In fact, I begged William
to show me what he was learning. But he stared at
me and shook his head. He didn't want to share any
of it.

Of course, Marty teased William about the hypnotism right from the start. Marty started calling him
"The Great Foodini," and he joked that William would
soon start making us all bark like dogs and cluck like
chickens. Then he'd start chasing William around,
barking at him, nipping at him like a crazed puppy.

We all thought it was funny. I don't think any of us
realized how seriously William took his hypnotism. I
could see that he tensed up when Marty started giving
him a hard time. But even I didn't realize what an

angry person William was becoming.

I didn't even pick up on it when Marty got the part-time job in that Italian restaurant, the job William had also interviewed for.

All five of us were studying at my house the night Marty got the job. I saw William's eyes go cold, as cold and clear as ice. But he didn't say anything until Marty left. Then he turned to me and said under his breath, "I really needed that job."

Erica overheard and quickly said, "So did Marty. His folks have been on his back for months to get a job."

"Why do you stick up for *him*?" William screamed at her. I was shocked by his sudden anger.

"I — I wasn't," Erica stammered.

"Give Erica a break," Stan said. He'd been twirling that Pete Rose bat of his in the corner, but he quickly came to her defense.

"Everyone gives Marty a break," William insisted with astonishing bitterness. "Why doesn't anyone ever give *me* a break?" Then he grabbed his jacket off the floor and stormed out without looking back, slamming the kitchen door behind him.

After that, things really changed. The five of us just weren't comfortable together anymore. Marty spent most nights working at the restaurant. I still saw Erica and Stan, but we didn't hang out as much as we used to. And William was spending more and more time in his attic, working on whatever it was he was working on.

I still cared about him a lot. He was so much more

interesting than other guys, so much . . . deeper. But I was really worried about how distant he was becoming. He seemed so unhappy.

One Friday night the four of us were at a local hangout called the Pizza Palace, and William seemed in a really good mood. Marty was working. We talked about driving over and surprising him. Then the subject got changed to William and his hypnotism. I guess we were all teasing him about it. But for once, William was laughing, too.

"Let's try an experiment," he suddenly suggested, smiling and jumping to his feet. He made Erica, Stan, and me squeeze together on one side of the booth. "Let's see if I really can hypnotize you," he said.

All three of us immediately started clucking like chickens. We were laughing and goofing around. I felt more than a little nervous. I mean, I wondered what it felt like to be hypnotized.

William held up a teaspoon and told us to relax and follow it with our eyes. Erica had to hold her hand over her mouth to stop giggling. I think she was nervous, too.

Eventually, we all settled down and followed William's instructions. He moved the teaspoon slowly from side to side, and we followed it with our eyes, trying to relax all of our muscles, trying to clear our minds, concentrating on the spoon.

After a while, William set down the spoon and stared at us expectantly. All three of us burst out laughing.

It hadn't worked.

We weren't the least bit hypnotized.

William sighed. His face fell. He was so disappointed. "Back to the drawing board," he muttered unhappily, shaking his head.

Of course, the jokes and wisecracks started to fly fast and furious. It would be a long time before anyone let William forget what a flop he was.

After that funny night, the four of us didn't get together again for a few weeks. I didn't see William much during that time, either.

Maybe the last night all five of us were together was the night in William's kitchen. It was a warm spring night, I remember. We were just hanging out. Marty was goofing on something or other. I think he was imitating Mr. Schein, our French teacher. Erica and Stan were being sort of lovey-dovey, smooching and kidding around at the kitchen table against the wall.

Then Marty had to leave. He was late for work at the restaurant.

After he left, it got sort of quiet. William seemed to be preoccupied. He barely said a word. "Maybe we should go, too," Stan suggested awkwardly. He and Erica stood up from the table.

"No, wait," William said. He glanced at me and smiled. Then he walked to the refrigerator and pulled a quart container of ice cream from the freezer.

"Hey — all right!" Stan declared. "What flavor?"

"Heath Bar Crunch," William replied. He took a silver ice cream scoop from the drawer and got some bowls out. I remember how the scoop seemed to glisten, catching the light from the low ceiling fixture.

The three of us stared at William as he scooped the

ice cream into the bowls. I guess we were surprised that he suddenly seemed cheerful and nice, like his old self.

"Here," William said, shoving the bowls across the counter toward us, the scoop still glistening in his hand. "Have some ice cream."

We started shoveling in the ice cream. It was hot in the kitchen, and it tasted really good.

But then Stan started teasing William about his hypnotism. I gave Stan a look, trying to signal to him to stop. But he didn't see me.

"Are you still into the 'Look deep into my eyes' stuff?" Stan asked. "Or have you moved on to pulling rabbits out of hats?"

Erica laughed, and, to my surprise, William chuckled, too.

Stan kept up the teasing — taking over Marty's role, I guess — begging William to show us some magic tricks, to levitate us, dumb stuff like that.

William took all the kidding good-naturedly. I hoped maybe he was returning to his old self.

Then he suggested the four of us go out for a walk. He put his arm around me as we went out the back door and headed around the house to the front. I sort of snuggled against him as we walked, feeling good about things.

It was only about nine o'clock but a lot of houses were already dark. The trees seemed to whisper in the soft, warm breeze, casting rolling shadows over the lawns.

We walked three blocks and reached Park Street. William squeezed my hand gently as a large oil truck roared past. Park Street is only two lanes. But it connects to the highway, and it is the main thoroughfare for trucks heading through town.

Several cars whirred by, and then a moving van, its enormous tires bouncing over the bumpy pavement. Everyone seemed to ignore the speed limit on this stretch of the road. Even this late at night, Park Street was hard to cross.

"Should we head back or keep going?" Erica asked, her long black hair billowing behind her as another large truck bombed past.

William squeezed my hand again, then turned to face Erica and Stan. "Go stand on the yellow line," he told them, "and don't move till I tell you."

"William!" I exclaimed, pulling my hand free.

I expected Erica and Stan to laugh at him. But to my shock, they didn't hesitate. Without even glancing to see if anything was coming, they both stepped into the street and walked to the yellow line that ran down the middle.

"William — what are you doing?" I cried.

A car roared past, swerving to the right and blasting its horn.

Erica and Stan didn't move. They stood on the yellow line. They didn't look frightened or alarmed. Their expressions were calm.

Down the road, I saw a huge semi zooming toward them.

"William — bring them back!" I shouted. Then I started screaming at Erica and Stan. "Come back! Get out of the street! Come back!"

The truck's horn drowned out my frantic cries. I could see the driver shaking his fist at us as he roared past without slowing.

I looked away. I couldn't bear to watch. When I turned back, Erica and Stan were still standing calmly in place in the center of the street.

"William — please! They're going to get killed! Please!" I pleaded with him, pulling his arm.

I hated the look on his face. His gray eyes seemed to glow. His whole face was lit up by his excitement. He was so . . . happy!

"Swear to me you won't tell them what happened," he said, leaning close, his strange eyes burning into mine.

"Huh?" I stared back at him.

"They won't remember any of it," William said, watching with pleasure as a station wagon swerved to miss Erica and Stan. "Swear to me you won't tell them — and I'll bring them back."

"I swear!" I cried eagerly. I would've sworn to anything.

"Come on back!" William shouted.

Smiling pleasantly, Erica and Stan walked together across the street and rejoined us. I was so relieved, I had tears running down my cheeks.

"What's wrong, Jennifer?" Erica asked me, seeing the tears.

I glanced at William, who was watching me intently.

"The wind blew something in my eye," I told her.

After that night, my life became something like a dream. Just bits of places and activities. A blur of faces and unconnected conversations. I'd go to school, do my homework, see my friends, talk to my parents, but everything seemed different, out of order, as if my life were a jigsaw puzzle that had been dropped on the floor, the pieces scattering everywhere.

I should have told someone — *anyone* — about what William did to Erica and Stan. But I didn't.

I can't explain why I didn't.

I really don't remember what I was thinking. My memory is so clouded.

I remember talking to Marty a few days later. School had just let out. We were standing in back near the student parking lot. The sky was solid gray, as gray as William's eyes.

I started to tell Marty that I was worried about William. He asked me why. "He's just become so . . . weird," I told him.

I don't know if I intended to tell Marty what William had done. Even if I had, I didn't get the chance. I suddenly realized that William was watching us. I saw him ducking down low, hiding behind the hood of a Honda Civic, spying on us.

I felt a cold stab of fear. "Listen, Marty, I've got to go," I said. Marty looked really surprised as I took off. He called after me, but I didn't stop.

William caught up with me a few blocks from my house. The sky was even darker now, and it started to drizzle. William grabbed my arm and pulled me behind the hedges of someone's yard. He looked very worked up, very angry.

"William — let go of my arm!" I cried. He was really hurting me.

He apologized but he didn't let go. "So you're on Marty's side, too," he said quietly. He looked very hurt, as if I had betrayed him.

For a moment, I felt sorry for him. He was just so mixed up. I wanted to comfort him. I wanted to tell him that everything was going to be okay. I wanted to see the old William again.

But I guess that was impossible. William loosened his grip on my arm. "There's no point in being on Marty's side," he said softly, staring into my eyes. "Marty is dead meat."

"Huh? William — what on earth — ?" He was scaring me now. He was really scaring me.

Why didn't I just run away? Why did I stay there and listen to him?

"Marty's going to die," William said, his face a blank, revealing no emotion at all. "Stan is going to do it."

"You're kidding — right?" I managed to say. "This is some kind of a joke?" This was too crazy. Too crazy.

"No," he said matter-of-factly. "Everyone is against me. Everyone is on Marty's side. I can't let that go on. You understand, Jennifer. I can't let everyone be on Marty's side. So, what can I do? What choice do I have? Stan is going to kill Marty. I'm going to hypnotize Stan and Erica. Then Stan will take his precious baseball bat and kill Marty."

"You can't!" I managed to cry, turning my head. I suddenly couldn't bear to look at William's face. Was this the same guy I had cared so much about?

He laughed. "Why can't I?" he demanded.

"You can't hypnotize someone to do something that's against their will. It won't work."

His expression turned thoughtful. He was silent for a while. My heart was pounding in my chest. The drizzle turned to rain. "I guess you're right," he said finally. "I guess it won't work."

He walked away.

I stood there for the longest time, the rain soaking my hair, soaking my clothes. I stood there watching him walk away, until he turned the corner and disappeared.

Why didn't I call the police? Or tell my parents? Or get help of any kind?

I can't explain it. My life was a dream. One scene ran into another. All a jumble.

I remember that I felt a little relieved knowing that you can't hypnotize someone and force them to do something against their will.

Knowing that made me feel a lot better.

William had even agreed with me on that.

But then I realized he had agreed much too quickly. I began to feel troubled again.

As soon as I got home, I changed into dry clothes, wrapped a towel around my wet hair, and phoned Erica. "Listen," I said before she could get a word in, "William is going to try to hypnotize you and Stan."

"Huh?" she cried. Stan must have been standing

right next to her. I could hear him asking her something in the background.

"William is going to try to hypnotize you," I repeated. "Don't let him. Just pretend to be hypnotized, okay?"

It took me a while to persuade Erica to believe me. Finally, she started to understand. "Let me get this straight, Jennifer. You want us to pretend to be hypnotized?"

"Yes," I told her. "Resist William with all your strength. You can't be hypnotized if you don't want to be. But go along with it. Afterwards, the three of us can figure out how to deal with William."

Erica agreed and hung up to explain things to Stan.

That made me feel a little better. William's plan cannot work, I told myself. No way.

I saw him in school the next day. He smiled at me across the room during third period study hall. The smile made me feel sad. It reminded me of how William used to be.

He called me that night, an hour after dinner. "Why don't you come over, Jennifer? Erica and Stan are already here. We're just hanging out."

Just hanging out.

I suddenly felt cold all over. And terribly heavy, as if I were made of stone. Heavy with dread, I guess.

But I knew I had to go over to William's. I had no choice.

The three of them were in the kitchen, seated around the table when I arrived. Erica gave me a nervous glance as I came in, then quickly looked away. Stan was giggling about something with William, a high-pitched, nervous giggle I'd never heard from him before.

It was obvious to me that Erica and Stan were both terribly nervous. This hypnotism thing really had them spooked. I said hi to everyone and tossed my jacket into a corner.

William, I could see, was the only calm one in the room. He was chatting playfully with Stan, telling him something that was making Stan utter that high-pitched giggle.

"How come you called us over tonight?" Erica asked William, interrupting whatever he was telling Stan. She glanced at her watch. "I've got a ton of homework to do. Miss Farrell really piled it on tonight."

William stood up, smiling pleasantly at her. "You said you were just finishing dinner when I called," he said, walking over to the fridge. "I thought you might like some dessert."

He removed a quart of ice cream from the freezer, then pulled the silver ice cream scoop from the drawer and held it up so that it sparkled under the kitchen light. He opened the carton and began scooping perfect ice cream balls into the bowls.

"Here. Have some ice cream," William said.

Then, leaving the bowls on the counter, he stepped to the head of the table and stood staring down at Stan and Erica. "Stan, when I finish talking to you, I want you and Erica to drive to your house and get your Pete Rose bat," he said softly, speaking slowly and distinctly.

Stan nodded in agreement.

William continued his instructions. "Every night just after ten o'clock, Marty hauls the garbage bags out the back entrance of the restaurant. He puts them in a Dumpster in the alley behind the restaurant. I want you two to drive to the alley. Park there. Be sure to turn off your headlights. Stan, you wait behind the Dumpster. When Marty comes out dragging the garbage bags, swing your bat at his head. I want you to hit him six times in the head. Do you understand? You swing the bat six times."

Stan and Erica both nodded.

Erica glanced at me. Her face was as expressionless as Stan's. Neither of them reacted to William's instructions in any way. But I could tell they were faking it. I could tell they were pretending to be hypnotized.

Thank god I reached them in time, I thought. Thank god I persuaded them to resist William.

"Okay, guys. Go get the bat," William instructed them in a low, calm voice.

Erica and Stan scooted their chairs back and climbed to their feet. Without saying a word, they headed toward the back door.

"Oh — one more thing," William called after them. They stopped at the door and looked back. "Stan, when you finish hitting Marty, be sure to leave the bat right next to him before you drive home."

Stan nodded in agreement. Then he and Erica disappeared out the door.

William gave me an odd, satisfied smile, then walked to the sink and began washing off the ice cream scoop.

He was humming cheerily to himself.

Too bad, William, I thought, staring hard at his back. But your hideous plan isn't going to work. Erica and Stan weren't hypnotized at all.

You're going to fail, William, I thought, standing up, picking up my jacket, preparing to leave. You're going to fail. And maybe after you fail, we can reach you again. Maybe we'll be able to help you.

He turned around. "Where are you going?" he asked, surprised to see me putting on my jacket.

"Home," I told him.

He shook his head. "No. You're coming with me." He looked up at the brass kitchen clock over the sink. "We're going for a ride a little later."

I sat back down. I didn't resist.

Time passed. I don't know how much.

We were in his parents' car, driving through the night. There was a full moon and a sky full of tiny white stars. It must have been pretty late. A lot of the houses we passed were dark. There were few cars on the road.

When William turned onto Madison Drive, I realized where we were going. To the restaurant. Where Marty worked.

William turned into the alley. I squeezed the door handle, gripped by fear. I had to force myself to breathe.

In a few seconds, we'd be behind the restaurant. And William would see that his plan had failed. What would he do then? Would he figure out that I had tipped off Stan and Erica?

What would William do? What would he do to me?

The car slid slowly through the alley, brick walls on both sides of us. I squeezed the door handle and stared straight ahead through the windshield.

In the white glare of the headlights I could see the back of the restaurant now. I could see the kitchen door, half open, a thin rectangle of gray fluorescent light escaping from inside.

I could see two metal trash cans lying on their sides, their lids beside them in the concrete alley. I could see a large green Dumpster. I could see a plastic garbage bag on the ground in front of the Dumpster, full, on its side, open, some of its contents having spilled to the ground.

And then the headlights seemed to focus on the body lying in front of the toppled garbage bag. It was Marty. Sprawled facedown in a round, dark puddle of blood. His arms and legs stretched out on the pavement. His head bashed in, still oozing blood. The baseball bat lying at his feet.

"No! No — no — no!"

Was that *me* screaming?

Something snapped. My mind suddenly felt so clear. As if a weight had been lifted. As if a heavy curtain had been pulled away.

"No — no — no!!"

Yes, it *was* me screaming.

And now I was pushing open the car door, running hard, my sneakers thudding on the hard alley concrete, gasping for breath. I was running away. I was escaping from William.

I was free. Finally free.

Everything was so clear.

Without slowing down, I glanced back. William wasn't coming after me. The car hadn't moved. He was still behind the wheel.

I was free. I was getting away.

I ran all the way home. It didn't take long. I knew what I had to do. I had to call the police.

Finally, I could call the police. Finally, I could get help.

I burst through the front door, calling my mom and dad. But no one was home. I stopped in the front hallway, leaned against the banister, rested my head on the railing. I waited for the throbbing in my temples to stop, waited for my breathing to return to normal.

Then I walked across the dark living room to the phone in the corner next to the couch. As I reached for the receiver, the phone rang.

A chill ran down my back. "Hello?"

"Hi, Jennifer. It's me." William.

"William — I have to talk to you," I said, unable to hide the fear in my voice.

"It's too late for talking," he replied calmly. "I have to come over now, Jennifer. I have to . . . deal with you."

"But, William — "

"I took care of Marty," he said, his voice low and steady. "I took care of Stan and Erica because they were on Marty's side. Now you're the only one left."

"But I don't understand," I cried, gripping the phone so hard my hand ached. "You *couldn't* have hypnotized them. I *told* them to resist. I told them just to pretend."

I could hear him chuckle on the other end of the line. It was the most frightening sound I had ever heard. "I didn't need to hypnotize them," he explained. "They were already hypnotized, Jennifer. I hypnotized all three of you that day at the Pizza Palace."

"No, you didn't!" I cried. "You failed — remember?"

"I made you think I failed."

"But, William, how — ?"

"Jennifer, haven't you ever heard of a posthypnotic suggestion? I hypnotized you at the pizza restaurant. I gave you all a posthypnotic suggestion. So there was never any need to hypnotize you again."

"But, William — "

"No more talking," he said abruptly. "I have no choice. I have to take care of you, too, Jennifer. I'm coming right over."

I realized I was trembling all over, trembling so hard, I nearly dropped the phone. "William — ?"

The line was silent for a moment. And then William said, "Here. Have some ice cream."

He hung up right after that.

And I'm sitting here in the dark in front of the phone.

I know I should call the police. Or run. Or *something*.

But I don't seem to be able to.

It's so dark in here. So quiet.

Oh, well. William will be here any minute.

Maybe he'll tell me what to do.

DEDICATED
TO THE
ONE I LOVE
Diane Hoh

Janie slid to her book bag.
The door opened.

MARLA MEDWICK'S BEDROOM REEKED OF THE ACRID smell of nail polish. Marla, her blonde head bent over cotton-separated bare toes, sat on one bed, concentrating on the careful application of Peach Pleasure. Lee Drum and Carrie Carbone, equally lost in the task at hand, occupied the bed's twin, opposite Marla. All three sang along with the music from the radio at Marla's right elbow.

"I love this song," Carrie said dreamily as she brought the tiny brush down toward her foot. "It's so romantic. Turn it up, Marla."

Red-haired Lee, the only one of the three with enough courage — or, as Marla put it, "bad taste" — to indulge in Frosted Fuchsia Frolic, made a gagging sound. "Romantic? It's just plain corny! All that garbage about true love! Makes me sick."

"Don't be bitter, Lee," Carrie said softly. "You sound like you're the only person in the world who's been stepped on. We've all been there, remember?"

Before Lee could reply, the voice of their favorite deejay, Bobby Gee, interrupted.

"This next song here on Kool-98, the place for all

your favorites, is dedicated to Carrie Carbone . . ."

Three heads snapped up; three pairs of ears sprang to attention like retrievers in a field of birds.

". . . by someone who loves her. Enjoy, Carrie!"

As the first strains of the song surrounded them, two pairs of eyes shot to Carrie Carbone, expecting to see pleased surprise on her face.

There was surprise.

But there was no pleasure apparent in Carrie's delicate features. Her skin was as white as the wall behind her, her brown eyes were wide with shock, and her lower lip trembled.

"Carrie, what's wrong?" Marla asked.

"That's . . ." Carrie swallowed and tried again. "That was *our* song. Richie's and mine. It's 'You Turn Me On.' " Her voice rose. "It was *our* song!"

Lee and Marla stared at her. Then Lee shook her head, tightened her lips, and said grimly, "We promised we weren't going to talk about *him*." She lay down on the bed, her long hair splayed out around her like a red cape. "So can it, Carrie."

"Lee, I loved him," Carrie said softly. Tears pooled in her eyes.

"Well, so did I! So did Marla. Which only goes to show how stupid this trio is."

"We weren't stupid," Marla said staunchly. "We trusted him, that's all. He told me it would be better if no one knew we were dating because he was older than me and my parents would object. I never guessed that it was really because he was dating you two at the same time." She sighed heavily. "It's probably the only time in our lives we didn't tell each other something, and look where it got us! We can't even talk about him without getting the shakes."

"*I* can," Lee disagreed. "He was a first-class jerk. No, I take that back. He wasn't even first-class. Just a jerk."

The look of shock on Carrie's face had been replaced by confusion. "But I never told anyone that was our song," she said nervously. "Richie wouldn't have told, either. It was our private song. How . . . how would anyone know that? And even if someone did, why would they dedicate it to me now, when Richie's . . . not around . . . to hear it?"

The three sat in an uneasy silence. Lee broke it by saying, "Well, if *you* didn't tell anyone, Richie must have. I mean, *he* couldn't have made the request — "

Marla interrupted by shaking her head and saying quickly, "Lee's right, Carrie. Richie told someone about your song. That has to be what happened." Then she was seized by a sudden chill and began trembling. She wrapped one of the blue blankets around her shoulders.

The evening ruined, Lee and Carrie went home soon after the last note of "You Turn Me On" had faded away.

Too upset to sleep, Carrie Carbone decided on a hot bath before bed. She tucked her radio under one arm, taking it into the bathroom with her.

As she placed it on the counter opposite the bathtub

and plugged it in, she sighed softly. "You're all I've got to 'turn on' now," she said, "now that Richie isn't . . . here."

As she turned to step into the tub, a warm breeze ruffled the curtains at the open window opposite the counter where the radio sat.

Lost in anger and sadness, Carrie didn't notice.

And because the window was behind her, she didn't see the small but rapidly widening blob of gray-green muck spreading across the white wooden sill.

Carrie stepped into the tub.

Marla was awakened the next morning by a phone call from a hysterical Lee.

"It's Carrie," she sobbed. "Oh, Marla, Carrie's dead!"

Marla pulled herself upright in bed. "Dead? Lee, that's not funny!"

"No, it's true." Lee could barely speak, she was so upset. "She was electrocuted last night. She was taking a bath, and . . . and she had her radio on the counter next to the tub. Her mother said she must have reached out to turn it on while she was still in the water. The radio fell into the tub, and . . ."

Marla sat frozen in shocked silence. Carrie? Carrie was dead? Her friend since fifth grade, the one who knew *everything* about her? She had been electrocuted? How could that be true?

"No," she whispered, "no, it's not true! Not Carrie!"

"It's true," Lee sobbed. "I can't believe it, either. I feel so awful . . . we argued on the way home from your house. She was so upset about hearing that song, and she kept babbling about Richie. I couldn't stand it. I yelled at her to shut up about him." Lee's voice fell to a harsh whisper. "I didn't even tell her good-bye when she got out of the car."

Lee's guilt tore at Marla, but she was too upset herself to find the comforting words she needed.

Unable to talk, they hung up in tears.

When the horror of Carrie's funeral service was behind them, Marla and Lee returned to school, white-faced and thoroughly shaken.

Although she didn't feel like talking to anyone, Marla couldn't help commenting at the crowded lunch table, "I think it's weird that someone requested a song for Carrie right before she died. Bobby Gee had never played a request for Carrie until that night." She glanced around the table with tear-swollen eyes. "Don't you all think that's weird?"

Toying disconsolately with her sandwich, Lee nodded glumly.

But Tina, who was sitting beside her, frowned and said, "Bobby Gee? The night Carrie died? He didn't play a song for her. I never heard a request for Carrie. I remember, because the next day when I heard what happened to her, I thought, Gee, there I was, just hanging out, listening to the radio, and poor Carrie was dying. Bizarre." Tina took a sip of her soda. "I'd remember if he'd played a song for her."

"I'm with Tina," a boy named Donald agreed. "Nobody played a song for Carrie that night."

Allen, opposite him, nodded. "Yeah. I was listening till after midnight. Bobby Gee never mentioned her name."

Marla stared at her friends. "You're kidding, right? That's mean!" Tears gathered in her eyes. "How can you joke now? About Carrie? Lee and I both *heard* that request!"

"We wouldn't joke about Carrie," Tina insisted, standing and gathering up her books. "Marla, Bobby Gee didn't play a song for her that night. You and Lee must have been listening to another station or something."

As everyone but Lee left the table, Marla questioned people sitting at other tables. "You heard it, didn't you?" she prodded repeatedly, her voice rising as her frustration and bewilderment grew.

But the answer was always the same. No one except she and Lee had heard the request for Carrie Carbone on the night she died.

"I don't believe this!" Marla cried, turning back to Lee. "How could they not have heard it?"

"They probably weren't even listening," Lee replied with a weary shrug. "How can they remember what they were doing that night?"

But Marla couldn't shrug off her confusion so easily. The strange fact that only she and Lee had heard the request nagged at her. How could that be? It seemed almost as bizarre as the way Carrie had died.

Marla had been thinking about Richie too much, maybe that was the problem. Maybe her mind was getting too tired . . . playing tricks on her. If only people would stop talking about Richie; and how he'd left town so suddenly, with just a note for his aunt and uncle. He hadn't even bothered to tell any of his friends good-bye.

"Well, that's Richie!" they'd say. "He never did want to be tied down."

She had to stop thinking about him.

But . . . she wasn't the only one who'd heard the request. Was Lee Drum hearing things, too?

The following night, Marla was trying to study in the quiet of her bedroom, when Lee called, shouting at Marla to turn on the radio.

"Get Bobby Gee!" she cried. "Someone's dedicating a song to me. Hurry up!"

Marla obeyed. Bobby Gee's deep, melodious voice filled the room.

". . . so here's 'Falling for You' for Lee Drum, requested by someone who loves her."

Marla's stomach did a somersault. And then Lee's enthusiasm faltered as the song's title was announced.

"This is really creepy, Marla. . . ."

Marla knew what Lee was going to say before the words crossed the telephone wire.

" 'Falling for You' was *our* song, mine and Richie's."

"Lee," Marla asked slowly, "did Bobby Gee have an open line tonight? I mean, did you *hear* the request made?"

"Yeah, I did. But — "

"But what?"

"Well, I didn't exactly recognize it. I mean, it was

real low, almost a whisper. But . . . but it sounded a little bit like . . . no, that's . . . you'll think I've lost it. It's too weird."

Marla drew in a deep breath. "Lee, *what*? Who *was* it?"

"It sounded a lot like . . . Richie's voice."

"Lee! That's impossible. Richie's . . . not around."

"I know. I *know*! It couldn't be. I *said* it was too strange. I just . . . it sounded like him, that's all."

Marla took another deep breath. "It was probably some sick joker trying to sound like Richie. Someone who's mad at him for leaving town without saying good-bye. What a rotten sense of humor!"

"Yeah, I guess. . . ." But Lee didn't sound convinced. Saying she might as well listen to the song, since it had been requested for her, Lee hung up.

Lee's remarks about the voice kept Marla tossing and turning in bed. If she asked around at school tomorrow, would the kids say they hadn't heard "Falling for You"? Would they insist that Bobby Gee hadn't played it tonight?

I'm not going to ask, she decided as she rolled over and buried her face in the pillow. Because I don't want to know if no one heard it but me and Lee. Sometimes it's better not to know. . . .

Sometime during the night, Lee Drum awoke in the darkness and felt her stomach growling. Knowing she wouldn't be able to go back to sleep until she'd grabbed a snack, she left her room in her flowered flannel pajamas and bare feet and headed for the stairs in the dark. She had made the trip countless times since her family had moved into the old Victorian house.

But when Lee reached the top of the steep, narrow staircase, her left foot suddenly slid out from under her, slipping on an unseen glob of slimy gray-green goo. She lost her balance and with a startled, murmured "Oh!" she catapulted forward. Her body tumbled head over heels in a graceless bundle from the top of the stairs to the bottom. When she hit the hardwood floor at the base of the staircase, there was one final thud.

Then silence.

Marla heard the news at school. She stopped breathing momentarily as a shocked friend said, "She's not dead, but something terrible happened to her spine. Mrs. Drum told my mother Lee might not walk again. She could be paralyzed for the rest of her life."

Lee Drum had studied ballet from the age of six. She had planned to make dancing her career. Now, the long, strong legs that she had laughingly called "Drum sticks" were useless.

Leaving school numbed with shock, her movements stiff and wooden, Marla remembered the night she'd discovered Lee and Richie . . . together. . . .

She was on her way home from the library. She was humming to a song on her car radio, the windows open to let in a warm autumn breeze. Lee's house was on her way home. The big yellow Victorian was, as always, bright with lights, including the one on the wide front porch.

Maybe I'll honk, Marla thought with a grin as she approached the Drum home. *I'll start honking now and lay on the horn all the way down the street. Lee will hear it up in her room and know it's me. She'll think it's funny.*

But just as she leaned forward, still grinning, the porch light illuminated two figures dancing, very close together, in front of the chain-suspended white swing. Marla saw the tall, leggy girl she knew so well and a taller, very cute boy, whose grin could light up a room. They were dancing so close together. She couldn't have slid even one thin dime between the two of them without touching the pale blue sweater or the plaid flannel shirt.

Lee and Richie . . . together. Her best friend and the only boy she'd ever cared about.

It wasn't Lee's fault. She didn't know Marla was dating Richie.

But . . . Richie *knew.*

And when Marla, in tears, went straight to Carrie's house and told her what had happened and mentioned Richie's name, Carrie's face had gone stark white.

"Who?" she whispered. "Who did you say he was?"

"Richie Creek. I didn't tell you because he said not to. He was afraid my parents would find out. He's older . . . I don't think you know him."

And then, for the second time that night, Marla reeled in shock as Carrie answered through tears of despair, "Yes, I do, Marla. I *do* know him. Oh, Marla! I've been dating him, too!"

The following night, after a long, painful session

together, the three friends confronted Richie with his treachery. Marla was the first to speak.

"What's going on, Richie?" she said quietly, while Lee fumed beside her, and Carrie, pale as a ghost, bit her lower lip nervously. "You've been dating all three of us at the same time? Don't you think that's pretty sleazy?"

And he laughed. Laughed! "Variety is the spice of life, sweetie," he said lightly. "Haven't you girls ever heard that?" He reached out and touched Marla's hair. "We had fun, didn't we? What's the problem?"

"You're a worm!" Lee burst out furiously. "Three-timer! Creep!"

"You said you loved me," Carrie said softly, "and I believed you. I feel so stupid!"

They all felt stupid. And they hated the feeling.

"I'm splitting this deadbeat town, anyway," Richie said. "Heading for the big city, where the action is. We had fun, but I gotta move on now. Feel like giving me a ride to the airport, saving me cab fare?"

Richie Creek sure did have nerve!

Remembering the way things had happened, Marla was as awash in tears as she'd been that night when she saw Lee on the porch with Richie. She had thought it was all behind them, but now . . .

What *was* happening now? Bobby Gee had played a song that had been special to Carrie and Richie, and Carrie had died. He had played a song special to Lee and Richie, and Lee had fallen. Carrie was gone forever; Lee paralyzed.

Why?

Her stomach turned over. Richie was the only other person who knew about the songs. If she didn't know better . . . no, that was impossible. Unless she really was losing her mind . . . was that it? Was she going crazy? Richie wasn't around to request songs, or to hurt them anymore.

Then who was doing it?

And *why?*

Food began to taste like mud to Marla. She slept fitfully, her dreams filled with shadowy, haunting images of Richie and Carrie and Lee. On more than one dark night she was jolted out of a tormented sleep by the strains of "You Turn Me On" or "Falling for You." Yet, when she checked, her radio was off, and the house completely silent.

Her jeans hung loosely on her hips, and dark shadows encircled her eyes, like bruises. When she tried to study, the words reshaped themselves into images of Richie, looking up at her from the page with mocking laughter in his eyes. Slamming the textbook shut failed to erase the image. It danced around the room, taunting her, teasing, until she put her head in her hands and wept.

She knew what was haunting her. It was the knowledge that all three of them had dated Richie, but only two had been attacked. Three people had loved him, shared a secret song with him . . . but only two had suffered terribly because of it.

Only *two*.

It wasn't finished. It couldn't be. Nothing terrible had happened to *her*.

Not . . . yet.

She picked the nail polish from her nails, forgot to wash her hair, and wore the same clothes to school two, sometimes three, days in a row. Her friends at school, uneasy about her appearance and behavior, began to avoid her. She missed Lee and Carrie fiercely, feeling lost and alone without them.

And she was terrified.

On a Saturday night after visiting Lee in the hospital, Marla was home alone, making a futile attempt at studying. Her parents had gone out. The house, set deep in a wooded area at the edge of town, was completely silent.

Marla was furious at herself for letting her parents leave. Why didn't I make them stay home? Marla asked herself.

Because I would have had to explain why I'm afraid. And I can't do that. *I can't.*

Giving up on her studies, she left the desk and crawled into her bed, burrowing under the covers for safety and comfort.

To break the silence, she reached out and turned on the radio.

"I want to request a song for Marla Medwick," a whisper breathed in her ear. "Play 'A Knife in My Heart' and dedicate it to Marla, the girl I love."

Marla froze. Oh, god, here it was! But . . . how could it be? That was her and Richie's song, and no one knew that except the two of them.

Images of Richie flooded her mind: smiling, talking about his plans to "see the world," bending his head to kiss her. Dressed in a sportcoat and tie, ready to leave town forever. Ready to leave her behind — forever.

That voice on the radio . . . she had to be mistaken. It couldn't be . . . how *could* it?

Now she was next. That was the way it worked: first the song that had once been so sweet, so special . . . then something terrible happened, leaving the victim dead . . . or worse. She was next.

It was *her* turn.

And the title of the songs told what was going to happen, Marla realized that now. Carrie's song had been "You Turn Me On," and she had been electrocuted. "Falling for You" had been played for Lee, and Lee had taken a terrible tumble down the stairs. What lay in store for someone whose special song had been, "A Knife in My Heart"?

Oh, God, she thought with sickening clarity, I'm going to be stabbed! Or have my face slashed, so that for the rest of my life people will turn away from me in disgust, or . . .

She began trembling violently as she tried to pull herself into a sitting position in bed, wrapping the blankets around her like a cocoon.

She had to stop it from happening. She *had* to.

. . . But she couldn't think straight. If only she could stop shaking, clear her mind. . . .

The police . . . they couldn't help her. Not with this. . . . There was too much she didn't understand, couldn't explain. They'd think she was crazy.

Wasn't there anyone who could help her?

Bobby Gee. This had all started with Kool-98.

Marla picked up the telephone with shaking fingers and dialed the radio station. It took her a few minutes to get through. "Oh come on, *come on*," she repeated anxiously to herself. "Pick up the phone."

"Name your choice," Bobby Gee said finally.

"No, no, this isn't a request," Marla said, trying in vain to control the panic in her voice. "I need help . . . you have to help me . . . he's going to *kill* me!"

"Kill you?" The disc jockey sounded amused. "Who's going to kill you, honey?"

"Richie. Richie Creek." Although the room was chilly, beads of sweat gathered on Marla's forehead.

"Who's Richie Creek?"

Marla was babbling, and she knew it. But she couldn't help it. There wasn't *time* to talk slowly. "He was my boyfriend. And Lee's. And Carrie's. Only none of us knew he was dating the other ones, not at first."

Bobby Gee's voice was patient. "Look, sweetie, I don't think some guy is going to put out your lights permanently just because you dumped him."

"No, no, it's not *like* that. We didn't dump him. We . . . oh, god, we *killed* him."

"Excuse me?"

"We killed him. Everyone thinks he left town and went to Los Angeles, but he didn't. He never got to the airport . . . because . . . because we killed him."

And Marla saw that night again, the night she had tried so hard to forget. . . .

When Richie asked for a ride to the airport, they were stunned by his gall. Of all the nerve! He'd broken their hearts, and now he wanted a ride. They couldn't believe it.

But then Lee turned to Marla, a sly smile on her face, and said, "Sure. Why not? Who better to see you off than the three girls who love you? When are you leaving?"

Richie looked surprised, but pleased. "Tomorrow night. Eight-fifteen."

"Pick you up at seven," Lee said, and dragged a dumbfounded Marla and Carrie back to her car.

Lee explained her plan during the ride home.

It seemed like simple justice to Marla. Carrie was less enthusiastic, but agreed to go along.

So, when they picked up Richie the following night, Lee sat in the backseat with Richie, while Marla drove, sharing the front seat with Carrie. And they didn't drive to the airport. They drove instead out to Blackberry Hill Road, a dirt road winding along a foul-smelling, brackish, grayish-green swamp.

Richie, in high spirits over his trip, chattered cheerfully about the new worlds he intended to conquer and what a great time he was going to have doing it. When he realized they were not on their way to the airport, he got mad. "I don't have time to fool around, you

guys," he said. "What are we doing out here?" He
peered out the car window into the wide pool of greenish scum dotted here and there with dead trees and
jagged logs. "God, it stinks!"

"Relax, Richie," Lee said. "This is a shortcut."

But Marla could see Richie's face in the rearview
mirror. He didn't take Lee's advice. He didn't relax.

A noise from downstairs interrupted Marla's
thoughts. She was alone in the house. There shouldn't
be any noise from downstairs.

Shivering, she eyed the door. It seemed, suddenly,
fragile, no stronger than a sheet of paper.

Marla dropped the phone, jumped out of bed, and
ran to her desk. Grabbing the chair, she dragged it
across the room and jammed the sturdy wooden back
up under the doorknob. Then she flipped the lock and
checked the doorknob to make sure the lock held. That
done, she ran back to the bed and retrieved the phone.

When the disc jockey spoke again, the patience was
gone from his voice. "Who *is* this?" he demanded. And
in an irritated aside, he muttered, "Jeez, isn't anybody
screening these calls?" To Marla, he added, "I don't
have time for jokes, kid."

"It's not a joke. This is Marla Medwick. Forty-four
forty-three Buskin Drive. Richie's going to kill me.
Tonight. I know it sounds crazy, but it's true. He's
going to stab me. You've *got* to believe me."

"I thought you said the guy was dead."

"He *is* dead. At least . . . we thought he . . . but
now . . ."

"Tell me about it," the disc jockey urged suddenly,

as if he had finally realized that the call *wasn't* a joke, and could be important.

All across town, listeners picked up the tone in his voice and stopped what they were doing. Pens remained poised in mid-air, textbooks lay ignored on desks, blow-driers fell silent, noisy water faucets were turned off, and countless radio volume dials were turned up.

Marla's eyes fastened on the chair-barricaded door. He was coming . . . she could feel it. . . . Her hands gripped the receiver so tightly the skin went bone-white to the wrist. "We were just going to leave him out there!" she cried, her voice rising precariously. "Make him walk or hitchhike back to town. We figured it would give him time to think about what he'd done to us. He had it coming, didn't he?" Her face flushed scarlet. "Well, *didn't* he?" she demanded angrily.

"Made you mad, did he?" Bobby Gee said gently.

There was another sound from downstairs. Marla sank down on the bed and pressed her back up against the wall.

"We made him get out of the car," Marla whispered into the phone, her breathing ragged and raspy. She never took her eyes off the door. "Lee had her little brother's toy gun. It looks real."

Lee forced him out of the car, and Richie stood there beside the swamp, his eyes wide with disbelief.

"You guys are nuts!" he yelled in fury. He grabbed for the door handle, yanked it open, tried to dive into the backseat.

But Lee kicked out at him. He grunted and fell

backward, and Lee pulled the door shut, slamming it hard.

"I was the one driving," Marla told the disc jockey breathlessly, "and when she yelled 'Go!' I took off, really fast."

"So is the guy still out there, or what?"

Marla swallowed hard. Her eyes remained glued to the bedroom door, waiting. . . .

"No. Lee was so upset she wasn't paying attention, or she'd have noticed the tie right away."

"The tie?"

Was that the sound of footsteps on the stairs? "Richie was all dressed up for the trip. I don't know who he was trying to impress. *We* weren't impressed." Her voice fell to a whisper again. "We'd only gone a few feet when Lee started screaming, 'His tie, his tie!' I thought she'd lost her mind."

"And had she?" At the radio station, Bobby Gee was sitting up very straight in his brown swivel chair, his ear glued to the telephone in his hand.

"No. Oh, god, no . . . she hadn't. It *was* Richie's tie. Stuck inside the back door. And . . ." — a sob of horror escaped Marla's lips — "he was still attached to it."

She could still see it so clearly. . . .

She slammed down on the brakes, hard, bringing the car to a shrieking standstill. They jumped out, and there he was . . . only . . . only it didn't look like Richie anymore, not after being dragged along that hard, stony road.

"Jeez, you *dragged* him?"

Wasn't the doorknob turning the tiniest bit? Marla

stood up. "We didn't know he was there," she moaned. "We *didn't*! We couldn't believe he was dead. I guess he was strangled, because his face was all purplish and his head hung funny." The phone cord, set in motion by her violent trembling, slapped crazily against the wooden bedside table.

Bobby Gee exhaled deeply. He raised a hand to the sound engineer in the booth, tracing a nine and two ones in the air. The engineer nodded and began dialing a telephone at his elbow.

The doorknob *was* turning. Marla, her eyes still on the door, began backing away from the bed, moving as far as possible from the door.

"When we saw what we'd done, we knew we couldn't take him back to town. No one would believe it was an accident. Everyone knew we were mad at him for what he'd done to us."

Remembering, Marla felt sick and faint. If it hadn't been for Lee, they'd have stood there screaming all night long. She'd made them snap out of it.

"We have to get rid of him," Lee said, bending down to take Richie's bleeding hands. "Help me." When Marla and Carrie, paralyzed with shock, didn't move, Lee screamed again, "Help me with him!"

"So what did you do?" Bobby Gee asked slowly.

"We . . ." Marla sobbed, "we put him in the swamp."

Their eyes clouded with horrified tears, the girls had dragged and pulled and tugged until Richie Creek sank like a stone into the disgusting greenish sludge.

"Gone forever," Lee said dully, watching the muck bubble up in protest over the new arrival.

But she had been wrong. Richie wasn't gone forever, after all.

"What else could we do?" Marla asked Bobby Gee, her voice a pitiful whine. "Everyone would have thought we'd killed him on purpose, to get even. And we hadn't! I swear, it was an accident!"

"Right."

"Lee said nothing ever comes back up out of the swamp, but she was wrong." Solid wall bumped up against her spine. She could move no further away from the door. "Richie did come back up. He's here *now*." In a thin, high-pitched voice, she said, "I *know* he is. I can *feel* it. You have to help me. He's going to *kill* me!"

"Is this for real?" the disc jockey asked her. "You dumped a body in the swamp out on Blackberry Hill Road?"

"We *had* to!" Marla shrieked, all control gone now. "We had no choice, can't you see that? *Can't* you?"

When the stench hit Marla's nostrils, so suddenly, so powerfully, her knees gave way, and she sank to the floor. That smell . . . she knew that horrid, unforgettable odor. Nothing else smelled like that.

"You have to help me," she sobbed, her eyes, wide with horror, fastened on the door. "You're the one who played the songs. If you hadn't done that — "

"Songs? What songs?"

"Our special songs with Richie. Lee's and Carrie's and mine. 'You Turn Me On' and 'Falling for You' and tonight you played 'A Knife in My Heart.' That was our song, mine and Richie's. That's how I knew he was coming to get me. You played it . . . a few minutes ago." It seemed like hours.

"Sorry, kiddo, you must have your stations mixed up. Haven't played any of those songs in ages. I mean, you *are* kind of confused, aren't you?"

Marla knew he meant "crazy." She didn't care. What difference did it make now? Richie had come for her, and there was nothing she could do to stop him. No one was going to help her. She was lost.

As she replaced the telephone receiver and tried to climb wearily to her feet, she heard the faint wail of a police siren approaching her house.

Her legs wouldn't work properly. She couldn't stand up.

The terrible stench was overpowering.

Her face swollen and tear-streaked, her body moving sluggishly, she crawled on her hands and knees to the door.

And saw, oozing in under the door, a thick, gooey puddle of grayish-green slime.

She knew what it was immediately. She had scrubbed and scrubbed that night, trying desperately to erase every last trace of the foul, stinking stuff from her hands and knees and from under her fingernails. She still awoke at night, terrified, thinking she was coated with the disgusting stuff. She knew the swamp sludge well.

Outside, car doors slammed, feet slapped up the sidewalk and onto the wooden porch, fists pounded on the door.

"Police, open up!" voices demanded.

I'm safe! Marla thought. They were here. She had made it. The terrible thing wasn't going to happen to her, like it had to Carrie and Lee. She was *safe*.

"Come on, open this door!" the voices shouted.

She would do that. She would go downstairs and open the front door and let the police in, let them save her.

"I'm coming!" she called out eagerly. Rising to her feet, she went to the door, and moved the chair. She was breathing more easily now. Careful to avoid the puddle of sludge, she put her hand on the doorknob and turned it. Let them put her in prison forever, she didn't care. At least she'd be safe there.

Straddling the slop of pale muck, she slowly pulled open the door and stepped out of the room.

Her sigh of relief became a shriek of terror as the glow from the ceiling light danced across the wide metal blade descending rapidly toward her throat.

The shriek ended in a shocked whisper as the blade met its target.

Eyes full of disbelief, Marla remained upright for a second or two, watching bright red streams of her own blood explode against the white walls, creating a brilliant scarlet design.

"No," she whispered, "no, Richie. . . ."

Then, in slow motion, she sank to the floor, her back against the wall. Her head slid sideways, resting on her shoulder.

After one final, weak gurgle of protest, Marla closed her eyes forever.

As the police broke down the front door and pounded

up the stairs, a thick pool of bright red blood crept across the floor and overtook the puddle of murky green.

With a soft, whispered sigh of satisfaction, the swamp sludge allowed itself to be absorbed by the bright red until there wasn't a trace of green anywhere in sight.

HACKER
Sinclair Smith

Every time I get near one of these things, something goes wrong, Violet wailed inwardly as she stared at the computer monitor. *ERROR ERROR ERROR* flashed over and over again, demanding her attention. Nothing she did seemed to help, though, and Violet was getting discouraged and exasperated.

She ruffled her short black hair and turned to peer out the classroom window. Rain was coming down in slanted sheets, splattering against the glass.

There are a lot of other places I'd rather be on a night like this than a computer class at a broken-down community college.

Still, her father had insisted. He thought it was important to learn about computers while you were still in high school.

But at least there was one good thing about the class ... there *was* Mr. Umberto, the teacher. Even though Mr. Umberto was too old for her — he'd probably been out of college for at least a year, she thought — he was fascinating.

She gazed at the teacher standing in front of the room and sighed. He was absorbed in pruning a plant

233

he had brought into the classroom. Mr. Umberto had told the class how much he loved flowers and indoor gardening — that plants had a special meaning for him. He even wore a rose in the buttonhole of his jacket every day. Violet thought this made him seem quite romantic — and sensitive.

She sighed again. If only the high school guys she knew were sophisticated like Mr. Umberto.

Too bad, though; thinking the computer teacher is fascinating isn't the same as thinking computers are. She looked at her Walkman with longing. Why not? she thought, glancing around the room. Everyone else was absorbed in practicing programming. Smiling, she slipped on the headphones and switched on some music.

Violet kept her eyes glued to the computer screen as she tapped her fingers in time with the beat. Suddenly an announcer broke in and interrupted the song with a special bulletin.

"Mr. Arthur Perez becomes the fourth victim missing and presumed dead in the ongoing series of bizarre disappearances that are leaving citizens terrified. Detectives on the scene believe the tragedy is once again the work of the serial killer whom newspapers are calling Hacker."

Violet sat up straighter. She had been following the case from the beginning, devouring every bit of information: mysterious disappearances, hardly any clues, and always a strange message found on the victim's home computer. Violet listened with rapt attention to the latest:

ROSES ARE RED
VIOLETS ARE BLUE
SUGAR IS SWEET
. . . TOODLEOOOO!

This time the message had been signed *EVERY-BODY'S FAVORITE CUT-UP*. Violet shuddered. She didn't like having her name used in the killer's message. Killer . . . if they hadn't found the bodies, what grisly clues were the detectives refusing to divulge that made them believe the victims had been murdered? And why did the killer choose only victims with home computers, and leave a message?

Imagine, the victims' computers had stored the death threat messages — for who knows how long. Maybe long after the victims themselves were gone. She gazed at the screen glowing in front of her as she eased off the headphones and turned off the Walkman.

"Problem?" someone whispered.

Violet turned quickly, startled, and looked up into Mr. Umberto's face. She hadn't heard him come up behind her.

How long has he been standing there? she wondered.

"I just don't seem to get these things," Violet laughed nervously.

"You know, you're allowed plenty of practice time after class — which I've noticed you don't take advantage of," he said rather sternly.

Suddenly Violet felt defensive. "This wasn't my idea. If I had to take a night course after school I'd rather take something fun like painting. This is boring. Besides, it's not like we're getting graded, anyway. This course is supposed to be for our own interest, and frankly, I'm not interested." She stopped suddenly as a flicker of annoyance froze on Mr. Umberto's face. He continued staring down at her, fingering the flower in his lapel.

Oh, no, it's that temper of yours again, she scolded herself. Rudeness was Mr. Umberto's pet peeve, and the only thing that really made him angry.

"I'm so sorry, I don't know what came over me, I didn't mean to be rude," she stammered. "I was planning to come in and practice — I guess I've just been procrastinating. It's a character flaw of mine, I guess," she finished looking down at her hands.

To her surprise, Mr. Umberto threw back his head and laughed. How could I have said those things to *him*, she asked herself, looking at his thick black hair and twinkling dark eyes.

"I think you're being too hard on yourself, Violet. Let's not say procrastination is a character flaw — let's just call it a bad habit. We all have those. Do you know what mine is?" Mr. Umberto asked confidentially.

Violet shook her head. Everyone thought Mr. Umberto was so clever, so good-looking, and so much fun to talk to. What bad habit could he possibly have?

"I'm a terrible practical joker," he confessed. "I have to watch myself all the time, because once I get started, I just can't stop!" He laughed again, and Violet laughed along with him.

"Tell you what, though. I wish you'd give computers another chance. I find them so — so very interesting."

Then I do, too, Violet almost blurted out. Then and there she vowed to practice on the computer, and to impress Mr. Umberto.

Why not start tonight? she thought later as she watched the other students leave. Violet hesitated. She had turned off her computer and she already had her coat on.

I'm going to stay, Violet told herself firmly. She took off her coat and sank into the chair in front of her terminal. Then she sat motionless for a few moments, staring at the screen and twisting a piece of hair at the back of her neck.

I could just get a candy bar and come back, she thought as she logged on to the computer. Suddenly she felt very hungry.

The prompt appeared on the screen asking for her password. Impulsively Violet closed her eyes, typed a few keys at random, pushed back her chair and stood up. I'll have to start all over when I come back, she sighed.

Oh, well, let's go get that candy bar.

You're *still* procrastinating, she told herself as she headed down the deserted hallway toward the vending machines. It looks like nobody stayed around, she thought, feeling a little uneasy. She kept glancing over her shoulder, hoping she'd see someone, but the whole floor looked deserted.

On the way back to the room, she stopped to read

the items on the bulletin board, and then stopped to check her makeup.

About fifteen minutes later she forced herself back to the computer. Okay, let's get started, she muttered as she entered the classroom.

But as she approached the terminal, she realized something was wrong.

There was a message on the screen.

As Violet read it, she felt an uneasy stirring in the pit of her stomach. The message — it was a lot like the rhymes she'd been reading in the newspaper the past few weeks.

> *ROSES BY THE HANDFUL*
> *VIOLETS BY THE BUNCH*
> *SHOULD I KILL YOU AFTER*
> *BREAKFAST*
> *. . . OR WAIT TILL AFTER LUNCH?*

Tightening her hands into fists so tight the knuckles whitened, Violet backed stiffly away from the screen. That's the kind of message Hacker writes, she thought trembling. And then she ran.

She didn't stop running until she reached the lobby. Thoughts were racing through her terrified mind. Was it a message for me? But why would he send a message here? The place was full of terminals, with several people using them each day.

Then another thought flashed into her mind, bringing her up short. She had closed her eyes when she typed in her password. She pressed her hand to her throat as the realization hit her.

Somehow, I've tapped into the Hacker's computer — and found a clue.

I've got to call the police.

Shaking, Violet walked across the lobby to the row of pay telephones. With trembling hands, she fumbled for a coin.

Just then she saw Mr. Umberto come striding across the lobby, pulling up the collar of his raincoat, and whistling a tune.

"Mr. Umberto — Mr. Umberto, WAIT!" Violet cried, rushing up to him as he pushed open the door.

Mr. Umberto stopped and smiled. "Violet? What are you doing here so late?"

"Mr. Umberto, it's so incredible. I stayed to practice, but somehow I got a strange message on the screen. It wasn't mine. I think I pressed the wrong keys, or did something — I don't know. The message on the screen — it was the Hacker's, I just know it. I must have accidentally entered his computer system." She quickly blurted out the rest of the story.

"Well, Violet, this is pretty amazing," said Mr. Umberto when Violet had finished. Then he eyed her suspiciously. "Are you playing a joke on me?"

Violet gasped. "A *joke*? About Hacker — about a murderer? How could anyone joke about that?"

"Well, the world is full of practical jokers, I can tell you that. And I'll bet one of your classmates is playing a joke on you. In fact, I'm certain of it."

"But why are you so sure?" Violet asked, confused.

"Because, Violet," replied Mr. Umberto, gently, "you aren't experienced enough to understand why breaking into someone's system by typing their password *accidentally* is such an improbable, and practically impossible, idea."

"Oh," Violet said softly, feeling a little foolish. "I guess you're right."

"Of course I am," Mr. Umberto said confidently.

Suddenly Violet had another thought. "But, Mr. Umberto — what if the Hacker sent the message *to me*?"

Mr. Umberto chuckled. "Don't let your imagination run away with you, Violet. Trust me. Someone just played a joke on you. And don't worry. Everything I've heard on TV or read in the papers says that Hacker always contacts his victims on their home computer. You don't even have one, so you can take it easy."

Mr. Umberto paused and glanced at his watch. "Shoot! I've got to go — I mustn't be late. Good night," he said abruptly. Then he was gone.

"Good night," Violet called after him, feeling suddenly drained. She collected her things and left the building. She always hated walking down the narrow winding path that led from the computer building. It was flanked on either side by tall trees tangled with overgrown shrubs. Lately she was sure she'd heard someone hiding there.

Tonight she was sure someone was there again. Violet hurried all the way home, glancing over her shoulder at every noise. A feeling of dread knotted the pit of her stomach, and she had the eerie sensation that she was being followed.

It's probably just that I've been thinking about the Hacker case too much, she thought as she reached her house and started up the walkway.

The house was dark.

What's wrong? she wondered, fidgeting nervously.

Calm down. Maybe Dad got called away on business at the last minute.

Violet sighed. Lately it seemed like he was always having to go away on mysterious, sudden trips. Well, he promised it wouldn't last much longer.

As Violet started to put the key in the door, her breath caught in her throat.

The door was open.

She knew she had locked it carefully before she left. Her father was a fanatic about such things. If you find the door open, never, never go into the house alone, he had told her over and over. Her heart pounded.

. . . But what if something had happened to Dad?

Panic seized her, and Violet gave the door a shove and lurched inside. She jumped as the umbrella stand fell to the floor with a crash. As she felt her way through the hall, she could hear the blood rushing through her head.

As her eyes adjusted to the darkness, she could make out an unfamiliar light coming from the living room. It was a weird greenish glow. She forced herself to keep moving closer until she could make out its shape. She gasped as she realized what it was.

It was a home computer! She bent down to read the message that lit up the screen.

> *SURPRISE!*
> *SORRY, HONEY, I WAS CALLED OUT OF TOWN AT THE LAST MINUTE. I HOPE TO BE BACK SOON BUT I'M NOT SURE WHEN. HERE'S A PRESENT TO KEEP YOU COMPANY WHILE I'M GONE. I'LL CALL YOU. LOVE, DAD.*

Violet sank weakly into a chair. Great, she thought. A home computer of my very own. Just what I've always wanted. She frowned.

The phone rang, startling Violet out of her thoughts. She jumped in her chair.

Relax, she told herself, feeling silly. It's probably Dad calling.

"Hi, is that you?" Violet said. But the voice on the other end was cold . . . a stranger.

"It's me. I guess you discovered me tonight. Now I've discovered you. It wasn't easy to find you — but I have my secret ways."

Violet felt a chill run through her as the voice laughed. It was a soft, threatening laugh. Her fingers tightened on the receiver.

"Sorry, I can't pay you a visit right now — too many other appointments." There was that laugh again. "I'll be in touch, though. I'll be seeing you."

The caller hung up. Violet hugged herself, in a panic.

She wished she weren't alone right now. Someone *was* following me home — whoever it was I've heard in the bushes outside the computer building. I knew I could feel someone there. And tonight they got here first, and opened the door. That's how they found my phone number.

Her heart pounded. She picked up the phone to call the police, but hesitated a moment before dialing. The voice had been really scary. But she remembered what Mr. Umberto had said about the world being full of practical jokers, and hung up.

The call probably was a prank, she told herself. After all — like Mr. Umberto said, Hacker left messages on the victims' home computers. He didn't make threatening phone calls — at least as far as anybody knew.

Violet walked through the house carefully checking all the doors and windows, and locking any she found open.

Then she went to bed and tossed and turned until morning, drifting in and out of sleep.

It's a good thing it's Saturday, Violet thought when she awoke late the next morning, feeling exhausted. Finally she got out of bed, padded over to the window, and peered out. The sky was a cold, steely gray.

Nice day, she frowned. Then an oddly shaped package on the porch caught her eye.

What on earth could it be? she wondered. She quickly threw on a robe and ran outside.

The package was huge — at least six feet tall, she

thought as she got close to it. It was wrapped in tissue paper, tied with a big red ribbon. She tore at the wrapping.

It was a large, flowering cactus. The blooms were brilliant red and orange.

Violet felt puzzled but pleased. What an odd sort of gift. The florist must have delivered it while I was still sleeping, she realized. After searching unsuccessfully for the card, Violet gave up and tugged the plant inside.

She had just finished placing it in the corner of the dining room and was admiring her handiwork, when the phone rang.

"Dad!" she said happily, grateful for the sound of his voice. They chatted a few minutes about nothing in particular, and then Violet forced herself to sound casual as she asked him, "Hey, Dad — did you have anything delivered to the house . . . like a cactus?"

"A cactus!" her father sounded surprised.

"Yes — I just brought it inside. It has flowers on it."

"Better phone the florist first and find out what's going on. Maybe it belongs to somebody and it's lost, or maybe you've got a secret admirer with unusual taste." Her dad chuckled. " 'Bye, hon. See you in a week or two."

Violet hung up and stared at the cactus. I can't call the florist because I don't know which one it is. There was no card, and no name on the wrapping.

Well, what could be dangerous about a cactus? Maybe it *is* from a secret admirer, she laughed to herself. I'd much rather have had flowers.

At the next class Violet mentioned the strange phone call to Mr. Umberto.

"I think you were smart not to fall for it, Violet. Whoever it was will probably get tired of his little joke and stop bothering you now," he told her.

He was right. Two weeks went by, and there were no more phone calls, and no more messages. Violet put the whole thing out of her mind and went on trying to improve her computer skills to impress the teacher. To her surprise, she began enjoying herself. She even became a member of a computer bulletin board and began to spend hours in front of her terminal at home, chatting with other members.

She was preparing to do just that one evening, but decided to check her E-mail messages first. One of them nearly scared her to death.

> *HI. I TOLD YOU I'D BE IN TOUCH. I'D LIKE TO BE FRIENDS. MOST OF MY FRIENDS DISAPPOINT ME, THOUGH, BY GOING TO THE POLICE. YOU KNOW WHAT HAPPENS THEN. YOU READ THE PAPERS. SO HERE IS A TEST TO SEE IF I CAN TRUST YOU. MY NEXT VICTIM IS GOING TO BE MR. BROWN. BUT DON'T GO TO THE POLICE, BE-CAUSE I'M ALWAYS WATCHING YOU.*

Violet sat staring at the screen for a moment, frozen

with fear. Then she forced herself to go to the phone. She had to tell the police what she had seen.

But just as she was about to dial, she stopped.

Wait a minute, she said to herself. If I tell the police that the next victim is going to be *Mr. Brown*, they'll think I'm crazy. There have to be hundreds of Mr. Browns in the phone book. This has to be a joke.

The next few hours were torture for Violet as she argued with herself, unable to decide whether or not to call the police.

It has to be a joke.

What if it isn't?

You're being foolish.

What if something happens?

You've got to call the police.

What if he's watching you?

Finally, feeling completely exhausted, Violet called the police and told them what she knew. A detective who sounded very weary assured her that messages like the one she had received had so far turned out to be pranks — and they had gotten hundreds of reports. Still, they thanked her and assured her they'd check it out.

As Violet hung up the phone, she thought she saw something outside her window.

A face?

No, she told herself, feeling much calmer now that she had called the police. You've been so upset — it's only your imagination.

"I know it was probably a trick, but I felt I had to

tell the police," she told Mr. Umberto the next time she saw him in class. "They didn't seem to mind. In fact — they said I did the right thing."

"Well then, I guess you did, Violet. It's always good to be on the safe side, I suppose."

That night, Violet had other things on her mind besides the Hacker case. It was the last class, and that meant Mr. Umberto would be leaving town soon. He told the class he was going away — and he didn't say where.

Violet was the only one who stayed after class. She hoped that he would say something — maybe tell her where he was going — but he had just gone to his office. You're being silly, she told herself, looking around at the empty classroom. Just go home.

Suddenly she sat up straight and blinked at the screen. *YOU HAVE MAIL* was flashing in front of her eyes. E-mail, she thought excitedly. Maybe Mr. Umberto had decided to send her a message.

She punched a few keys to close the file she was working on, typed in *MAIL*, and hit return. *YOU HAVE ONE MESSAGE* sprang up on the screen. Violet hit return and waited.

She froze as the message appeared.

I KNOW YOU WENT TO THE POLICE.
I SAW YOU MAKE THE CALL. TOO BAD.
DAISIES IN THE GARDEN
POSIES ON YOUR GRAVE
WHEN YOU'RE FALLING OUT THE
WINDOW

. . . DON'T FORGET TO WAVE!
I'M RIGHT BEHIND YOU I'M RIGHT BE-
HIND YOU I'M RIGHT BEHIND YOU I'M
RIGHT BEHIND YOU. . . .

Violet sat still, as if hypnotized, while *I'M RIGHT BEHIND YOU* filled the entire screen. Then she stood up slowly and began backing away. She was afraid to turn around.

The classroom door slammed shut behind her, followed by the sound of running feet in the hallway.

Violet drew in her breath sharply and listened, straining to hear the smallest sound, as the *thud-thud-thud* faded farther and farther away, growing fainter and fainter. She didn't know how long she stood there in the silence, or what snapped her out of the trance she was in, but finally she snatched her coat and her purse and ran from the room. She was going to find Mr. Umberto.

His office door was open, she saw from the stairs. Yet when she reached the room at the end of the hallway, no one was there. The computer was on, though — every teacher's office had one. She started toward it curiously, when she felt a hand on her arm.

"Looking for something?"

"Oh!" squeaked Violet. "I was looking for you."

"And here I am." Mr. Umberto smiled. He looked strange, Violet thought . . . not himself. But she was about to begin her story, when something stopped her — something she saw on his computer that made her voice freeze in her throat. She couldn't stop staring.

Mr. Umberto followed her gaze to the terminal, where *I'M RIGHT BEHIND YOU* still lit up the screen. "So you see," he said slowly, "someone need not be right behind you to send you a message saying that they are — that's the beauty of computer communication. I see you've found me out."

Violet looked around the room frantically, gasping in disbelief as she saw the entire wall covered with newspaper clippings about Hacker. On some of them were drawn little smiley faces. "Why?" she whispered.

"Why?" Mr. Umberto smiled, and twirled the flower in his lapel. When he spoke Violet had the eerie sensation of listening to a TV advertisement for a product like mouthwash or a tummy toner. "Well, don't look so glum. You know, I used to be an old gloomy gus myself — a regular party pooper," he chuckled. "People looked at me, and you could almost feel them saying, 'Uh-oh, here *he* comes.' "

Mr. Umberto shrugged. "People were rude to me, and it really got me down. But now I know how to chase those blues away." He patted the computer terminal. "The computer tells me what to do. As long as they've got a computer, I can put them in their place." He paused and gazed fondly at the rubber tree in the corner of the room for a moment. He turned back to Violet.

"And do you know the wonderful simplicity of it all?" he asked, raising his eyebrows.

Violet shook her head helplessly.

"No matter what the problem, and no matter what computer — any old one will do — the answer is always the same. Nasty neighbor getting you down? ELIMINATE HIM! Snubbed by the 'IN' crowd? GET RID OF THEM!

"Now when snubs and slights from rude waiters and sales people — or students — put me in a bad mood, I do something about it. Now I'm so cheerful, my social calendar is always full." Mr. Umberto looked thoughtful and knitted his brows. "I suppose I shouldn't keep doing it — killing people after I leave a message on their computer." Then he laughed. "Maybe I could send them a fax!"

"But what if someone . . . puts you in a bad mood and they don't have a computer?" she squeaked.

Mr. Umberto waved his hand lazily and looked at her as if he couldn't imagine such a silly question.

"Well, that's no problem. I just pick out someone who *does*. Anyone will do, really — it all balances out."

Now Violet realized a new terror. He seemed to really believe that there was logic in what he was saying.

Violet was paralyzed with fear. Mr. Umberto was smiling broadly, obviously pleased with himself.

"If you're the Hacker, then what do you do with the bodies?" she asked weakly.

Mr. Umberto's eyes twinkled. "I put them in potted plants — however many it takes. Say it with flowers, that's my motto! And of course, there's the added advantage that they're always guaranteed flowers on their grave — well, for part of the year, anyway.

"Of course, I can't use flowering plants exclusively — you can see how impractical that would be. Most of them are just too small. So I use a few flowering plants — and throw in a couple of rubber trees or maybe some potted palms. It makes for a nice arrangement."

Violet felt horror overtaking her. He was completely, utterly insane she realized. She had been edging toward the door slowly as he spoke — but her knees felt almost too weak to hold her. Now, in a burst of energy, she flew out the door and raced down the steps. She could hear Mr. Umberto's crazy laughter following her down the hall.

She reached the main lobby running so hard people turned around, startled, and stared at her.

She heard Mr. Umberto, calling after her, "Violet, wait! Wait!"

She paused for a moment, out of breath, and aware that she was safe in a lobby filled with people. Still, she backed away warily as the teacher moved toward her.

Suddenly he stopped in front of her and doubled over with laughter. He laughed so hard tears were running down his cheeks.

"Can't you take a joke?" he grunted out, between spasms of laughter.

Violet stared in surprise. This made Mr. Umberto start laughing all over again. "You should see the look on your face!" he gasped. "You fell for the whole thing! This is one of the best gags I've ever pulled."

Finally he straightened up and contained himself, with difficulty. "That day in class, when you were kind of rude — I saw that you stayed to practice, and I thought I'd play a little joke on you. When I saw you walk away, I couldn't resist going over and typing a message on your screen.

"But when you came back — you got so scared I couldn't believe it. And then when you thought you'd actually gotten into Hacker's system — well, it was just too much."

Once again, Mr. Umberto was seized with a laughing fit. He squeezed the flower in his lapel and a stream of water shot out and squirted Violet in the face. "Say it with flowers, that's my motto!" he shrieked.

She jumped back, flabbergasted. She couldn't believe that a grown man could act this way. Mr. Umberto looked like an immature, bratty little boy, laughing over a dirty trick.

"You're ridiculous," she snapped, and strode out the door. Mr. Umberto's laughter echoed in her ears.

Well, I guess the joke's on me, all right, she thought angrily as she strode down the path that led from the building.

But something nagged at her, something that wouldn't let her walk away.

I don't believe him, said a little voice inside her head. He did everything he could to make me believe this was all part of a big joke — but he's lying. I just know it.

Violet slowed her steps. Looking around to make sure Mr. Umberto wasn't behind her, she left the path and cut into the tangle of trees and shrubs. Her thoughts were racing.

Of course! she thought. Those poems Hacker sends to his victims. They're not like death threats anyone would take seriously. They're more like — jokes.

In a few moments, Violet saw Mr. Umberto leave the building, laughing to himself. When he got in his car and drove away, she went back inside.

Soon she was back in the computer room, sitting in front of a terminal. There was a way to prove that Mr. Umberto was the Hacker — if she could do it. She was going to have to get into his computer system for real this time. And now she had learned enough to know how difficult that would be.

I've got to find out the secret password he uses somehow, she told herself desperately. It could be anything, she knew.

Think.

People often use a word that means something special to them — such as a pet's name, or — of course — a favorite flower.

The prompt appeared on the screen, asking for the password, and Violet typed in *ORCHID*.

INCORRECT PASSWORD appeared on the screen.

She tried using just plain *FLOWER* this time.

INCORRECT PASSWORD.

For the next half hour Violet typed in all the names of flowers and plants she could think of, with no luck.

What's the matter with me? she thought suddenly. I haven't tried the most obvious one of all.

Hurriedly she typed *ROSES*.

ROSES ARE RED VIOLETS ARE BLUE appeared on the screen.

She had gotten into the system.

Next she typed *DIR* and hit the return key.

A directory of all the files in the system appeared on the screen. Working quickly, Violet began to read the one labeled *Hacker*.

One by one, the rhymes she had seen in the newspaper articles about Hacker appeared before her eyes. Finally Violet came to a new message she hadn't seen in the papers — yet. It was followed by a name and computer address.

> *ROSES IN RIBBONS*
> *VIOLETS IN LACE*
> *IT'S TOUGH TO BREATHE*
> *WITH A PILLOW ON YOUR FACE*

The message was for a Mr. Bart Brown. Hacker could be on his way to Mr. Brown's house right now, Violet thought, in a panic. Then she had an even worse idea. He could have visited Mr. Brown already, some time earlier. She didn't want to think about that.

Violet rushed to type a message of her own for Mr. Brown.

> *I'M GIVING YOU A CHANCE TO SAVE YOURSELF, BUT YOU'D BETTER HURRY. I'M COMING TO KILL YOU.*
> *HACKER.*

She typed *SEND*, then made a hard copy of the Hacker's file and put the paper in her purse. This time, she had a *real* clue for the police.

It was several weeks before Violet was able to go near her computer again. The police had caught the Hacker hiding near Mr. Brown's home two days after she showed them the copy of the file she had made. It was Mr. Umberto, all right. He confessed to everything. The bodies were right where Mr. Umberto told her they'd be, too — in potted plants.

Mr. Brown told police that he had received Hacker's rhyme, but had assumed it was a joke. When he received the message Violet had sent, however, he became alarmed and contacted his local precinct. Thanks to Violet, Mr. Brown was unharmed.

In the course of the investigation, detectives were able to piece together something of Mr. Umberto's — Hacker's — strategy. He'd bury a body in various potted plants, and then send one of the plants to a few of his next intended victims. Following that theory they were able to track down all of the missing bodies.

They found the remains of Arthur Perez in Mr. Umberto's private greenhouse, in the rubber tree in his office, in several potted geraniums at Bart Brown's house — and underneath the flowering cactus in the corner of Violet's dining room.

Poo Lee kicked out at him. He grunted and fell

DEATHFLASH
A. Bates

It COULDN'T GET YOU IN THE LIGHT.

It couldn't get you if you held completely still.

It couldn't get you if you were totally covered up, including your head.

Marissa pulled the sheet over her head. I don't think it will work this time, she thought.

She remembered the absolute, overwhelming terror she'd felt as a child, waking suddenly from a bad dream — a terror so raw and immediate it could only be caused by something waiting in the darkness . . . waiting for her. If she moved, *it* would get her. If she didn't move, she couldn't cover her head, and *it* would get her anyway.

She had recognized the dilemma even as a child — a dilemma so impossible and so horrible that she'd been certain she would die of fear and indecision whether *it* got her or not.

Now, she shuddered. In the still, hot darkness she could almost hear the sweat as it rolled across her face.

Only this isn't a nightmare, she told herself starkly. This is real. The rules only work for nightmares.

It's going to get me.

Unless I get *it* first.

The idea startled her, and she sat up beneath the sheet, careful to keep herself fully covered. If I get *it* first? How could I?

The thought of stalking *it* made her laugh, though she immediately wished she hadn't. The laugh sounded forced, hollow, too loud for the fragile illusion of safety she'd carried beneath her sheet.

She thought back to when she'd first seen *it*, trying to see the events in a new light . . . to find some kind of weakness in *it*, perhaps . . . a weakness she might use to fight *it*.

She'd left the high school late that Thursday because she'd stopped for help with her math. She had to pick up her little brother at the junior high and take him to soccer practice at the Y, so she'd taken the back roads — the shortest way. The back roads led through the old part of town — the crumbling buildings, the trash-strewn alleys, boarded windows, and people who always looked pinched and cold.

Third Street seemed even darker than the others when she turned onto it, dark as if night had fallen early — or as if daylight couldn't quite penetrate the grime. Dusk hung like a mist. Marissa leaned forward, peering intently through the windshield. Alley entrances loomed suddenly, stark and eerie in the dimness, and it was difficult to see where gutters left off and sidewalks began. She drove carefully, but quickly, eager to leave the area and its mist behind.

Headlights would help, she thought, reaching for

the switch. From the corner of her eye she caught the streak of motion and turned her head in time to see two cats leaping from an alley, yowling, leaping as if propelled, straight in front of the car. The thump was sickening. Marissa knew she'd hit at least one of the cats.

Her legs shook as she braked. Her hands shook as she turned off the engine. "Oh, no, oh, no," she chanted, pleading. "No. I didn't mean . . ."

She jumped from the car, begging the cats to be okay — but at least one of them was not okay. A huge black-and-white tom was howling in pain, rolling and thrashing, aiming itself in a mindless, crippled scurry away from the alley. The other cat was nowhere to be seen.

Lie still! Why won't you lie still? Marissa thought helplessly. She glanced unwillingly at the alley, almost expecting something to emerge . . . something the cat seemed determined to get away from as it thrashed toward a dark doorway.

Sobbing quietly she started to follow. A vet, she thought. If he'll hold still I can catch him. Take him to a vet.

And then *it* came, slipping silently from the alley behind the cat.

A small *it*, shadowy and vague, thin and gray, but with a pale face that was avid with hunger and intent on the cat.

*It*s intention was clear. On all fours *it* stalked the cat, creeping, focused, *it*s intensity that of a cat itself, stalking a prey of its own.

Horrified, Marissa looked for something — a stick or rock — thinking vaguely of defense for herself or the cat or both, knowing even as she grubbed through the piles of trash that the shadowy *it* would not be stopped by one person, with or without a stick or rock.

She knelt, scrabbling through newspaper, grimy rags, rotten bits of filth. Her mouth dry and her hands shaking, she hurried, needing a weapon even if it was useless.

She glanced up. *It* had almost reached the cat, *it*s concentration so intense that *it* had not even noticed her.

Then she heard *it* hiss.

It was a hiss of glee, of anticipation, and it iced her blood. Her heart beat frantically, trying to force the cold fluid through her veins. She wanted to shout, "No! I hurt him and I will save him. I will take him to a vet, and he will live!"

But the fear *it* cast with *it*s hiss had chilled her speech, had frozen her tongue and her words. It was the same fear she'd felt alone in the dark when she was a child. She felt not only chilled, but marked, somehow . . . as if the ice inside made her more transparent, more shadowy and vague like *it* was.

Dumbly, she watched. They were in profile to her, the dying cat and *it*.

The cat spasmed, and *it*s face glowed in anticipation. Marissa could have sworn *it* was humming to the animal in a crooning hiss, a kind of grotesque lullaby, and she felt clogged — choking with horror, with the cat's pain that she had caused, with the shifting, shadowy *it*-ness.

It waited, motionless. The cat spasmed again, then lay still. *It* hovered, *it*s face rapt. There was a sudden, small flash of light, a tiny, yet brilliant cat-shaped glow that seemed to be released from the animal as it died. The *it* pounced, mouth open, swallowing the light.

Marissa's stomach heaved. Horrible, she thought. That was . . . horrible. I . . .

Sudden grayness replaced the icy hold she had felt, and she fell forward in a faint, waking facedown in a pile of trash.

She looked, but *it* was gone. The cat's body lay empty where it had died. The icy shadow *it* cast still hung over the alley, but the strength of it was less immediate. She could think again.

Marissa remembered her brother. She glanced at her watch, unable to believe that barely fifteen minutes had passed since she'd run over the cat.

She wanted to bury it, but she couldn't even bring herself to touch it. Finally she upended a trash bin to cover the shrunken body and gave a small scream as the other cat, an orange cat, jumped out from beneath the bin. Without pausing to think, she grabbed it, ignoring its struggles to escape as she placed the bin over the other, dead cat.

I can't leave you here, she thought. She ran to her car, wrapped the orange cat in her jacket, and leaped into the driver's seat, squealing her tires in her haste to get away.

She felt soiled, contaminated . . . marked by something worse than filth. Her knees felt Jell-O-ed, and it was an effort to move her foot from the floor to the clutch when she had to shift gears.

"You're late!" Robbie announced, clambering into the car in a flurry of elbows, knees, and noisy energy. "Wait'll I tell Mom. . . . What's the matter with you?"

"I . . . I ran over a cat," Marissa whispered, and suddenly she was sobbing aloud, tears running down her face.

"This cat?" Robbie unwrapped the orange cat, stroking it gently, murmuring to it. "This guy's fine," he said. "Scared, but fine. You must not have hit it."

"A different one," Marissa said. "A big one. He . . . he ran right under the wheel, but I think *it* scared him into running so he would die and then *it, it* — "

"You killed him?" Robbie's eyes darkened with the thought. "No wonder you were late." He patted the orange cat. "She's purring," he announced. "Did you see the other cat die?" he asked Marissa. "Did you see anything come out of him? A cloud, maybe?"

"What do you mean?" Marissa asked sharply.

"You don't have to yell," Robbie said. "We were just talking — in science, you know? The teacher said some scientists believe if you have the right equipment you can measure death. I just wondered if you could see something, too. Do you think we could drive now? To practice? Coach is going to yell at me for being late."

Marissa started the car and drove them from the lot. "How can you measure death?" she asked. "You mean that machine that keeps track of the heartbeat and beeps when they get a flat line?"

Robbie shook his head impatiently. "Not hospital machines!" he said, his tone saying, Dummy! "Like radiation measuring machines."

Marissa glanced at her brother. "I remember reading something about that. I think I still have the magazine." She turned the corner, moved into the right-hand lane. Her insides were shuddering as she remembered *it*, the avid expression, swallowing.

She pulled up in front of the Y, and Robbie hopped out of the car. "Mom's going to pick me up. Thanks for the ride." He ran off, shouting, " 'Bye!" as he headed for the door of the Y.

Marissa waited until he was safely inside, then drove home.

She rewrapped the cat in her jacket and carried it inside. It seemed calmer now than it had by the alley. Robbie had that effect on animals. But when she put the cat on the kitchen floor it stiffened again, its eyes wide and frightened, ears quivering. Quickly Marissa poured a saucer of milk and tore up some bologna slices. The cat gulped the food, then slunk from the kitchen, darting quick glances in all directions, hugging the walls as it headed down the hall in search of a hiding place.

It sniffed at doorways, stopping finally at the door to Robbie's bedroom. It looked up at Marissa.

"I guess he won't mind," Marissa said, opening the door. The cat scurried inside and under the bed.

Marissa found two boxes. She lined one with old doll blankets, the other with a plastic garbage bag. She shovelled a few scoops of dirt into the plastic-lined box and set the improvised litter pan near Robbie's desk. The box bed she placed near Robbie's bed.

Then she lugged a carton of papers, books, and magazines from the basement to her bedroom and sat down to read.

She had a pile of books and magazines in front of her when she finally found the article. As she read, her stomach knotted; her lungs froze. A sense of unreality enfolded her as she digested the words. She threw the magazine from her, knocking over her stack, and left the house quickly, almost running as if she could run away from the information.

"Okay," she told herself, forcing herself to slow down and walk calmly up the street, toward the park. "Summarize it. Translate. Put it in English. Okay . . . things that are alive send out currents. Like electricity or radiation. With little things like turtles or mice, there isn't much. Say . . . a current or two, but it's constant. Everything that's alive is always sending it out. There are machines that can measure it.

"The bigger the animal, the stronger the current. Like, say, five for rabbits, cats, small dogs, seven for bigger animals like deer. Only it's not just size. It's intelligence, and power, too. The smarter the animal, the stronger the current. So people have the strongest current. At death, the body lets go of all the stored-up electricity at once and there's a flash . . . maybe one hundred to one thousand times stronger than the constant current. It's called a deathflash.

"That's why Robbie wondered if I'd seen a cloud or something. He wondered if it was strong enough to see. But the article said it was invisible. They've learned to measure it, but it can't be seen."

But I saw it! she thought, walking faster, walking home again. And that thing . . . *it* swallowed the flash.

She shuddered. *It* wasn't like an animal killing for food, she thought. *It* didn't even kill the cat. But it was horrible. It was worse . . . even worse than if *it* had done the killing. I can't think of words bad enough to describe what *it* did. It wasn't torture. It wasn't murder. It was worse.

It was worse because . . . because the flash of life was meant to escape. Even murderers don't swallow the life out of their victims. What I saw . . . what *it* did . . . was worse, worse than the most horrible evil I could ever imagine!

At home — with dinner on the table, her parents brightly discussing the events of their day, the lights shining, TV news in the background, coffee gurgling — everything was so normal Marissa could only laugh at herself. My imagination clicked into overtime, she thought, that's all.

Still, she didn't taste the food she ate, and she felt cold all evening — a deep cold that no blanket could reach. At night in her bed, she shivered. She got all the extra blankets and the sleeping bags and put them on her bed and still she shivered. The cold was too deep.

When she saw *it* again, *it* was much bigger.

She never drove by the alley, going blocks out of her way to pick up Robbie, but she saw *it* anyway. She stopped at a red light and *it* walked in front of her, full of glowing, recognizable shapes. She slipped down behind the wheel, but it was too late. She'd been staring at *it*, horrified by what she could see inside of *it*. Somehow *it* felt the intensity of her gaze. Slowly, *it* turned and returned her stare, smiling, *it*s teeth gleaming dully in *it*s avid, shadowed face.

She couldn't move, not even to roll up her window or lock the doors. If *it* had wanted to, *it* could have climbed right in beside her. . . . Did *it* whisper "Soon," or was it the wind?

No, she thought. *It* didn't whisper. *It* hissed.

It walked on, across the street, up the curb, across the sidewalk, fading into the crowd. Why aren't people screaming? Marissa wondered. Why aren't they running from *it*? Can't they see what *it* is? Don't they see what's inside of *it*? I can't be the only one who can see inside *it*!

She jumped in shock when the car behind her honked. The light was green. She drove, somehow ending up at home where she sat in her car with her head resting on the steering wheel, telling herself she'd only imagined the shapes she'd seen in *it*s vagueness, only imagined the glowing energy of *it*s victims imprisoned inside of *it*.

"The cat," she said aloud. "I did not see a cat inside of *it*. I did not see birds or dogs or the snake or the raccoon. Most of all, I did not see a person. No.

"NO! I did not see a person, and I did not see a hand."

A human hand, twisted in frantic plea.

No!

"It's so gross!" Robbie said.

"If it's gross, maybe you should wait till after dinner to mention it," their mother suggested.

"Jeff's dad!" Robbie went on, looking awed at his own news. "He works at this plant, see? Works the night shift. So last night he was working and suddenly all the lights went out. This crane slipped in the dark. And there was this pile of lumber all stacked up. The crane hit the lumber, and the whole stack fell on his dad and another guy! Jeff's dad is going to be okay, but the other guy died! He got mashed flat."

"I just read about that in the paper," their mother said, flipping back through the pages. "I didn't know it was your friend's father."

"He's not really a friend," Robbie said, shrugging. "He's just this kid at school."

Marissa watched as he casually dropped a lump of meat loaf into his lap. For the cat, she thought. So far Mom hasn't complained about it. Of course, the cat stays in Robbie's room. I don't think it has ever come out.

"Here's the article," their mother said. "It says the man probably died of massive internal injuries." She read silently for a minute, then said, "Listen. The paper says the other employees 'wish to extend their thanks to the anonymous passerby who stopped to give the man mouth-to-mouth resuscitation.' They didn't get the passerby's name. How nice of him to stop and help!"

The rest of the conversation swirled around Marissa but she didn't hear it. She put her hands on the table, needing a solid support to keep from fainting. The gray roared in her ears.

Anonymous. Passerby. That wasn't someone who stopped to help! she thought. It was that thing . . . that *it*. *It* was waiting — waiting for the deathflash.

She tried to tell her family. The words formed, fumbled, fell back inside without being spoken. Even her thoughts fell back without completing themselves, landing inside as gray clumps. All of her thoughts were gray except one — *it* will want me.

It wasn't very big or strong at first, she thought. *It* started small, with animals. But now. . . .

She thought back to when she'd seen *it* at the stoplight, when *it* stared right at her and hissed. *It* had never seen me before, she realized, and the realization was like a blanket of ice dropped over her. She shivered. *It* came when I was little, but I hid under the sheet. *It* didn't see me. In the alley *it* couldn't see anything but the cat. But now *it* knows. *It* knows that I saw *it* . . . recognized what *it* was. Nobody else saw what *it* was, but I did. *It* knows.

That thought was red, glowing, burning. *It* will want me.

She went to bed, feeling better in the morning. She felt better every day that she did not see *it*.

A few weeks later, Robbie came to her room at bedtime, bringing the cat, looking troubled. "She's got something wrong with her," he said. "She's getting fat. I think she's eating herself sick. Sometimes she cries when I pick her up, like her stomach hurts."

"Uh-oh," Marissa said, reaching over to feel the cat's stomach. "She's going to have kittens, Robbie. Mom's not going to be too happy about that."

Robbie's face brightened momentarily, but then he looked troubled again. "And she never goes out of my room. I try and try to get her outside for some fresh air, but she just fluffs all up and looks terrified. Could she remember the other cat getting run over?"

Marissa looked at the orange cat, purring under Robbie's petting. She remembers *it*, she thought.

"It's like she has bad dreams, too," he went on. "She cries in her sleep sometimes. I'm really worried about her. Do you think cats can go crazy? I think she might be crazy, Marissa. She's okay as long as I'm there with her, but when I come home from school she's always huddled up with her fur fluffed out, like she's been standing like that all day! But why? Why would she be so scared? Even remembering the other cat getting run over wouldn't make her afraid in my room."

"It's more than just the other cat getting run over." Marissa took a deep breath and told him . . . about the alley, the *it*, the stoplight — her words coming reluctantly at first, then spilling out.

"I was terrified when I saw *it*," she said. "And I'm

a thinking, intelligent human being. A cat would be more than terrified."

Robbie shrugged. Marissa thought he looked as if he half disbelieved her story, as if he thought she were telling ghost stories like she used to when he was little, to scare him into obeying and going to sleep when she had to baby-sit.

"I'm not making this up," she told her brother.

"It's pretty weird," Robbie said.

"I know. But look how your cat behaves. We saw the same thing, Robbie. *It* scared me! And I'm never scared!" Except by things that wait for me in the dark, she admitted silently. "I'm not a chicken, Robbie. But this scared me. I mean, *really* scared me!"

Robbie frowned, but he looked more believing. "Well . . . what is *it*, then?" he asked. "Is *it* a person?"

This time Marissa shrugged. "I don't know," she said. "But I think *it*'s been after me since I was little. Remember all those stories I told you? They were real. They were about *it*."

"Marissa?" Robbie took her hand, looking shy. "At the stoplight? You said other people didn't run from *it*. Do you think they couldn't see *it*? I mean, they could see *it*, but do you think they couldn't see what *it* really was?"

"I don't know what to think," Marissa admitted. "I know what I saw. I know that no one else seemed to see *it* for what *it* is. If they'd seen the shapes inside of *it* they'd have screamed. They didn't scream. They didn't run. So they can't have seen *it* the same way I did."

"Marissa." Robbie looked troubled again. "I've been thinking. Did you ever notice how some people are special, sometimes? Some people seem to be born with great minds for science. Some people have just the right bodies to be famous athletes. You could have been born able to see things like that . . . evil things, and recognize them. If you could see *it*, if you're special somehow . . . and if *it* noticed . . . is *it* going to come and get you? What I mean is, I'll help you. If you're in danger, let me know. I'll help."

So now, here she was, hiding in bed, huddled beneath the covers, waiting.

It wants me. The thought was red, glowing, burning. *It* wants me.

Thinking back hadn't told her anything new — nothing that would help her fight *it*.

Instead of freezing in bed, Marissa roasted. The knowledge that *it* had seen her cooked her, and sweating, she struggled up in bed, burning. She threw the covers aside, kicked them until they slumped in a pile next to the bed. Now she was only covered by the sheet.

Sweating, trembling, trying to quiet the rustle of the sheet, she waited for *it* to come.

The absolute, overwhelming terror of childhood bathed her, a terror so raw and immediate it could only be caused by *it*, waiting in the darkness . . . waiting for her . . . waiting as *it* had waited when she was a child. She was certain she would die of fear whether *it* came for her or not.

She straightened her body beneath the sheet, listening, stretching her awareness. *It* was not in the room.

It was near, though, she could tell. *It* had marked her. *It* knew she'd seen the shapes inside. *It* knew now, for sure, who she was.

It had whispered "Soon."

Tonight, Marissa thought numbly. *It* will come tonight. I can't stalk *it*. It's too late for that. *It*'s stalking me.

Her thoughts began tumbling: *It* didn't kill the cat; I did. But *it* made the cat run under my car so it would be dying and *it* could swallow the deathflash. *It* made the lights go out so the men couldn't see what they were doing so they hit the stack of lumber and *it* could get another deathflash. *It* doesn't exactly kill; *it* arranges death.

It'll do something — scare me to death, probably. Then *it*'ll feed on me. And after that . . . after *it*'s grown stronger, *it*'ll go after more.

Marissa shook her head, interrupting the wild thoughts. Sweat ran into her eyes, stinging. The sheets were sodden with sweat. Her nightgown was drenched.

It only makes death possible; *it* doesn't kill. I'm not lost. I won't let myself be lost. I'll do something. Only fear keeps me from doing something. I just won't be afraid. What are the rules?

It can't get you in the light.

It can't get you if you hold completely still.

It can't get you if you are totally covered up, including your head.

A sudden calm stole over her. Maybe I can beat *it*. She peeked out from under the sheet. Then she reached out and snapped on the lamp on her nightstand. She stepped across the pile of blankets and turned on her overhead light. It *can't get you in the light*.

The rules. They had worked before. *It* didn't get me before. It's true that *it* was weaker then, but so was I. I'm not a child anymore. I am stronger, now, too. The rules might still be enough.

She surveyed her room, her eyes resting on her desk, her teddy bear, the posters, the wooden shelf that ran across the end of her room in front of the window. Her plants sat in pots on the shelf, their leaves trailing and tangling in a pleasing mass of greens. Near the orange pot — a flashlight! Marissa grabbed it.

I can at least try to beat *it*. Maybe if I shine the light at *it* . . . maybe the wrong kind of light will hurt *it*.

She stretched her awareness, sensing *it*. *It* was nearer. *It* was very near. *It* was in the house.

Marissa grabbed her damp sheet from her bed. She draped it over her head. Now I'm completely covered up, she thought. And it's light. I'm in the light. I have a light ready. I will hold completely still. Then *it* can't get me.

She heard her door open, and she held her breath.

"Marissa?" It was Robbie. "There's really something wrong with this cat."

Marissa yanked the sheet down and screamed, "Robbie! Get in here! Get under the covers! *It's* coming!"

She had time to register Robbie's face as it whitened, as his eyes grew huge. He dove under the sheet with the cat, and she yanked it up over both of their heads.

"Don't move!" she hissed. "Don't say a word."

It came.

She could feel *it* in the room . . . standing over them.

Suddenly the lights snapped off, and Marissa thought, of course. *It* made the lights go out in the factory. *It* makes *its* own darkness.

The sheet rustled as they breathed, and suddenly Marissa realized that no one can hold completely still. People have to breathe, she thought.

We're still covered up, she thought numbly.

But we can't stay here forever.

She waited. The cat seemed to be having convulsions of some kind, but Marissa couldn't worry about a cat . . . not when Robbie was huddled next to her and a shadowy, evil *it* lurked inches away, waiting.

Waiting.

She weighed her options. Sooner or later we have to come out, she realized. We can't stay covered up forever. If we don't come down in the morning, Mom and Dad will come up to see what's wrong, and *it*'ll get them. We don't have any more choices. I have to try the flashlight. Maybe light will kill *it*, if it's aimed right at *it* . . . right when *it* thinks *it* will get our flash. . . .

She pulled the sheet from her head, flipping on the flashlight at the same time.

Nothing happened. There was no beam of light from the flash. Dully she thought, dead batteries. Dead us. She could barely see *it*, illuminated only by the glowing shapes *it* held captive inside, but she could feel *it*, *it*s mouth gaping and the horrid dread, the evil emanating from *it*.

Her heart pounded so hard she thought it would burst right out of her throat. So this is what it feels like to die of fright, Marissa thought, her breath coming fast and shallow. I just wish Robbie weren't here, too.

Suddenly there was a beam of light . . . a light that illuminated the *it* as *it*s jaws opened wide and *it* swallowed avidly. For an instant there was a gleam of triumph in *it*s eyes.

And then *it* screamed in agony.

It writhed, retching and coughing. *It* fell to the floor and burned, lit from within by the softest, most beautiful glow Marissa had ever seen. Then *it* flashed . . . giving off *it*s own deathflash. The captive shapes flashed, too, in rapid sequence like miniature fireworks as they escaped. The *it* withered to ashes on the floor of her bedroom . . . ashes that glowed softly, then faded.

"What happened?" Robbie whispered. "I didn't see."

He didn't see, Marissa thought. He didn't see any of it! "Our cat," she said, looking down at the glowing animal and the tiny, shining forms that struggled to find their mother's soft belly. "She had babies. She gave birth. Life . . . " Marissa sighed happily, joyful tears stinging her eyes. "Life has its own flash, and I guess it's stronger than evil. Stronger than death. *It* tried to eat a *life*flash, Robbie. But life ate *it*, instead.

"Mom's going to have to let us keep these kittens. All of them. We'll give them light names like Sunshine and Sparkle and . . ."

She smiled, reaching out to turn on the light on her nightstand.

THE BOY
NEXT DOOR
Ellen Emerson
White

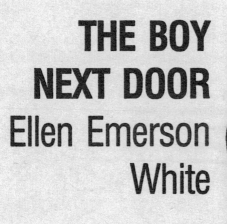

WINTER, IN NEW ENGLAND, WAS MUCH TOO COLD for ice cream. But the show must go on, the store must stay open, and Dorothy was working from four to nine. The closing shift. It was boring to work by herself, but they weren't getting enough business for her boss to justify paying extra staff.

It was *very* boring.

A few parents — divorced fathers, mostly — brought their kids for pre-bedtime cones; some sorority girls from the university rushed in to get a cake for a birthday that had been forgotten. She talked them into the twelve-inch, instead of the nine, because — they were supposed to sell up. When someone asked for a cone of chocolate chip, or whatever, she was supposed to say, "Yes, sir, would that be a medium?" Because suggesting a *large* cone would make customers nervous, and inclined to say, "No, no, just a small." But "medium" sounded so — so *harmless*. So average.

The same way a dollar ninety-nine sounded so much less expensive than two dollars.

As memory served, W. C. Fields had a theory about that.

Two couples came in, double-dating. The girls were, quite vocally, watching their weights, so they decided on small diet Cokes. The guys didn't seem too happy about that, and there was a lot of discussion before all four of them finally ordered sundaes. "No nuts on mine," one of the girls added, quickly, which would be a not-inconsiderable savings in calories, considering that they were butter-toasted — but a rather paltry saving, in the scheme of the overall sundae.

Dorothy, however, just kept her mouth shut, and made the sundaes. Rang them up. Gave back the change. Rinsed the two scoops she'd used.

Business was slow, and dull. Although there were worse things than getting paid minimum wage for doing physics homework.

Around seven-thirty, her friend Jill came in. Best friend, actually. They had met in kindergarten, and become instantly inseparable because they were the only two in the class who could read, and looking at d-o-g and c-a-t flashcards was dull. "Ennui," Jill had said, more than once. "Our friendship is *founded* on ennui."

Not that she had a flair for the dramatic or anything.

In many ways, they were exact opposites — Jill was tall, she was short; Jill was blonde, she had dark hair; Jill liked art, she liked science — but by the time they had gotten around to noticing that they had very little in common, they were already such close friends that it didn't matter.

"So," Jill said, leaning heavily against the counter. "What do I get free?"

Dorothy grinned and pointed in the direction of the drinking fountain.

"Think I'll pass," Jill said and took off her mittens. Lumpy looking mittens, but then again, she'd made them herself, and Dorothy had to give points for that. "It's really *cold* out — are people actually coming in here?"

Dorothy shook her head. "No."

Jill hung over the glass counter, looking at the various tubs. "Is that one new?" she asked, pointing.

"Yeah, Licorice." Dorothy reached for a little wooden paddle. "Want to try it? It's even worse than Pumpkin."

Jill tasted the spoonful, then nodded. "It's almost as bad as Cinnamon Crunch."

Dorothy nodded, took the paddle back, and threw it away.

Jill unzipped her jacket slightly, then zipped it back up. "I was kind of surprised there were so many people," she said.

The funeral. "Small town," Dorothy said. Almost everyone knew everyone else, so when someone died — or was born — or played Little League — or had a yard sale — a lot of people showed up. So even though Mrs. Creighton had been an absolutely *terrible* teacher — a complete terror, when you got right down to it — the church had been packed. The funeral had been over the weekend — but that didn't mean that everyone wasn't still talking about it.

"Yeah," Jill said and frowned. "I'm just always surprised. I mean, no one likes you while you're alive, but then you *die*, and suddenly, everyone's lining up to give eulogies. It's strange."

Dorothy nodded. Very strange.

"I really don't *like* funerals," Jill said.

Dorothy nodded. No argument there.

"Well." Jill straightened up. "Think you'll get out of here in time for 'Miss America'?"

Dorothy looked around the empty store. "Unless I get a rush."

"Right." Jill grinned; and also looked around. "Well, if you do, come by, or call me up — I have a feeling it's Miss Rhode Island's year."

Highly unlikely. "I'm going with the Pacific Northwest," Dorothy said. Miss — Oregon, maybe. Not that she had any idea of what any of the contestants looked like. Or, really, even cared much.

"Not a chance," Jill said. "Unless they have really good talent." She paused. "I can't remember why we wait all year to watch it."

Well — not for the baton twirling. "Because we each, secretly, want to be Miss Congeniality," Dorothy said.

"Oh. Right." Jill put her mittens back on and headed for the door. "Don't work too hard."

Dorothy nodded and, finished with her physics homework, reached for her calculus book.

The store manager, Howard, stopped by at eight-thirty, to grumble about the lack of money in the register, and take most of it back to the safe. Then, he came back out to remind her about turning off the heat under the hot fudge and butterscotch, being sure to rotate the ice-cream sandwiches when she restocked, and to remember to turn on the alarm system before she left.

She nodded, already at work refilling the jimmies. Sprinkles. Ants. Everyone who came *in* had a different name for them.

By the time she'd locked up, promptly at nine o'clock, she only had to tip the chairs up on top of the tables, mop the floor, and spray-clean the glass on the display cases.

Howard hated fingerprints. Small children sometimes even left *face* prints.

It was ten after nine when someone knocked on the door. She pointed to the CLOSED sign, then saw that it was Matt Wilson — who she had known since third grade. They had even gone on a date — once — to the movies. Freddy Krueger. Not exactly her idea of a thrill, although Matt had liked it just fine. She had kissed him, pleasantly, good night, and since then, they had treated each other with mutual, vague disinterest. Had some of the same classes, ended up at the same football parties, said hi if they ran into each other at the mall. Other than that, they rarely spoke.

She didn't particularly want to let him in — but if she didn't, it was the sort of thing that would get around school, and everyone would think she was a — do you really *care* what people think, Jill would say. And she would probably answer that she did more than she didn't.

Besides, it was pretty cold out there.

"Hi," she said, unlocking the door. "I kind of have to close up."

Matt nodded, coming in. Since she remembered him as a skinny ten-year-old in maroon Toughskins jeans, it was always sort of a shock to realize that he was six feet tall now, had a much deeper voice — and possibly even shaved. Hard to believe it was the same guy who had thrown up on the bus — all *over* the bus — when they had gone on a field trip to the aquarium in the sixth grade.

"You want anything?" she asked. "Before I finish scooping down?" She went back behind the counter — and back to the Chocolate Walnut Fudge, which was frozen rock-solid and unyielding.

"They make you work alone?" he asked.

"Well — we aren't exactly thriving lately," she said, gesturing toward the empty parking lot. Well, empty except for her parents' station wagon.

Matt nodded, looking around. Shifting his weight from one high-top to the other. Looking around some more.

Call her prescient, but she was getting a bad feeling here. "Uh, Matt?" she said. "I can make you something fast, but then I really have to lock up."

Now he looked at her, and — his eyes seemed a little funny. Too bright, or — too *something*. Jumpy. "I want to see what it's like," he said, quietly.

Make that a *very* bad feeling. "Oh, yeah?" she said. "The thing is, my manager's going to show up, and if you're in here, I'm going to get in trouble."

He shook his head.

"Come on." She started to move out from behind the counter again. "I don't want to lose my job."

He shook his head. "I saw him. He already left."

He'd been watching. Great. And her car was the only one out there, so he must have parked somewhere else. Must have been *planning* this. Whatever it was.

She glanced down at the little metal ice-cream spatula she was holding — it wasn't much, as weapons went — then glanced in the direction of the wall phone. A good fifteen feet. And it had a *dial*, not push buttons, so it would take her longer to get an operator.

Well, gosh.

Time to be distracting. After all, she'd known the guy since *third grade*. How dangerous could he really be? "Matt, if you don't take off," she said, "I'm never going to make it home in time for 'Miss America.' "

He just looked at her.

"And — neither are you," she said.

He didn't say anything.

Keep talking. "Well, okay, I see your point," she said, nodding. "You've probably already missed the swimsuits."

He looked at her with very little expression. Slight eagerness, maybe. "Open the register."

She stared at him. "What?"

"*Open* the register," he said.

This was scary — but this was also weird. "What do you mean?" she asked. "There's almost nothing in there. No one buys ice cream in weather like this."

"*Open* the damn register," he said.

"Oh, and give you the whole twenty dollars?" she asked. "If there's even that much."

His fist came out, unexpectedly, and knocked the glass donation jar off the counter. It landed with a shattering crash, change rolling all over the floor. Which was scary, but it made her a little mad, too.

"That's for crippled children," she said. "You really going to take money from *crippled children*?"

He looked at her with the same strange — blank — expression.

"On top of which," she said, "I *just* swept."

He came over the counter with an easy athletic motion, landing right in front of her. And, under the circumstances, it occurred to her that six feet was pretty big. A good ten inches — and at least eighty pounds — bigger than she was.

The small metal spatula probably wasn't going to tip the odds.

Not that it wouldn't be worth a try. But — she would keep it as a trump card.

"Matt, this is really weird," she said. "Are Nicky and Fred and all those guys outside, and you're all just pulling my leg here? Because I *really* want to close up."

He reached into his jacket pocket — expensive Goretex — and brought out a gun. A handgun. Which he pointed at her. "I want to know what it's like," he said.

Well, this was just going from bad to worse, wasn't it. "Why don't you help yourself to the twenty," she said, indicating the register. "Take the money for Muscular Dystrophy, too. In fact," she pulled a five-dollar bill out of her jeans, "take this. Get yourself a couple of Big Macs."

He didn't even seem to hear that, holding the gun, and smiling slightly. "I've *always* wanted to know what it's like," he said. This had moved beyond weird, past ominous, and straight to dire. The thing to do, was stay calm. "I don't know, Matt," Dorothy said, putting the five-dollar bill back. "This is turning into a bad *Afterschool Special*, know what I mean?"

Since he was just standing there, smiling — he probably didn't know what she meant.

Okay. Time to go into a holding pattern. Since she *really* wasn't enjoying looking at a gun that might — might not? — be loaded. "Well," she said. "I think I'll — "

He stuck the gun into the back of her uniform shirt. "I think you'll shut up."

Okay. She shut up.

"I'll take the money," he said, and twisted the spatula out of her hand. It fell into the ice-cream case, out of reach. "After. To make it look like a robbery."

"Okay," she said, checking the quiet street outside. Since everything was closed, there wasn't much reason for anyone to drive by. Even one of the few town police cars. "But you'd better hurry, because my father's going to be coming to pick me up."

He jabbed the gun into her back, then pointed with it at her car, out in the snowy parking lot.

"I know," she said. "Dead battery."

He jabbed her, harder, with the gun. "Shut up."

Well — it had been worth a try. She shrugged, and

shut up. There was going to be a point at which she was going to have to take this situation a little more seriously — start *panicking* — but she wasn't there yet. This was, after all, a guy who had always tried, and failed, to cheat off her in eighth-grade earth science.

"I'm going to kill you," he said.

There it was — her cue to take this seriously.

"See" — his smile widened a little — "I've always wondered what it would be like — you know, to kill someone — so, I'm going to do it. Find out. And, the police'll just think it's a robbery, see?"

Unh-hunh. She edged a step away from him.

"I really want to. Always have," he said. "I've been thinking about it for a long time, and — you know, what it would *feel* like — and I think — " He grinned, a little. "I've been planning this, you know?"

Well — she certainly knew now. "Boy," she said, keeping her voice calm, "and people say it isn't dangerous for MTV to show all those violent images."

He didn't seem to think that was funny. Somehow, she wasn't surprised.

"Look, I don't know if you're kidding, Matt," she said, "but, either way, I think you should consider *intensive* psychotherapy."

He didn't seem to think that was funny, either.

"Okay if I sit down for a minute, Matt?" she asked. "Considering how long we've known each other?"

"Sure." He laughed again. "We got at least thirty minutes, an hour, I figure, before anyone thinks it's funny the lights are still on in here."

It would also probably be that long before her parents got worried enough to call, or show up. They didn't like the idea that she closed up alone, on weeknights. They were always afraid that something — bad — might happen.

In the future, she was going to have to take those sorts of concerns more seriously.

"On the floor," he said. "So no one will see us if they go by. Right there." He indicated for her to sit down against the counter, and then he sat down too, looking pleased with himself, his back resting against the soft-ice-cream machine.

Her head hurt, in a numb sort of way. "Want a dish of Cinnamon Crunch?" she asked. "It's really good."

He scowled at her. "You'd better start being scared. It's not as fun if you're not scared."

Exactly. She resisted the urge to rub her temples. "So, if you're a robber, how'd you get in? Would I really have opened the door?"

He gestured with the gun. "I'll break the glass, on my way out."

Oh. "Wouldn't I have heard you?" she asked.

"I'll turn the radio up," he said.

Oh.

"See," his eyes brightened even more, "it looks *fun*. When they do it. When you see films of it, and all. So, I want to see what it's like. To do it."

What had he been doing, sitting at home watching reenactments on *America's Most Wanted*? Taping shows like that so he could watch them over and over? He seemed so normal, the neighbors would say. So polite. The boy next door. "Shouldn't you work your way up?" she asked. "Start off by — I don't know — throwing rocks at sea gulls?"

He smiled. "I killed a dog."

Oh. She rubbed her hand across her forehead. Thought thoughts about aspirin.

"But, you know, I didn't *feel* anything," he said. "I didn't feel good, or bad, or — maybe 'cause I used a car. Maybe if I'd really *done* it, myself, I — so I'm really going to *do* this. And — then I'll know."

The thing she had to keep in mind here, was that Matt Wilson wasn't exactly the brightest guy she had ever known. So — keep him talking. "Did we really have *that* bad a time on our date?" she asked.

He didn't say anything, just stood there, looking at her, holding the gun with great confidence. Familiarity. Pleasure.

Well, "Quick on the uptake" wasn't going to go on *his* tombstone. "I don't want to be trite," she said, "but, why me?" Such a nice boy, the elderly neighbor would tell Maury Povich. Always shoveled my walk.

"Because — you're not special," he said.

Oh. Not exactly the answer she had expected. Her breath got stuck somewhere inside her throat, and it was an effort to swallow.

"You know what I mean?" he said, leaning forward. "You're just — you're just *there*. Like, I know you, and I see you around, but — I don't give you any thought. Like, if you *weren't* there, I don't think I'd really notice." He frowned. "I don't think anyone really will. After the first couple weeks, or — maybe not even *that* long. You know?"

"The feeling's mutual," she said stiffly. Nice to have her entire existence reduced to a footnote. A Memorial Page in the yearbook. *If* that.

"Like," he didn't even seem to hear her, too far into his own crazed little reverie, "they'll be sad, at school, at *first*, and they'll have, you know, counselors come, so everyone can *talk* about how sad they are, and then — " He snapped his fingers. "Next thing you know, spring training'll be starting."

The fact that he just might be right was almost more terrifying than the rest of this. People's lives *were* getting pretty disposable these days. Even if you died in a really *interesting* way, you *still* might not make the evening news.

"So, I do you," he said, "and — big deal. They shouldn't've had you working here alone at night. 'Cause — you got robbed by some hopped-up junkie with a" — he made his hand shake on the gun — "quick trigger finger."

He *had* been thinking about this. What a waste of limited brain power. Because — it *would* look like a robbery gone bad. Like her mother always said, plenty of bad things happened in small towns, not just big cities, but the difference was, in the small town, you *knew* the people.

Her head hurt. She wanted to go home. The floor was filthy. "What about fingerprints?" she asked.

He grinned. "Haven't touched anything. And if I do

have to — " With his free hand, he took a pair of winter gloves out of his pocket to show her.

"Well." She leaned back against the cold white counter. There was a small chocolate smudge, maybe knee-high. "That's good. You've thought of — almost everything."

"I've thought of *everything*," he said, and glanced at his watch. "I want you to lie down now. Hands behind your head."

Oh, great. Execution-style. He must have been renting gangster movies. It was important to keep in mind that she really was smarter than he was. Maybe not *special*, but definitely smarter. "What you haven't thought about," she said, "is what it's *really* like to kill someone. It *is* easy, but it's pointless. Even if it's personal."

He scowled at her. "Shut up. I'm getting tired of you."

"Yeah, but" — she lowered her voice, carefully, as though there were someone else around to hear — "I know what I'm talking about."

He scowled at her, but uneasily.

Okay, good. Keep it up. "Even if the person probably *should* die," she said. "Even if you have a *serious* grudge against them, it doesn't seem to matter. Because, it doesn't change anything. You do it, and you don't feel better, you just feel — nothing. Like with the dog. You feel — it's a waste. You risk so much, and you don't get anything back."

"What do *you* know about it?" he asked — but at least he was listening.

Okay, she'd gotten his attention. Time to bring out the big guns. "I know more than you think," she said. "But — we have to have a deal. If I tell you, you have to leave here, and no one'll ever know about this. Because we'll each have something to hold over each other, so — we can just keep it to ourselves."

He frowned at her suspiciously. "You just don't want me to kill you."

God, he was dense. "Well, *obviously*," she said. "Would I really be stupid enough to tell you about this, otherwise?"

He frowned. Pointed the gun. "Tell me what?"

Dorothy took a deep breath, then let it out. "I killed Mrs. Creighton."

He sat up straighter, then shook his head. "Oh, yeah, *right*. Nice try. You're just like, *stalling*."

No, she was trolling her line out, trying to get him hooked. "You want to hear what it was like?" she asked. "Stuff *nobody* else knows?"

He didn't say yes, but she could tell he was starting to get a little curious. Intrigued.

"Think about it, Matt," she said. "We were all in her class together." Fifth grade. "Think about what a terrible teacher she was. She was really *mean* to me — remember?"

He frowned. "No. Like, she was mean to everyone."

"Yeah, well, I didn't like it." She paused. For great effect. "And I waited a *long* time to get back at her."

It was quiet for a few seconds, the hum of the freezers sounding loud.

"She was in an accident," Matt said. "Just a dumb accident on the ice."

Dorothy nodded. "That's right. I *wanted* it to look like an accident. The same way you want *this* to look like an accident." Hooked? Or still just nibbling at the bait?

He glanced at his watch, then looked back at her, grinning. "Okay," he said. "Let's see how far you can take this, hunh?"

Hooked. "First, promise not to tell anyone," she said.

He laughed. "Like I'm really going to tell anyone what you *said* while I was *killing* you?"

Okay, so she wasn't making as many inroads as she'd thought. "I'm not kidding, Matt," she said. "I'm making a deal here. And — admit it. You want to hear about it."

"I'm the one holding the gun," he said. "*I'm* the only one who can make deals."

"Fine." She folded her arms across her chest. "Go ahead and shoot. Before you run out of time."

He shook his head, looking very amused. Stupidly amused. "No. I want to hear about your big-wow murder plot, first."

Well, it was the only hand she had, so she might as well play it out. Go for broke. "You know how the road curves there?" she said. Everyone in *town* knew about that curve. "Above the ocean? And that's the way she would *have* to drive. To get home. And, well, I know what her car looks like, right? Same way you know that's my parents' car out there in the parking lot."

He frowned, but he *was* still listening.

No matter what a story was about, the important thing was to *tell* it well. With *conviction*. "So, I waited," she said. "In the bushes, there, just around the curve. More than one afternoon, if you want to know the truth. Because — she had to go by — and I figured the best time was right after dusk."

He shook his head, scornfully — but didn't, she noticed, interrupt.

"So no one would see me, and so she wouldn't have time to react." She was getting a little stiff, and would have stretched, but didn't want to do anything to distract him. "It's a funny thing about that curve," she said. "It really is dangerous, but everyone always drives pretty fast around it. I guess because they know it's there, and don't think about it much. I mean, *I* go fast around that curve, don't you?"

He nodded, then frowned and pointed the gun.

Play it out. "So, I waited," she said. "I had a pretty good view, because I wanted to be able to see her coming in plenty of time. And I was trying to think, how could I be *sure* she would turn out of the way fast? Be *sure* she'd go right over onto the rocks there."

He wasn't looking at her now, so much as *watching* her.

"Because — I was only going to get one chance," she said.

He watched her.

"A baby carriage," she said. And paused. "I don't care who you are, no matter where you are — even if it doesn't make sense — if you see a *baby carriage* come out in front of your car, you're going to try not to hit it. Right? Makes sense, doesn't it?"

Matt nodded a little.

"Right," she said. Press on. "So, I waited. And, I waited. And Thursday afternoon, right after dark, *who* should come speeding along?" She paused, then nodded significantly. "Yeah. So, I timed it. Wanted to be sure she'd *see* it, but only after it was too late. I *timed* it, and then I pushed the carriage out there, and — " She let herself grin with exquisite slowness. "And she swerved, and she went *right off the road*, just like I thought she would."

Matt was watching her with his mouth hanging open, although he probably wasn't aware of it.

Good. Keep going. "I didn't bother looking down over what was left of the guardrail," Dorothy said. "In case she *hadn't* been killed, and only — maimed — or something, and was looking up. I just went out to the middle of the road, got the baby carriage, and carried it back, through the bushes, to my car, so I could get rid of it." She paused. Slightly longer than briefly. "Evidence — right?"

She checked Matt's expression; he was frowning.

"But, here's the problem," she said. "The problem for you. I *really* didn't like her. I had it *in* for her. And yeah, she ran off the road, and yeah, it was because of me, and — it didn't seem to matter. It wasn't a kick. It was just like, so what? I mean, you're right — you and I have absolutely no opinion about each other. So, if you *waste* it on me, take the chance, it's just — stupid. If you have to do it, make it someone you *hate*. Try to make it worth your time and trouble. Make it worth the *risk*."

It was quiet again.

"Nice story," he said, then cocked the gun. "Now, put your hands behind your head."

She'd really thought she'd had him going along there. "I can *prove* it," she said, as he started to get up.

He stopped.

"Because" — keep that brain working quickly — "even when you're sure you've thought of everything, you haven't."

He eased back down, but kept the gun cocked. "So, prove it."

"She *hit* the carriage," Dorothy said. "So, if the police or, I don't know, whoever, checked the bumper, they'd find paint or metal chips that *weren't* from the guardrail."

He shrugged. "So?"

Slap down the last card. Full force. "I'll tell you where the carriage *is*," she said. "So, if I went to the police, and said you came in here and threatened me, *you* could, easily, tell them I was lying about it, because you knew about Mrs. Creighton."

He narrowed his eyes at her.

"It's *perfect*," she said. "This way, we're both off the hook. We can both go home, and — pretend this never happened."

"Yeah, right," he said. "Like I'm going to fall for *that*."

Yes. He was. "I threw it off the bridge," she said.

"Up near the Point? Because, even when the tide goes out, and it's just marshy, there's so much junk down there, I knew no one would notice."

He frowned, but indecisively. "I know you're lying."

"We can drive up there," she said. "After school tomorrow. I can *show* you." She almost had him here — she could feel it. So, she paused again. "And, if you want," she paused again, "I'll tell you about the others."

There was no question but that his eyes widened. "The *others*?"

Hook, line, *and* sinker. "Seems to me," she said, "that there's been more than one accident in this town, in the last couple of years." Remember to pause. "I can tell you all about them."

"I *know* you're lying," he said, but without much assurance.

She shook her head. "No, you don't. Admit it. You *know* I'm telling the truth."

He looked at her. *Studied* her.

"You know I am," she said quietly.

There was another long silence, and then, finally, he nodded.

Next stop, National Poker Championships. "Yeah," she said. "I'll tell you about all of them, and then — maybe you and I can do another. *Together*."

He looked at her. Started to grin.

"What the hell," she said. "Maybe it would be more fun that way. If you had someone to *share* it with."

The phone rang, suddenly, and they both jumped.

"What's that?" he asked nervously.

She checked her watch. "My parents. Because I'm running late."

The phone rang again.

"Look, get out of here," she said. "You can't do anything now, because they'll *know* it wasn't a robber. Get out of here, and we can talk at school tomorrow."

The phone had rung again, and then again.

"*Go*," she said. "Don't be stupid."

A fifth ring.

He nodded, getting up, and she got up, too, answering the phone. Indeed, her mother.

"Oh, hi, Mom," she said. "Yeah, I was down in the basement, getting straws and napkins and all." She motioned toward the door, and Matt nodded.

"Tomorrow?" he said.

She nodded; *he* nodded; and he left.

Left.

All right! Nice *talking*, Tex.

She explained to her mother that she was still cleaning up, was almost done, and got permission to stop by Jill's to watch the end of "Miss America." Then, once she'd hung up, she went over and locked the door. Took the keys, and put them in her pocket. Lowered the lights.

She should probably call the police — or have told her mother, but — tell them *what*? That the right tackle on the football team suffered from psychosis? Had a violent fantasy life? Was just plain *wacko*? That he'd broken the Muscular Dystrophy jar? That he

had — all she wanted to do right now, was get out of
here. Then, she could worry about how to handle the
situation.

She swept up the glass and pennies. Left a note for
Howard that the jar had fallen, and put the change in
an empty box that had once held cans of whipped
cream. She took up the chairs, mopped the floor,
turned the lights off, and the alarm *on*.

It was ten-fifteen. Seemed later.

She went out to the parking lot, and sat in the car.
Sat, taking deep breaths, seeing her hands still shaking with reaction trembling.

That, had been scary. Really, really *scary*. Unbe-
lievable, in fact. And — she wasn't quite sure what to
do. If she should just go home, or — she started the
car, and pulled out of the parking lot, driving slowly
and cautiously, on the ice. Headed toward Jill's house.

Jill's little brother, Timmy, let her in.

"You're late," he said cheerfully. "You missed the
question-and-answer section."

Dorothy nodded. "Yeah, I know. She in the den?"

"Yup," he said, and offered her his bag of Doritos.

"No, thanks," she said, and headed for the den.

Jill was sitting in there, alone, wearing her reading
glasses, her French book open — and completely ignored — on her lap. "Hi," she said.

Dorothy nodded, and sat down in the easy chair.

"Miss Nebraska had a really nice gown," Jill said.

Dorothy nodded, trying to figure out exactly how to
explain what had happened tonight. Exactly what to
say.

"But her hair was stupid." Jill glanced over for a second. "You all right?"

"Yeah, I — " No. "Um, tonight, uh — while I was closing up, um — " She should just start. Tell her the whole twisted story. "Look, uh — " She let out her breath. "We have to do it again."

Now, Jill looked away from the television. "*What?*"

"Yeah," Dorothy said.

Jill glanced at the television, then took her glasses off. "We can't. She was going to be the last one."

"Yeah, I know, but — " Dorothy sighed. "*This* will be the last one, okay?"

Jill sighed, too. "You sure?"

Dorothy nodded.

"Okay," Jill said, and closed her French book. "When?"

Preferably, an hour ago. "After school tomorrow?" Dorothy said.

Jill thought about that, then nodded. "Okay. Who is it, anyway?"

"Matt Wilson," Dorothy said.

Jill grinned. "Whoa. *That* must be a long story."

Very long. Dorothy nodded.

"Well — tell me at the commercial," Jill said, then looked at her. "This *is* going to be the last one, right?"

Dorothy nodded.

"Good," Jill said, and put her glasses back on.

Then, they both looked at the television.

COLLECT CALL
II:
THE BLACK
WALKER
Christopher Pike

IT WAS ALMOST A MONTH AFTER THE DEATH OF JA-
nice Adams that Caroline Spencer went out on a date
with the mysterious and handsome Bobby Walker. The
date was Caroline's first trip into the world since the
horrible accident that had put her in the hospital. She
was still not fully recovered. Headaches as violent as
volcanoes frequently gripped her, and her supposedly
mended ribs screamed every time she bent the wrong
way. Yet when Bobby Walker called and asked if she
wanted to go to the movies with him — even before
she had returned to school — she said yes. Caroline
disliked lying around the house, and Bobby was, of
course, awfully cute. She thought it would be fun.

Bobby picked her up in a '59 Chevy convertible, a
car considerably older than Caroline herself, which
nevertheless shone white and bright in the crisp autumn moonlight. Bobby wore blue jeans, a dark
T-shirt, and his usual black leather jacket. He opened
the car door for her as she came out of the house,
although he had not come to the door of the house to
get her, simply pressing on his vintage horn to an-
nounce his arrival. Her parents had not approved —

they liked to meet any guy she dated. But neither had
followed her outside to interrogate Bobby, and Caroline was relieved. It would not have been the first
time her parents had pulled such a stunt.

"How are you doing, babe?" Bobby asked as he
helped her into his vehicle. Even though it was a convertible, the rich smell of the leather seats filled the
air. Caroline had only a light-green windbreaker over
her white blouse and slacks, and worried she would
be cold. For an instant she considered returning inside
the house for a sweater, but a glance into Bobby's
strong face made her change her mind.

"Great," she said, climbing inside. "How about you?"

"I've never looked better," he replied as he returned
to the driver's side. She thought she saw him grin at
his own joke, but could not be sure. He stared at her
as he settled beside her, his dark eyes penetrating,
unblinking. "What do you want to do?" he asked.

She giggled. She always giggled when she was nervous, and she was pretty much always nervous around
people. She was head cheerleader, used to dancing and
shouting in front of large audiences, but she was terribly insecure.

"I'll do whatever you want to do," she said.

Bobby Walker slowly smiled. It was a curious affair.
His lips seemed to crawl off his beautiful teeth rather
than simply move into an expression of pleasure. They
crawled like something slimy in the night, and Caroline
shivered involuntarily, for what she thought was no
reason.

"I'd like to see the dead come back to life," Bobby

said. "I'd like to see the living lay down with the dead."

Caroline missed a couple of beats. "Pardon?"

Now his grin widened, sweet and fun-loving. "There's a horror movie at the theater called *The Listeners*. I want to see it."

Caroline nodded. "That's good. Is it gory? I don't like gory stuff."

Bobby stopped smiling. "Why not?"

"It scares me."

"Why does it scare you?"

She shrugged. "It just does. I guess I'm a coward."

"The movie's full of blood. It's about a lizard monster from the past who reincarnates in a twin's body and then begins to rip people apart." Bobby nodded. "I've seen it twice already."

"Why do you want to see it again?"

He started the car. "Because I like it."

"OK," Caroline said without enthusiasm.

There were few people at the theater. It was a Tuesday night, and apparently the movie had received poor reviews. Bobby did not have to go to the window to buy tickets. He had purchased them earlier, he explained. Caroline glanced over as he pulled a wad of them from his tight jean pocket. It looked as if he had bought tickets for tomorrow's show as well, and the next day's.

Caroline had not eaten dinner and wanted popcorn and a drink. Bobby said fine, but did not offer to buy the refreshments. Feeling embarrassed, but also hungry, she got them herself, while Bobby stood nearby, staring blankly into the distance.

"Would you like some popcorn?" she asked as they went into the theater, offering him her medium-sized tub. But he shook his head.

"No, thank you."

"You don't like butter on it?" she asked. Actually, she did not like butter, either, and had only asked for it because she thought Bobby would want it. She understood that most people did like butter. She was hoping to loosen Bobby up. He didn't seem to be enjoying himself.

"I never eat before midnight," he said.

She laughed. "You really are a horror movie fan."

He looked over at her. He was taller than she remembered. "You know it, babe."

They watched the movie, and at first it was OK. But then the lizard monster from the past entered the body of the pretty red-haired twin and she began to kill people, and swallow people, and Caroline had to close her eyes. But now Bobby was having a great time. He laughed as if he were watching a comedy, slapping his knee whenever the victims screamed for mercy. And it made her wonder, just a tiny bit, if Bobby wasn't a little sick in the head.

When the film was over, and the lights had come on, Bobby glanced over at her. "Did you like it?" he asked.

"I told you, I'm a chicken. I had my eyes closed half the time."

"Then we should watch it again."

"What?" she said.

"Let's stay for the ten o'clock show."

Caroline cleared her throat. "I'd rather not. I'm feeling a little tired. You know, I'm still recovering from the accident."

Bobby nodded. "The accident is why you should watch it again."

"What do you mean?"

He turned away from her, staring once more at the screen. "Keep your eyes open this time and you'll see."

"But . . ."

"Just do as I say."

Caroline could hardly believe it, but they watched the entire movie again. They were the only ones left in the theater. This time she kept her eyes open at all the bloody parts. She had to. Whenever the monster was about to tear someone apart, Bobby would glance over to make sure she was taking it all in. And the look on his face — it was as if he would do something to her if she turned away. What that something was, she didn't know, but it scared her. She was definitely not having a good time.

There was one part in particular in the movie that spooked her, a part she hadn't fully registered the first time. Before the evil lizard monster from the past genetically changed the twin, the two twin girls hypnotized each other, and led one another back into the past, through their childhood, and then back into other lives, into the ancient past, when monsters walked the earth. As Caroline watched, she felt herself slipping back in time also, not so far as another age, but back to the night of the accident. The impact of the crash had knocked her unconscious, of that there was no doubt, yet suddenly she could see how the interior of the car had looked immediately after the crash. The shattered glass. The crumpled metal. The blood — everywhere, hers as well as Janice's.

But I was thrown from the car.

Suddenly Caroline could even remember how Janice had climbed out of the car, and then climbed back in, and dragged her into the driver's seat. Yet she knew none of those things had happened. Janice had never left the car. Only the smoke from her burning ashes had escaped.

I am not remembering, I'm dreaming.

But she had this feeling that what was coming back to her was the truth. Minus one big important element.

What had happened before they had crashed?

Something. Something bad.

"Fun, huh?" Bobby whispered in her ear as the cute red-haired lizard monster bent a young man's finger back too far. Snap, crackle, pop, and my don't these taste good? The monster took off the guy's head next.

"Oh, yeah," Caroline muttered, cringing.

Finally, thankfully, the movie ended. Not many of the actors were left alive. Caroline practically jumped out of her seat with relief. She had a headache. Her ribs throbbed from sitting still for so long. She wanted to go home and go to bed. She wanted to get away from Bobby Walker. He might have been cute, but she was more convinced than ever that he had a screw loose. He practically licked his lips as they walked toward the exit.

"Did you like the part at the end when she squished

the guy's skull as flat as a pancake?" he asked.

"The special effects were amazing," she said.

He stopped her, grabbing her arm, just as they stepped out into the deserted parking lot. "How do you know it wasn't real?"

"Bobby?"

"Do you even know what's real?"

"It was just a stupid movie, for god's sake." She pulled her arm back. His grip had been unpleasantly strong. "I don't know how you can enjoy crap like that, anyway."

His face darkened. "What did you say?"

"You heard what I said." She met his gaze, no small feat. He was incredibly handsome, but there was a cruelty in the lines of his face that she found hard to believe she had not recognized before. His eyes blazed at her as if they wanted to burn her, the way Janice had burned. Yet just as soon as she saw the look in his eyes, it vanished, and he smiled sweetly. She wondered if she had seen it at all, if it was not simply something else she had imagined. Bobby spoke gently.

"I'm sorry," he said. "To each his own. I guess I sometimes forget that. Hey, you haven't had much fun tonight. Let me make it up to you. Let me take you some place special."

She checked her watch. It was almost midnight. "I don't know. It's late. The doctor says I've still got to get plenty of rest."

His face showed concern. "The bang on the head still got you down?"

"Yeah, a little. I get headaches."

He nodded. "I remember how you looked that morning in the hospital. Your face was ten different colors."

She smiled briefly, softening inside a little. A handsome face worked miracles on her. She may have been too quick to judge him so harshly.

"It was nice of you to wait all night at the hospital to see how I was," she said. Of course, he hadn't called her since that morning. Except yesterday, to ask her out.

"That's just the kind of guy I am," he said.

"Bobby, when I woke up in the hospital after the accident there was a message on my machine from you. Do you remember leaving it?"

"Sure do, babe."

"Did you leave the message before you heard about the accident, or after?"

"Hi, Carol, this is Bobby. Wanted to know if you loved the tape. If it did something for you. I'll see you soon, if you're still alive, that is."

She hated being called Carol. Or babe, for that matter.

He was watching her closely. "Before. Why?"

She thought for a moment. "It's nothing. Where is it you want to go?"

He offered her his arm. "You'll see when you get there, Carol."

She hesitated. Then took his arm.

They drove out of Chesterock, into the surrounding country. The cold had deepened, and Caroline shivered in the front seat. But Bobby was not inclined to put up the roof, despite her repeated requests for him to do so. He laughed and said he liked his women cold.

They parked a mile off the road behind a cluster of thick trees.

Caroline looked around in the dark. "Why are we here?" she asked.

Bobby jumped out of the car and opened the trunk. "I have to show you what's real," he said.

Caroline climbed out uneasily, clasping her arms close to her chest. "I don't understand," she said.

"You will."

She looked up at the tall trees. In the cold white light of the moon they looked like silver sentinels standing guard at the edge of a forbidden land. And they looked familiar. She had been to this spot before, not that long ago. Only she could not remember . . .

"Where are we?" she asked.

Bobby shut the hood of the trunk and walked toward her. In his hands he carried a portable stereo and a shovel. "Home," he said.

A stab of fear shot through her, thin but sharp. "I want to go home," she said suddenly.

Bobby came closer. "Didn't you hear me? You're already there."

"What are you doing with that shovel?"

He tossed it higher into his right hand, holding the flat of the metal above his head. "Nothing," he said.

"Bobby."

He moved to within arm's reach. She could feel his breath on her cheek, and it was like the light of the moon. Cold and distant. "What are you afraid of?" he asked.

She shook her head. "I'm not afraid. I'm just tired. Take me back, please?"

His flesh looked so lifeless in the silver light. "But we have to visit Janice."

"Janice?"

He cocked his head to the side and gestured with his shovel, to the sky, the ground. His voice came out like a grumble in a deep well. "She's here. Right here."

Caroline reached for the car door, opening it. "Bobby, I'm serious, I want to go now. Oh!"

He had slammed the car door shut with the heel of his boot, almost taking off her hand. "You're coming with me. I'm serious."

Caroline swallowed and nodded. She could see just how serious he was. For the first time, she wondered if he meant to harm her. Now she was afraid, boy, was she afraid.

They went through the thick of the trees, with her walking in front. The way was dark, shot through with shafts of unholy white rays. She could feel the evilness of the place even before the trees thinned and the tombstones became visible. She recognized in an instant why the place had looked familiar. She had come here only a couple of weeks ago, with flowers in her hands. They had taken the back entrance into the cemetery where Janice had been buried.

"What is left of her was buried here," Bobby remarked, coming up at her side, reading her mind. He surveyed the cemetery for a moment before turning toward her, the blade of his shovel turning with his head. "Do you know how long the car burnt before the police arrived, the firemen?"

Caroline shook her head. Bobby leaned close again, to her ear, her hair. "A long time," he said softly. "She burned a long time."

Caroline trembled. "What do you want with me?"

Bobby took in a sharp breath, then he seemed to relax. He leaned back. He held up his stereo. "I just want to play you a song."

A tear rolled over Caroline's cheek. He was insane, and she was trapped in a cemetery late at night with him. "Then will you take me home?" she asked pitifully.

He laughed softly. "Sure, babe."

He led her out into the cemetery, where all the dead people were laid out in plots of grass and weeds. All except one. The lawn had yet to grow over Janice's remains, and perhaps for that reason Bobby had no trouble finding the grave site. Yet Caroline suspected he knew exactly where it was because he had been there many times before, as he had gone many times before to the same horror movie.

"I bought fresh batteries for tonight," Bobby said as he set the stereo on top of Janice's tombstone, a low, simple affair with only Janice's name and the years of her short life inscribed above the note: *BELOVED DAUGHTER*.

"What's so special about tonight?" Caroline asked miserably.

"It's a night of song," Bobby said. He turned on the tape player.

"I come from the past.
I eat the night.
I knew you when you were young.
I tell you my story.
But I sleep with a gun.
This is my night, this is your night.
I'm a black walker, babe.
Touch me softly and you get a fright.
The stars are holes in the sky.
The moon is a thorn in the dark.
It drips white light.
Give me the knife.
Let's cut out our eyes.
Yeah, this is our night, this is what's right.
I'm a black walker, babe.
Brush my lips and I bleed you white."

Bobby turned off the tape and stared at her. He looked as real as the tombstone he stood beside. Real as rock. "What do you think, babe?"

"Oh, god," she whispered. Suddenly she remembered new things, terrible things — the song in the car, the eerie rhythms, the argument on the dark road, the two of them fighting over who was going to get Mr. Bobby Walker. Then the slap in the face.

She had hit Janice in the face.

She had made Janice drive off the road.

Bobby took a step toward her, carrying his shovel. "I didn't quite catch that," he said. Caroline just looked at him.

"You know," she whispered.

He grinned a red mouth full of white teeth. "I know many things."

"I killed Janice."

He nodded. "You did what the Black Walker told you to do."

"Who is the Black Walker?"

"Who am I?"

"Bobby Walker." She nodded. "I knew it all along."

He raised an surprised eyebrow. "Had you known you wouldn't have come here. But that's beside the point. What should we do with you, now that we know you killed a girl?"

Caroline stood perfectly still, although her eyes darted to the right and left, trying to find the best direction to run. He intended to kill her, she could see that now. He thought he was the Black Walker, after all. Why was it that the cutest guys always turned out to be the psychopaths?

"I think we should go to the police," she said.

That made him laugh. "I think we should go to Janice."

She began to cry again, to shake. "I don't understand."

Bobby caressed the shaft of the shovel. "You and Janice have to get together, talk out your problems."

Caroline glanced at the grave site, the unsettled mud. He had brought a shovel. The ground was still loose; it would be easy to dig up. It was as if she could read his mind. Her and Janice together, under the ground.

"You're a monster," she swore.

And with that she turned and ran. But she was only a cheerleader, still recovering from a serious accident. She leapt over one grave, two plots. The moist grass slipped beneath her sneakers. She did not get far. A cruel metal hand struck her on the back of her head.

She went down, into the grass, sprawling in the dark. The white light of the moon turned an ugly shade of red, and the grim rows of tombstones twisted into dwarfish green gremlins, laughing at her. Rough hands grabbed her from behind, and pain shot from the base of her skull into her guts. Bobby dragged her to her feet by her hair.

"You have to stay," he said, breathing into her face as he pulled her back toward Janice's grave. "It's after midnight. The Black Walker wants to meet you."

Caroline was too dazed to fight back. Blood seeped down the back of her neck, soaking her blouse. The cemetery continued to dance as her eyes went in and out of focus. He threw her against a tree and then grabbed her once more as she toppled to the side of the gnarled trunk. From his pocket he drew forth a thin length of black rope. Her arms were yanked behind her back. Another wave of pain shot through her body. He began to tie her to the tree, talking all the while.

"I'm glad the Black Walker gets the two of you," he said. "Two such pretty things. He will be pleased, and when he's pleased, I'm pleased." Bobby paused in his knot, trying to press his mouth against her cheek. His teeth scratched across her soft flesh. "You don't know how close we are, babe."

Caroline coughed, fighting to remain conscious. Her brain felt as if it had been immersed in acid. "But I thought you were the same," she gasped.

Bobby took a step back and let out a cruel laugh. Just like a demon. A walker of the black path. His face was suddenly animated with a life from another world. His limbs twitched with strings pulled out of another dimension. He began to circle the tree restlessly. Caroline's head cleared somewhat. She strained against her binds. The twine cut into her wrists. She was trapped.

"We are the same as our reflections," he said. "When he looked out of the void he asked me to be his mirror. He told me to turn off the light and let his music come into the place of the dead. Then he sang to me, and let me use his voice. You see how beautifully we get along?"

"I don't know what you're talking about," Caroline said, not that she wanted to know. Struggling with her binds was not helping. She went limp, trying to relax, to think. Bobby continued to rave.

"You can tape the voices of the dead," he said gleefully. "I read about it in a magazine. A published journal on occult investigations. You put a microphone in a deserted place. You put in a blank tape and push the record button. You catch the sounds of the wind, the distant train. But you also catch *their* whispers. He spoke softly to me, and I listened. I recorded his song."

Caroline frowned, curious in spite of herself. "Are you serious?"

Bobby stopped in front of her. "It can be done.

did it. I contacted the dead. I got the master, who walks past the lines of dead. He chose me. He gave me his song. He gave me his power."

"And what power is that?"

He threw his head back and cackled again. He was really losing it. "I have the power to make nightmares come alive! Janice found that out. She spent the whole night in a dream. She didn't even know she was dead!"

"Janice died in a car crash."

"She died because the Black Walker wanted her! He wants you, and that's why you're going to die. I bring him pretty girls, and he brings me the song of power."

"What power?" Caroline asked again. She was beginning to think she understood. Bobby Walker was "possessed" by the Black Walker.

"I'll show you. Listen, and you will feel it." Bobby hurried over to Janice's tombstone — fifteen feet away — and returned with the stereo. He began to rewind the tape. He was beside himself with excitement, panting like a dog in the midst of a rabid frenzy, his cold breath a gray smoke before his insane face. He set the stereo in the grass at her feet. "You listen while I dig," he said, reaching for the play button.

"What are you digging?" she shrieked, her worst fear confirmed. Bobby took back his hand and stood and grabbed the sides of her head. He kissed her hard on the lips. His touch was like sharp ice, and she tasted blood inside her mouth.

"She burned for so long god knows there'll be room for you in the box," he told her as he let go, making it sound like a promise. Tears poured over Caroline's face, blood poured 1down her neck, but she managed to spit in his face.

"You will not get away with this," she swore.

He wiped off the spit as if he were sorry to see it go. He grinned again wickedly. "I've gotten away with it in a dozen towns," he said. "You're only one of many. And there will be many to come." He leaned over and pressed the button on the player. "Enjoy the music, Carol."

"I come from the past.
I eat the night.
I knew you when you were young.
I tell you my story.
But I sleep with a gun. . . ."

Bobby returned to Janice's grave and began to dig. He was strong. The damp earth flew over his head and landed in a steadily expanding pile at his back. But it seemed he preferred to work to the music of his god, and he kept returning again and again to the ghetto blaster to rewind the tape. There appeared to be only one copy of the song on the cassette. When the music finished there would be nothing but an eerie hiss: The sound of a lost wind blowing over a foresaken land. The Black Walker's land. If only Janice and she had not turned off the tape so quickly in the car the night of the party. Then they would have known the present had been no normal gift from the record store.

Yet Bobby would sometimes allow a minute to go by before resetting the tape, sometimes two. In fact, the deeper he dug, the more the possibility of reaching Janice's coffin took priority over the tape.

"I can hardly wait to open the box!" he called to her, already hip-deep in the ground.

"Damn you," Caroline whispered. The power of the song was lost on her. It only worsened her already throbbing head. She was no clever heroine; she had never even been good at extricating herself from problems at school. She was a wimp, she thought, a flake. How was she supposed to outwit an experienced psycho? She struggled fiercely with the binds on her wrists, cutting herself worse. Bobby ran over, shovel in hand, to rewind the tape. He was covered with mud.

"I love the full moon," he breathed. "It brings out the best in me."

"My parents will have called the police by now," she cried. "They'll catch you. They'll put you in jail."

Bobby shook his shovel before him as if it were a spear of power. "I'll be long gone by sunlight. And you'll be buried so deep even the memory of you will fade." He laughed. "Then it will be another school, another pretty thing. The Black Walker will walk across the country." He reached down and pressed the play button. "Why don't you sing along, Carol," he suggested.

"It's Caroline," she said bitterly. The bitterness helped. It made her cry less, and think more. Still, no good ideas came to her. She was alone in a cemetery, tied to a tree beside an opening grave. There were not a lot of options.

Bobby continued to dig. He was getting down there.

He shouted over to her that he would be hitting home any second. He let the song run out and did not return to rewind it. The hiss sung in Caroline's ears, hypnotic in its horrible loneliness. Then she heard the faintest of sighs, or, thought she did. A word spoken in a lost wave of dry dust.

"Record."

"Hello?" Caroline said quietly. "Is someone there? Hello?"

The hiss continued to blow. Then another sigh, a whisper from unseen lips. *"Record."* Followed by a longer stretch of emptiness, then another word, slightly louder. *"Button."* Spoken with a female ring to it.

"Jesus," Caroline moaned.

"Hi, Caroline, this is Janice. You called me so I'm calling you. But don't try calling me back. I can't answer the phone. The fire burned off my hands. But don't worry, I'll be in touch . . . soon."

It sounded like Janice.

But Janice was dead.

Then again, if she believed Bobby, so was the Black Walker.

Record. Button.

Bobby and his goddamn song of power. How many copies did he have?

Looked like maybe only one.

It was a chance.

"I'm there!" Bobby howled from deep in his h . "Can't wait to see how she smells! You're going smell the same way!"

Quickly Caroline worked her tennis sneakers and socks off and reached out with her feet for the stereo. It was just out of her reach, but by sliding her bent arms down the trunk of the tree she was able to stretch out and snatch it between her big toes. She pulled the player close and stood back up. The buttons were big, well lit up by the light of the moon. She pushed the stop button followed by the rewind button. The tape spun its ugly thread once more.

"Just got to get the dirt out of the way and then we can see how Janice is doing!" Bobby called.

The tape stopped. Caroline pressed the stop button once more. Then her big toe reached for record. It was harder to push down than the others, but go down it did. Now the speakers of the stereo were listening, not talking. They were the microphone now, hungry perhaps, for once, for the voice of the living instead of the dead.

Softly, so that Bobby could not hear, Caroline began to sing.

" 'Silent night, holy night. All is calm, all is bright. Round yon virgin mother and child. Holy infant so tender and mild. Sleep in heavenly peace, sleep in heavenly peace. . . . Silent night, holy night. All is calm, all is bright . . .' "

Caroline did not know all the verses.

She just kept singing the same one.

A few minutes passed.

Bobby stood up in the grave, probably on top of the exposed coffin. He shook his head as if shaking off a hangover. He looked over at her.

"What are you singing?" he growled.

"Prayers," she said, shutting up. She had sung "Silent Night" five times, enough times to wipe out the Black Walker tune. Bobby climbed slowly out of the hole, with effort. Caroline reached down and clicked off the record button. Bobby walked wearily toward her. He had been digging hard, of course, yet his sudden fatigue struck her as a favorable sign. The lines on his face sagged as he stood before her.

"How come the tape is off?" he demanded.

Caroline shrugged as best as she could with her arms tied behind her back around a tree. "It just ran out."

Bobby knelt beside the stereo. "But it shouldn't have gone off." He noticed her bare feet. "You turned it off."

"I am very sorry," she said sarcastically.

He stood back up and slapped her across the face. The blow made her cringe, yet he did not hit her hard. Not really.

"Shut up," he said. "I'm putting you in the hole now. I don't want any trouble."

"Sure, why would I want to give you trouble?" she said, sounding more like Janice than herself. She watched as Bobby leaned over once more and rewound the tape. He did not start the song again, however, not immediately. He stepped to the back of the tree instead, and undid her binds, clasping her right wrist as he did so, in case she should suddenly bolt when she was loose. He still felt strong enough, certainly stronger than herself. The binds fell away, and the blood rushed back into her aching arms. Bobby grabbed her tightly and pulled her off the tree. Then he reached down with his free hand and turned the tape back on. Because there was normally a few seconds' delay before the song came on, he noticed nothing amiss. His mood had changed for the worse.

"You're a bitch, you know that?" he said.

"And you're a fine upstanding young man."

He slapped her again and began to drag her toward the hole. "I'm going to enjoy throwing the dirt back on top of you," he said.

"It's you that's going in the hole!" she screamed at him, fighting him all the way to the grave. But she could not get free. He hauled her to the edge of the pit before he threw her down into the pile of mud at the edge of the grave. It was his turn to spit on her and kick her in the gut. The wind went out of her in a hot red gasp. She doubled up in pain, rolling on the ground. He still had the edge on her in muscle, his erased power tape notwithstanding. She noted out of the corner of her eye that Janice had been buried in a pink coffin. He had yet to open the box. Thankfully.

"I don't want to hurt you too bad before I put you inside," he said, his face savage. He reached for his shovel. "I like to hear a girl kick as the mud settles on top of her."

Caroline crawled onto her knees, gasping for air. "I'm sure you'll have fun burying me to the new song I recorded for you."

Bobby froze. "What new song?"

Caroline smiled. "Listen."

From the direction of the tree the gentle strands of

"Silent Night" wafted toward the grave.

"I've been taking singing lessons since I was a little girl," she said. "I hope you like it."

Bobby dropped the shovel and screamed. Then he swore at her, his face contorted into a thing that might have been dead a thousand centuries. *"You!"*

Caroline clapped her hands together. "That's me."

Bobby whirled and ran toward the tape. Caroline jumped to her feet, picked up the dropped shovel, and ran after him. He was down on his knees beside the stereo when she came up at his back. She had slowed down by then. The monster had been transformed into a mouse. "Silent Night" was the only thing playing, and that made Bobby Walker very sad. He actually turned to her with tears in his eyes.

"I never even got to hear it on MTV," he complained.

"I thought the Black Walker didn't prostitute himself," Caroline said. Then she belted him in the face with the shovel, the edge of the blade catching him clean on the lovely line of his handsome jaw. A fat line of blood split his expression in two and he went down. She raised the shovel again and brought it down hard on the back of his skull. He let out a muffled grunt and went still. "Neither of you is ever going to be on TV," she assured him.

There was only one thing left to do and then she could go home. She dragged Bobby to the edge of the open grave and jumped down beside Janice's closed coffin. She closed her eyes, her nose, and tried to close her mind as she reached down to pull away the lid. It came up easily in her hands; she suspected Bobby had already loosened it. Yet no foul smell assailed her, and as she cracked open one eye, no gruesome remains jumped out to grab her.

Janice's parents had had their daughter cremated. A small porcelain urn containing the ashes was all that rested in the center of the casket. Caroline sighed with relief. She leaned over and placed the urn in a corner of the coffin and then reached up for Bobby's hand. It was cold, limp. She had hit him hard. He toppled into the coffin without a sound of complaint. She reached into his pocket and removed his car keys. She reclosed the lid of the coffin and climbed out. She had to walk back to the tree for the shovel. Then she rewound the tape of her song and pushed the play button. She thought the music would help finish the job quicker.

When three feet of the mud had been piled back on top of the coffin, and the grave was half full, she heard Bobby start to kick. Cheerleading had not prepared her for such things; it was hard on her nerves to listen. Quickly she turned up the volume on the tape, hoping to drown out his growing screams. And suddenly, miraculously, the music sounded fuller, richer, as if another voice had joined hers, singing about the bright angels rather than the black walkers. It almost sounded as if Janice were singing beside her.

After a while the hole was full, and the kicking and the screaming stopped. Caroline brushed herself off, left the cemetery, and drove to within three blocks of her house. Then she parked the car and walked home. She heard no more from the handsome Bobby Walker.

About the Authors

D.E. ATHKINS was born and raised in the haunted South, and spent a wasted childhood trying to catch Santa Claus, the Easter Bunny, the Tooth Fairy, and the ghost in a women's dormitory at a local Methodist college. Upon reaching adulthood, Athkins moved to the prosaic North and eventually took up horror writing as a way to fill the gap left by a dearth of supernatural beings.

The author enjoys reading true-crime accounts, criminal case law, murder mysteries, and mail-order catalogs. Athkins will not go to scary movies, is afraid of blood, and believes that there is much more to this world than meets the eye. (What else are cats looking for all of the time?) In free moments, Athkins enjoys horrorticulture — accumulating, by fair means or foul, plants for a horror garden at the edge of the woods behind the author's house, where baby's breath and deadly nightshade thrive.

Look for D.E. Athkins' horror novel, *Sister Dearest*.

Little is known about **A. BATES** except that she brings fresh insight and mystery to the suspense genre. She confesses to being a student of human nature, intrigued by the dark depths that allow people to prey upon each other. "What's truly terrifying to me," she says, "is what people are actually capable of doing."

She believes every person is a labyrinth of secrets, a mystery of passions and possibilities. That some of these passions could erupt in violence is what creates tension in life and fiction. Long fascinated by the unanswerable questions of existence — questions like why are we here, and what other forces might exist unseen — the author submits for your approval a tale about the ultimate struggle: good versus evil.

Horror novels by A. BATES:

Party Line
Final Exam
Mother's Helper

JAY BENNETT is the critically and popularly acclaimed author of such books as *The Killing Tree*; *The Executioner*; *I Never Said I Loved You*; and *Deathman, Do Not Follow Me*. He has twice won the Edgar Award for Best Juvenile Mystery and is also the author of successful adult novels, plays, and television scripts.

Bennett's professed aim in his young-adult novels is "to write honest books that speak about violent times . . . but throughout the books, and in every word I write, there is a cry against violence."

Bennett lives in New Jersey.

CAROLINE B. COONEY is a master at writing about the eerie and the intangible. She manages to create an atmosphere of evil from ordinary events, without blood or violence. Only Cooney could successfully turn something as harmless as a deer into an image evoking fear and dread, as she does in "Where the Deer Are." As she explains, "You can be walking through the forest, with no sense of another living creature nearby, when suddenly there's this huge animal, *staring* at you. I think it's very creepy the way they seem to materialize out of nowhere. And then other times you don't see them at all. *Where are they?*"

Cooney lives in a small seacoast village in Connecticut, with three children and two pianos. She writes every day on a word processor. She also plays the piano for school music programs, is learning jazz, reads a mystery novel a night, and does a lot of embroidery.

Horror novels by CAROLINE B. COONEY:

> *The Cheerleader*
> *The Fog*
> *The Snow*
> *The Fire*

CAROL ELLIS is the author of more than fifteen books for young people, including *My Secret Admirer*. While Ellis doesn't read horror books herself, some of her favorite reading is mystery and suspense, especially those books in which an ordinary, innocent person becomes caught up in something strange and frightening.

Ellis calls herself a procrastinator, who tends to do her best writing under the pressure of a deadline. She rewards herself a few days before she finishes writing by buying a book she's been wanting to read and enjoying it as soon as she's done with her own.

Carol Ellis lives in New York with her husband and ten-year-old son, a dog, and two cats. While her son isn't yet old enough to read her books, he and his friends do find it hard to understand that the same person who supplies the chocolate-chip cookies also writes horror books.

"Writing tales of horror makes it hard to convince people that I'm a nice, gentle person," says **DIANE HOH**. "I love rainbows and wildflowers and butterflies and babies, and I wouldn't swat a fly unless it was diving directly into my fruit salad.

"So what's a nice woman like me doing scaring people?

"Having the time of my life. Discovering the fearful side of life: what makes the heart pound, the adrenaline flow, the pulse throb, the breath catch in the throat. And hoping always that the reader is having a frightfully good time, too."

Diane Hoh grew up in Warren, Pennsylvania, "a lovely small town on the Allegheny River." Since then, she has lived in New York, Colorado, and North Carolina, before settling in Austin, Texas, where she plans to stay. "Reading and writing take up most of my life," says Hoh, "along with family, music, and gardening."

Horror novels by DIANE HOH:

Funhouse
The Accident
The Invitation

LAEL LITTKE's town of Lake Isadora is based on a real town that was moved when the nearby river was dammed and the valley flooded. Littke read an article about it and went to see the foundations of the old town, which emerged as the waters receded. She was fascinated by the eerie remains of the buildings, and the willows growing beside the still-paved streets. She knew it was the perfect setting for a horror story. And so "Lucinda" was born.

Littke grew up in Mink Creek, Idaho. While she rode her horse over the hills to fetch the cows, she dreamed of becoming a writer. Her mother read *Dracula* to her and her brother, sitting in front of the old kitchen stove on cold winter nights. But she never imagined that one day she might write tales of horror.

Littke went on to study writing at Utah State University. After she was married, she took writing classes wherever she lived — Denver, New York City, Washington, D.C., and Pasadena, California, where she now lives with seven cats, two dogs, and her daughter, Lori, nearby.

Lael Littke has published approximately seventy-five short stories of all types, and several books for young people, including *Prom Dress*.

CHRISTOPHER PIKE is America's best-selling author of young-adult fiction. He started writing when he was twenty-one and had his first novel, *Slumber Party*, published when he was twenty-eight. He is the author of over a dozen teen books, and his first adult novel, *Sati*, is now in paperback. He currently lives in Los Angeles with his muse and word processor.

When asked where he gets his ideas, Pike responds, "I don't know." But he does plan to continue to write for teenagers. In fact, he says, he has twenty young-adult titles in the works. At present he is also writing a major adult horror novel, *The Season of Passage*, which will be available the beginning of 1992. For recreation Pike scuba dives, meditates, runs, and tries to convince teenagers in local bookstores that he really is Christopher Pike.

Horror novels by CHRISTOPHER PIKE:

Slumber Party
See You Later
Fall into Darkness
Remember Me
Scavenger Hunt
Spellbound

SINCLAIR SMITH was born in New York City, but spent an unusual childhood growing up in Las Vegas, Nevada. "One day I looked out our apartment window and there was a lion in the swimming pool," recalls the author. "It's my favorite childhood memory."

Smith's stories are based on real-life experiences. "Strange things happen to me just about every day," says Smith, adding that "while the supernatural may give you goose bumps, reality really scares my socks off." The author loves horror novels and movies and also enjoys running.

While visiting the famous Madame Tussaud's wax museum in London, **J.B. STAMPER** was terrified while walking through the Chamber of Horrors. Luckily the exit door was open. But her imagination never forgot how it felt to be surrounded by those eerie, wax bodies. And in her story, she made sure the exit door was locked.

J.B. Stamper lives in the shadowy outskirts of New York City, was married on Halloween, and enjoys reading mysteries past the midnight hour. She has written a popular series of horror stories: *Tales for the Midnight Hour*; *More Tales for the Midnight Hour*; *Still More Tales for the Midnight Hour*; and *Even More Tales for the Midnight Hour*.

R.L. STINE has written more than a dozen scary thrillers for young adults. One of the things he loves about writing for young people is the wonderful mail he gets from readers. Stine mentions a letter he received recently from a boy who, while reading one of the author's books, started screaming so loud his parents came running to see what was the matter. "That made me feel really proud," Stine recalls.

Where does this author get his ideas from? According to Stine, everything in his scary novels is true. "It all actually happened to me," he explains. "You can't imagine what a *horrifying* life I've led. But at least I've been able to get a few books out of it."

R.L. Stine lives in New York City with his wife, Jane, and his son, Matt.

Horror novels by R.L. STINE:

The Snowman
The Boyfriend
Beach Party
The Baby-sitter
The Baby-sitter II
Twisted
Blind Date

ELLEN EMERSON WHITE grew up in Narragansett, Rhode Island, and often has nightmares that take place in this New England-type setting. White is the first to admit she is easily scared. To this day, she is still afraid to go up into an attic after dark and relies heavily on her pets for protection. "If the animals are acting normal," she comments, "you're probably safe."

Like Dorothy in "The Boy Next Door," the author once worked in a Carvel ice-cream store while in high school. According to White, when it comes to horror there's nothing like working at Carvel. "Fudgie the Whale and Cookie Puss are *just terrifying*," she explains.

Ellen Emerson White lives in New York City.

PATRICIA WINDSOR was born in New York City but now lives in Savannah, Georgia, where she claims there are a lot more ghosts. For this award-winning novelist, the historic old South is certainly a breeding ground for new material when it comes to horror.

A longtime horror movie fan, Windsor is very rarely scared by anything she sees on the big screen. While the rest of the audience cowers in their seats, this author is the one with her eyes wide open. However, Windsor is quick to point out she is not interested in blood-and-guts and slasher-type flicks. Her all-time favorite horror story, "The Turn of the Screw" by Henry James, is the kind of in-depth horror/mystery she prefers. And, believe it or not, she even likes horror books with nice endings!

Horror novels by PATRICIA WINDSOR:

> *The Christmas Killer*
> *The Sandman's Eyes*